VENGEANCE

By

USA Today Best Selling Author

Kathy Coopmans

Vicky
Vengeance
Kathy Coopmans
XoXo

VENGEANCE
© 2018 Kathy Coopmans
Cover Design- Ellie McLove
Editing done by Ellie McLove
Proofreader- Cat Parisi.
Formatting- Small Town Girl Books

Dedication-
To new beginnings...Amy McGlone this one is for you!

Vengeance is a story with triggers. This means there will be hard to read scenes of abuse. I promise you there will be an HEA. Cade and Ivy will get the Vengeance they need. There is so much happy to this story that I hope you will pull for these two characters who have been wronged by one person they trusted. Thank you for reading this story.

Forever Grateful,

Kathy

Prologue
Cade
Eighteen Years Old

Loud voices shouted from downstairs as I pulled my earbuds out and jumped out of bed.

Terror swelled in my head.

I heard my mother's tortured screaming. My father crying out in an unhinged voice pierced with pain. Both repeating one question.

Why?

Before I could bring my tired mind to comprehend what the hell was going on, two gunshots went off from downstairs; they swirled around the confusion with the sudden flames and smoke that began ripping and roaring through the floorboards of my bedroom.

I froze.

Everything went silent except the unimaginable rushing thoughts in my head, the pounding of my heart and the crackling sound of fire as it licked and twisted itself into my room. Thick black clouds choked the air as I shoved open my window to catch my breath.

Panic twined around my legs.

Death whirled within my twitchy finger reach.

I needed to get to my sister and brother whose rooms were across the hall. Except, the dirty fuckers who set the house on fire didn't leave me a choice. I had just swung in the direction of my door when it blew off its hinges nearly knocking me on my ass from the combustion as pieces of incinerated wood sailed through the air.

I ducked, but I couldn't avoid the bits and pieces of burned wood that pelted and stung my skin.

"Move Cade. Save your family."

I wasn't giving up. I was shocked. Confused and scared. I had to get to them. Save them all even if I died doing it.

I took a step and the floor shifted underneath my feet.

With a scream so loud it should have woken the dead, and with the guilt of leaving them behind, I did the only thing I could do. I flung my body out my window, skimmed down the trellis and hid in the shadows. Body shaking, hot salty tears burning behind my lids.

I couldn't move to see if any of them made it out alive.

I watched it burn as choking clouds of toxic smoke pilfered through the chimney, crinkling flames torching the roof. The smell of gasoline so fierce it burned my nose. An out of control inferno. Ash floating to the ground like flakes of snow while I sat there wondering who in the hell would do this.

Gripping handfuls of my hair did nothing to dull the ache in my chest as my gaze traveled to my neighbors standing on the sidewalk across the street. My eyes scanning for my family.

None of them were there.

I searched the crowd, body shaking, mind not quite catching on to what was happening and there in the middle of everyone stood my girl all wrapped up in her father's arms. I started to stand, to let them know I was alive when I heard my older brother Drew and a few of his friends whispering just a few feet away from me.

My heart leaped knowing he was alive.

I started to move toward them when something was said that rooted me in my spot.

I heard Drew ask which one of his friends had my dad's life insurance policy. I squatted, crawled through the grass like a snake ready to strike, shaking my head to clear the misunderstanding I surely thought I heard. The closer I snuck, the more bile rose in my throat.

"We need to get the hell out of here," one of them said.

"Give me the policy and two minutes to watch them burn," my brother demanded with laughter trailing those words that will forever haunt me.

"Fairly certain they're all dead, man. You shot your parents in the head. These two pussies watched for your brother's bitch to sneak over. I took care of your sister real fucking good before I choked the life out of her, and there isn't a chance in hell Cade

made it out of his room. You made certain of that."

Want to bet you, rotten piece of shit.

I didn't hear a goddamn thing wrong. My brother and his friends killed our parents and little sister.

The way they laughed about certain things they had done before executing their well-thought-out-plan made numbness take over my brain.

I pressed a hand against my heart while vowing to the Gods of Vengeance I was going to get mine. I'd strike when they least expected.

Watching your family go up in flames, wanting to put a bullet through your own brother's head, the guilt of not being able to help save them did all kinds of fucked up shit to my mind. It tempered inside until the silent vow of putting them in the ground defeated my every thought.

Knew I had to go rogue. So I fled. I left leaving my brother to believe I had died. Left my girlfriend Ivy McCarthy who I loved more than anything behind.

For ten years, vengeance has shaded my soul from gray to black. It's feasted throughout my entire system, shutting down my state of mind, and becoming the focal point of my existence.

Once I started to plan their deaths, the imagined ways and inhuman actions on how I wanted to kill them ticked at my jaw and dripped like poison through my veins.

More times than I could count while I pulled the trigger and put a bullet through hundreds of enemies' heads, my mind would tip in the other direction, and that loose wire would trip up in my brain. The one that gives a vivid image of happy memories, what ifs, and what could have been.

And goddamnit all to hell when I thought about them, wishing they were here, wondering what kind of woman my sister Rachel would have turned out to be if it didn't leave me wondering if my soul would still be painted black, would I still want to pull the trigger and blow my brother's fucking face off.

Then again, I remembered who I'd become, and why I'd spent years hiding in the shadows, and vengeance once again became a deadly virus in my mind.

It's been left unsettled, it's festered, leaving me balancing somewhere between Heaven and Hell.

Chapter One
Cade

When I was a kid, my parents used to drill holes in my head doing their best to teach me and my sibling's right from wrong. They taught us to respect others, treat them the way you wanted to be treated, all the typical things a parent does to raise a decent human.

Regrettably, I've been plotting too many years to take their teachings and live by them. It's an easy decision to make when my brother and the men who done them wrong went about their lives as if they didn't take them away. It drove an arrow of retaliation into my heart. Charred it coal black, and left me with zero fucks except seeking revenge.

I was the one always getting in trouble, listening to that lecture about duty, honor, and respect when it turns out my brother who never did a goddamn thing wrong killed our family for money.

Greed. The thing that makes our world go round.

Our beautiful mom who stayed at home, cooked our meals, stroked our egos and worshipped the ground we walked on. A sixteen-year-old sister who loved animals, and dreamed of becoming a cowgirl living on a ranch. A father who sacrificed his life for his family and citizens every day he walked out the door. A cop. Twenty-two years he'd worked for the NYPD busting heads, arresting thieves, rapists, murderers, and he loved it. He never took a bribe, never turned his head. The man walked the straight and narrow and brought it home to his family.

I had plans to be just like him. But life doesn't always work out according to what we plan. So here I am, on the opposite end of the law. A grown man my father would detest. My life, my family's lives, would all be different if Drew wouldn't have done the unthinkable over greed.

The blood money man has a lot of lives he has to atone for. Too damn bad, it won't be by asking for forgiveness to a priest.

Fucking greed. It not only spins us around, it's what makes

people toxic. The slide of a dirty hand under the table stuffed with cash.

A promise that's usually broken.

Men who can't keep their dicks to home and women who spread their legs for someone other than the one who slipped a ring on her finger. There are many definitions of the word. Doesn't matter how you spin it, you choose to be greedy with me it's going to cost you.

With your life.

An eye for an eye.

A tooth for a tooth.

A brother for a brother.

Pain shoots up my arm when I look to where my hands are wrapped around the steering wheel of my Suburban. The word vengeance scrawled across the knuckles of both my hands. A black heart on my pinky. Detailed Ivy, which most people misconstrue as the plant when in all actuality its poison Ivy twined around a long-stemmed deep purple tulip. It begins at my wrists and winds up my arms. A deadly reminder of who I am, what I've lost, what I've become, and the beginning of the end of my nightmare.

The irony has never been lost on me that my brother took the land our parents owned along with three other homes surrounding it, plowed them down and built himself a nice little club, named BURN of all things, right in the middle that seems to be quite popular, loud and lively. Except he didn't have to demolish our parents' home, because it was already sitting in a pile of ash and rubble; our families bodies charred to the bone and buried somewhere within.

The filthy little cunt is a big hot shot lawyer. A dirty dealer who has a love-hate relationship with a lot of people. He has no idea how much I'm about to drive an arrow full of hate through his heart.

"Wonder how fast it would take the fire department to get here," I ask out loud, more to myself than the man sitting next to me. Doubt very long, not with the pull my brother seems to have in this safe suburbia borough of the city. Definitely not as long as it took them to get to our house the night he burned it down.

Pisses me off that the screwed up shit about living in certain areas of New York is, house fires, burglaries, and murders are a dime a dozen. Half of them go unreported, and the other half get swept under dirty-greedy cops dishonored feet. Got the proof that's what happened with the investigation of my family. Lies, betrayal, and a despicable waste of human space from my brother's lying mouth caused them to close the case.

Such a vicious scam of a cycle filled with his greed and deceit.

Don't fucking matter no more, cause at the end of the day, disloyalty due to greediness has made my job a hell of a lot easier for me.

You ain't the only one with connections in this town, brother.

I've mastered my own goddamn web of destruction by becoming a heartless killer. I've weaved it so well that there's no escaping the downfall of the men who brought out the monster in me. You won't find a man like me in the Yellow Pages or see my face on craigslist if you're looking to off your cheating spouse. Asking me to kill a woman or child could cost you a bullet in your head. In fact, it's cost a few dirty dealers already. You want to reach me; you call one man. Roan Diamond. The boss of a Mafia Empire. The man who would take my name to his grave.

Today, and every day since my family died, I've been strumming up a plan while I became a sharpshooting lethal weapon to my country. I never miss a target. I've perfected it so well that I'd bet a free kill if you measured from one side of the skull to the other, the bullet would be dead even.

My brother Drew St. James, and his friends are going to suffer the same kind of slow and painful death that I've suffered every day and night before I end their lives.

As I sit here, I can feel the first kill of vengeance slithering through my veins, the slippery, lethal, harsh vines of death. Years ago, it rooted in my tendons and twisted around the connecting bones. It knotted up my muscles, and not one of them will survive.

A chill runs down my arms and hits my twitchy trigger finger when sleet pelts the windows, my gaze moving up toward my brother's mansion. Outbreaks of shitty winter weather erupt through the fast moving clouds as it progressively makes its way from here to the city.

New York City. The most populated city in the states. Used to love this place along with this time of year. The holiday season. A time for family and celebration. I'll be celebrating alright; it just won't be for the reason everyone else does.

It's early afternoon, but the cold hard sleet turning to snow, the increasing howls of the wind remind me of the night my family died.

Persistent pain eats into my flesh. Recollections so goddamn vivid of our house torched in flames, the heavy curl of smoldering smoke from water hitting fire rattles the cavity in my chest.

It's been ten years. Ten years I've been fighting against the raging beast inside of me. The one who dies a little more each day to get his revenge.

Vengeance.

The word was coming to a boiling point in my head, a steady simmer of punishing those pricks has kept me alive. It holds more meaning for me than any other thing in my life.

"Count your days, motherfuckers. This crafty man you made crazy is coming for you. This city they call Gotham is mine."

All I need to do is kill my first victim, and then the walls they've built will crumble under their own weight once they realize who it is. I'll make them regret the day they placed an invisible rope around my neck, pulling the bitch until I choked.

I wandered the streets for a few days after the night I lost everyone I loved. Pieces of my soul were dropping on the sidewalk with each step I took. I missed them so damn bad I could barely breathe. My mind kept spinning about their funeral. Head and heart kept on about my girlfriend Ivy. I've loved that girl ever since the day she moved in across the street a few years before the night that changed my course of life. Black as night hair, eyes shaded as green as dew filled grass. At first, she was shy, a pocket full of sunshine with a smile so wide you couldn't help but want to drop to your knees.

It didn't take me long to convince her to go out with me. Didn't take long for the true her to surface either. The girl was feisty and stubborn. We'd been together since. But I couldn't go back, not with what raged inside of me.

The money I knew my brother would collect didn't mean a goddamn thing to me. I wanted him dead. After several days of freezing half to death, pissing, taking a shit, and vomiting next to where I slept, I knew I had to do something.

Couldn't have been more than an hour later when I walked past a recruiting office. I stood outside that office for all of ten minutes before I strolled in and enlisted. It took a few days to scrounge up enough money to get a copy of my birth certificate. After that, it played out perfectly in my hands.

I thought it was the best fucking decision until halfway through my first tour I was called into my sergeant's office. I was left with no choice but to tell him the truth about my family when he slid my death certificate across his desk. I told him I ran scared and as messed up as my story was, he let me go with a warning to stay in line. I left with a nod and constant worry he'd turn me in or think I was running from a crime I didn't commit. Worse, I wasn't ready for my brother to find me.

But I blocked it out. Busted my ass and trained to kill. Fought against the demons that corroded my brain. Took my vengeance out on the enemy and became one fucked up man set out to be the best. That quench to kill beat out the desire for a cold drink while I sat in the desert sweating my balls off. It made my dick harder than screwing a woman in her tight little ass.

And to this day, I often wonder if my brother knows I'm alive. In a way, I hope he does, because that means he knows I'm coming.

Glancing to the passenger seat, I make eye contact with one of the few men I trust with my life, Chaz Mayhew. Cold-blooded killer. A computer genius. My old sergeant. He investigated my families closed and unsolved murders without my knowledge. Found out I had a brother alive, hacked into his bank account, his investments and put two and two together.

One night he pulled me to the side. Told me what he found out and right there we made a vow that we'd stand by each other's side in and out of the war. All we both had to do was make it back to the states alive.

In his search, he found several people who were willing to give us the low down about my brother and his friend's whereabouts. Over the years, the sneaky bastard has done more than the cops ever did to track down killers. Works for me being that I want to destroy them myself.

It wasn't until several months later that I found out why he took the information he found about me and dealt with it in his own way. A way to this day I'll take to my grave.

Chaz, along with, Nick Williams, my lookout man I met on tour, and me, formed an untouchable bond that's filled with plans and plotting. They both been dealt a shitty hand in life. Lived through hell before the army saved them. Both with a desire embedded in their bones to seek vengeance. And soon, I'll be by their sides when they get it.

"You make the phone call?" I finally speak to the poor dude who's been sitting here with me night after night. I reach for my pipe, pack the tobacco, light up and fill my lungs with the sweet-smelling flavor. My dad used to smoke a pipe. My mom hated it, but there was always something about the aroma I loved, so I tried it. Ended up becoming a habit. It's the only damn thing I picked up from him. A reminder I feed into my lungs that I'm his son.

"Yeah. Asshole was eager to meet me. Listen, Cade, I know you're hurting man, but come the hell on. What good is sitting out here doing for you besides torturing you more? Besides, it's colder than the bitch I banged last night." I chuckle. Most bitches around here are definitely frigid.

All except one. She's fire to my ice.

Prying my face from the house in front of me, I ask myself the same question. I've been sitting here every night for weeks, hoping I'd get a peek at Ivy. My perfect gift. One close-up that isn't from a picture, or seeing her from a distance. She's the icing on my cake of vengeance.

The woman Drew stole from me.

I can't think of how to answer. Except, awareness sizzles underneath my skin like it always did when she was near me.

Ain't no different for my cock either. I sit here with him raging like a hungry goddamn beast whose been jacked up for years on an experimental drug that makes you wanna fuck the woman of your dreams, and nothing will tame him until you slide into her slick wet heat. Not even the nameless bitches with a snug cunt will do.

"Don't know. Whenever I've seen her from a distance, it doesn't make me feel as screwed up in the head. Like maybe there's a chance she wasn't part of it. Like there might be something good for me after this is all over." Doubt if that's true. For one, she's the only riddle I haven't figured out. And two, I'm not sure I can forgive her for marrying my brother.

The one person I'm not sure was part of the plan to kill my family. Plus, whenever I do see her from a distance, she never smiles. Not one damn time.

The idea of *my* Ivy sleeping in the same bed as Drew, letting him touch her, kiss her, fuck her, and caress her silky smooth skin is enough for me to want to fuck her up right before I kill her. Make me the last face she sees before she slips down the hole of betrayal. Not sure I'll ever forgive her for marrying him.

The thing is, there's no proof she was or wasn't part of Drew's plan all along. If she was, she's the last person my twitchy finger will murder.

Chapter Two
Ivy

It's Friday, which means I should have been home an hour ago. Today it won't matter if I'd been sitting there waiting for him with my legs spread wide, he's still going to come at me with all he's got. It won't matter to him that we live in a city where we get rain and sleet one day, snow falling like crazy the next. It won't matter to him that I'm late because I'd rather not kill myself driving to rush home from getting my thick mane of hair straightened to perfection just the way he likes it. And, it won't matter to him that I'm doing this right along with millions of people trying to bust their asses to get out of this town. Because today, like every year when this day rolls around, he'll still take it out on me with his fists and weapon, and I'm the stupid, stupid woman who puts up with it.

His violence is unrestrained, and at times comes out of nowhere. But today, he's going to make me suffer for still loving a dead man. Little does he know I've been suffering every day since the man I'll always love died. There are times my suffering surfaces with a sudden burst of ferocity. It's a combination of every emotion you can think of. It burns, it shatters, sweeps me away and engulfs me in so much despair that I feel as if I'm drowning.

My torturous husband may be known as one of the city's most ruthless attorneys but to me the woman who knows him better than anyone, he's a sick twisted man. All bogus grins to the cameras, voice deep and powerful. He's a loyal man to his business partners, a hard as stone statue in the courtroom. A genius who will twist a story to his advantage. A manipulator. However, the minute he steps through our door, he becomes a vile, self-seeking man. One with sharp teeth and claws that can strip you bare, bruise your soul and leave you wishing the last final blow from his fists to your face is the one that ends you right there. That the torment he has caused you over the years stops your bleeding heart from pumping, and for you to just die.

Daily, I've worried if I'd wake and wonder would that day be the day I would take my last breath. There were times I wanted it to be. Times I felt like I was, but I needed to hold on. Needed to push through the pain for the man who helped bring me into this world.

My father.

My father is the reason why I've stayed. I needed him to be taken care of, and God rest his soul because if the man would've been in the right frame of mind, he would have killed the monster I live with before disowning me for the things I allowed Drew to do. I've kept up with his violent and near-deadly violence in order to keep my father in one of the best assisted living facilities in the state.

My father raised me on his own. Took me home from the hospital two months after I was born to a junkie of a mother who passed her drug addiction down to me before I took my first breath.

From the stories, he used to tell me. They were hooked on heroin when they found out she was pregnant. They sought help, cleaned up their act for the sake of her pregnancy during which my growth was monitored. My father stayed clean. Obviously, she didn't. She gave birth, signed off her rights and walked away leaving a newborn to fight for her life and a man who did everything to make sure I survived.

My dad worked his fingers to the bone to provide for the two of us. One week after I graduated from high school, he had a stroke which caused our roles to reverse. With a broken heart over losing my boyfriend in a house fire not long before that, I took over and became the parent. Skipped out on going to college and taking a job as a waitress in a run-down truck stop a few miles over the Washington Bridge in New Jersey while Drew and my next door neighbor helped me out. At times, it was too much for all of us, but somehow we managed.

Inhaling a deep breath, I toss back the ibuprofen I pulled from my black Hermes leather bag; the new one Drew bought me and pull into our drive. The idiot thinks I need to be decked out in all things designer. He also thinks my favorite color is black when it's actually purple. The color of the bruises he loves to leave on my body. It's rather disgusting to love that color. However, it's a part of my past memories involving Cade, my recollections are the only part the Antichrist I live with can't take away from me.

Clutching my hand to my chest, I push the garage door open, pull in and clench my teeth when I see Drew's SUV parked in his spot. I know what's coming so I sit and let the main reason why today he's going to hurt me sink into my bones.

Briefly closing my eyes to avoid crying when the face of the young boy I loved flashes in front of me. I take a deep breath and remember what today is. Cade's birthday. Twenty-eight-years-old he would have been today.

God, I'll never forget the day I met him, fascination tumbled around me like a hypnotic force.

The day we met tremors rolled through my body, and they didn't have a thing to do with the shivers I kept getting from our recent move from a small town in Michigan to New York City where my dad's job transferred. No, those tremors came from the teenage boy across the street. They glided effortlessly over the icy road as he stood there shoveling snow. When he turned around and looked at me, his smile was filled with something so potent it blasted warmth across my flesh that was tucked underneath my winter's coat. Our instant attraction zinged and soared through the frosty air. Sticking to my skin, mixing with the snow and begging me to act on it.

My heart sputtered. He kept looking at me in that way a teenage girl dreams of a boy looking at her. Like he wanted to crawl inside and never come out. Fascinated. Bewildered.

His attention solely on me as he stared at me from where he stood beside a car. He made the thin wintry air thick. My freezing body turned scorching hot.

I felt longing. Desire. Lust and need.

It all rattled the thumping beat in my chest.

There's no use putting this off any further, so I tuck my memories away and grab the few bags of groceries I picked up earlier off the front seat. I shut the garage door, climb out, bump my door closed with my hip and step inside the tomb of a home I live in. I place the bags on the counter, my coat in the closet, slip off my shoes and make my way through the house and up the stairs to my bedroom.

Hello darling, your Stepford wife is home.

A cold hand grasps my throat as I step through the bedroom door. My body tightens and locks. My throat bobs and goes desert dry as I wait for the blow that is sure to come.

"You're late. Grieving time for you is over, Ivy. Get on your goddamn knees. You need a reminder of who owns you." The familiar voice I hate flows down my spine, slowing my blood flow to my beating heart. There isn't anything he could order me to do that he hasn't done already. Still, what he wants me to do is enough to break my spirit. The one the person I've been grieving over would want me to fight to have.

I've gathered internal scars from my husband's hands, feet, and belt. A heart that's floating somewhere in the Hudson River and determination to make it out of here alive now that I don't need him anymore. I just need to figure out a place to go. A place where he and his zombies he calls bodyguards can't find me. It's been two weeks since the death of my father. Drew knew I'd do anything to assure my father had everything he needed to live comfortably. Since he's passed, Drew has left me alone, and now the son of a bitch is on a riff to put me through hell.

Over the years, I've been beaten to within an inch of my life from the man I grew close to after the horrific death of his family. I mean, we were always friends, but I was in love with his brother, Cade. I've never loved Drew, not the way I did Cade. He and his family's lives ended much too soon. The only one who survived was Drew, and he's the one who wouldn't be missed if he'd died.

Drew though, he knows I feel this way, knows I'm still in love with his brother; he's used it right along with his threats to cut my father off to retain his power over me. A power I wish I would have been strong enough not to let him have.

I've allowed my scum of a husband to beat and rape me over and over. His threats of not paying for my dad's care whispered in a menacing voice while he punched me, took me by force and ordered me to keep my mouth shut.

Drew was all I had left of the man I loved. The good-looking friend who promised me so much if I'd give him a chance to prove he loved me. He swept the naïve girl in me away, all the while knowing I would never fully get over Cade. Once he received the millions of dollars from his parents' life insurance he asked me to marry him, placed my dad in a facility where they took great care of him and the minute he slipped a ring on my finger, said I do, he made me quit my job, shoved me past the gates of Hell and straight into it.

"I thought we were going out tonight."

"I am. You're not. And if you try leaving, you know I'll track you down. Now get on your knees. Don't make me ask you again," he grits out, his expression cold, his eyes filled with rage.

I study him. He and Cade look so much alike, it's scary. Only I know the difference between the two, it's in the way they both looked and touched me. Cade would never have treated me this way. I used to wonder what could possess Drew to treat me the way he does. Make me do some of the things he makes me do. Every time I tried, I came up with how sick and twisted his mind has to be. How he gets off on debasing me in a way a sane person will never understand.

Panic shoots through my body. The sensation is making my stomach queasy. Drew hasn't forced me to do this in a long time. The day we buried my father he told me I had a few weeks to pull my shit together. Even with my heart hurting, they've been the most peaceful weeks of my life. Before that, it's been weeks since he's touched me sexually. That's his typical sign he's screwing someone new. I live for those times, wish they'd come more often. Sleeping with someone else doesn't stop him from raising his hand to keep me in line though.

"No," I gasp out, fear gripping my throat when he squeezes my neck hard enough that it seizes and closes my air supply until I'm left with no choice but to drop to my knees and glare up at the hard feral eyes of the man who promised to love, honor, and cherish me. He's done none of those things. What he's done is degrade, humiliate, and make me wish the one and only time I tried to kill him by slicing his thigh with a knife, I would have succeeded.

I learned my lesson the day I tried to kill him. He dragged me through the house, up the stairs by my hair, blood dripping all over the floor and made me suck him off with a gun to my head. The minute I was done, he broke my hand by stomping on it. Bones crunched while I screamed out in pain and before he took me to the hospital, he had me clean up his blood, treat his wound and concocted the biggest lie to the doctors by telling them I fell from a ladder.

With his free hand, he undoes his belt, the hissing sound of his zipper going down brings bile up my throat. Internally I yell and scream at myself. I should have run the day I buried my father. I knew he was getting weaker, knew I didn't have much time left with him and yet I stayed. I have no one to blame for what's about to happen but myself.

"You'll do it the way I like it."

"Please don't do this, Drew. I'm your wife; you don't have to make me do this, please." My voice sways around my heavy breathing. I'd rather him fuck me than make me do this.

"But I do. I'm not fucking stupid, Ivy. You despise me. I see it written all over your face. Hear it in your tone whenever you speak to me. The thing is, you can suck dick like a porn star when you're scared. Open up and don't you dare stop until I've come down your throat. Don't be thinking of him when you have my cock in your mouth. My brother is dead. Six feet under, probably burning in hell. He isn't coming back to save you."

God, how I wish he would save me. Rise from the dead and cut out this man's heart.

Every year when Cade's birthday rolls around, he beats me worse. It's his sick and twisted way of reminding me of what I lost. He lost them too, and for the life of me, I'll never understand why he doesn't bring any of them up except his brother. It's his jealousy over a dead man. Funny how when he brings him up it's okay, but whenever anyone else does, he turns into a raging lunatic and takes it out on me. Bringing Cade's name up is just one of the many lessons I've learned the hard way not to do.

"My God, why would you say such a thing? He's your brother. You lost your entire family. When was the last time you went to their graves, huh?" He's never gone as far as I know.

I'm going to pay worse for that remark. But I don't care.

Hearing him talk about Cade that way for some reason, sets

my soul on fire, it bursts into flames like a burning stake driving into my soul. Meant to destroy the remorse, the humiliation and the weakness I've let stay alive inside of me for far too long.

"Shut the fuck up about my family. You know the rules. You don't bring them up, ever. I've allowed you to break too many of them since your father died. You will do what I say by crawling to the end of the bed and kneeling the way you were taught. Put that goddamn pretty little mouth to use and suck my dick. On second thought..." I have no time to register his words because the next thing I know his fist flies and connects with the side of my head. My body wobbles sideways, and my vision blurs as I topple over. Doesn't stop him from pressing his shoe to my throat, applying pressure until my eyes bulge. I knew I was pushing him, and now I'm paying for it.

"Fuck, if I didn't need you to give me a son I'd crush your windpipe." I will not give him a son. One of his many flings can. How I wish one of them would. Although, I don't wish this kind of torture on another human. I swear me not getting pregnant is the only prayer the gods who hate me have answered.

He grabs me under my arms and drags me up his body, spits in my face and strikes me hard enough with the back of his hand that my teeth rattle.

The next punch to my face sends the hatred I have for this man to fly to the forefront of my mind. I press a finger to my lips when a thin trickle of blood seeps out of a corner of my mouth.

I need the little effect the ibuprofen brings to kick in because I've not ever gotten used to the pain this unhinged man has inflicted on me. I don't think a person ever truly can.

My blurry eyes travel down the length of his dress pants, his dick bulging and swollen.

Beating me always makes him hard.

I watch as his eyes turn pitch black, hatred and in charge as he lifts off my throat, grabs my hair and drags me across the carpet to the bed. My knees scream in protest. The carpet peeling away a layer of my skin.

Numbness takes over when he positions himself on the edge of the bed, pulls out his dick and points to where he wants me to sit back on my haunches like he's training a dog.

"Suck, you worthless cunt." He shoves my face in his lap; his disgusting musky scent is the last thing I inhale before the next breath I take has him tapping the head of his dick on my lips forcing me to open my mouth.

I'd love nothing more than to resist and have him beat me instead, but I've no doubt more of that is coming too.

Closing my eyes, I drift to the only place my mind goes when Drew does this to me. I think of Cade and the way he encouraged me on when I'd take him in my mouth. He might have been rough, and in control when we were in bed, but not once did he make me feel like I wasn't worth everything to him. We were just two young teenagers in love. Learning how to please each other. I wanted to please him in every way.

"Harder, goddamnit. Suck me off." He grips both sides of my head, thrusts up into me causing me to gag. "Vomit on me bitch, and I'll beat you worse. Now take it. All of it. Suck my cock hard and deep, Ivy." I dig deep into the marrow of my bones for the courage to make me keep going instead of begging him to end my life. I almost do until I remember he'd killed the woman I'd been, with the first punch to the gut.

Tears leak from the corner of my eyes as he forces me to open wider, sliding in until he's hitting the back of my throat. "That's good, yeah like that."

I squeeze my eyes shut, trying to pretend he's Cade. The good brother, the one who treated me with respect. The one who brought me purple tulips. His young face spiraling through my mind. Falling from my skull, cutting through my body like a sweet torment.

My hands dig into the threads of the carpet as the force of his drives threatens to knock me onto my back. My vision blurs, and my brain screams for relief as he presses his hands harder into my scalp. It feels like he's going to snap my head off from my neck.

His thrusts quicken, his moans of pleasure growing louder. I suck harder, the taste of salty pre-cum sliding across my tongue.

Reaching up with shaky fingers, I gently take hold of his balls and roll them around with my hand the way I know he likes. Seems to get him off faster. One long moan, the sudden stillness of his demanding thrusts and he's coming down my throat with satisfaction smeared all over his face.

"I'll take care of our dinner guests tonight. Let them know you have a headache." He sneers. "Anthony will be downstairs; I'm taking your phone and the keys to your car. Try to leave, and he'll kill you." He stuffs himself back into his boxers, does up his pants and levels himself so we're eye to eye.

I close my eyes; I know what's coming. I have no choice but to take it.

"This is for telling me no and bringing up his name. Happy fucking birthday, little brother. It's a damn shame he isn't here to see I've ruined his gift. That's what he used to call you, isn't it Ivy. His perfect gift."

What a sick bastard.

I crumple to the floor as a hard punch comes in contact with the lower part of my stomach. It knocks all the air out of my lungs. My breathing becomes choppy as blow after blow lands in my gut. Kick after kick raining down on my ribs. I cry out. My brain on the edge of turning black. Every blow to my head, every kick sends an intense piercing jar of never-ending agony throughout my whole body. The pitch of nothingness summons to me.

I want to run and hide when he pauses and grabs the item I didn't see sitting on the edge of the bed. The one thing he uses on me every year this day rolls around. His eyes are hungry as he studies the smooth edge of the blade.

My ears cry out in agony as he uses the sharp edge to cut away my pants, I finally give in to the darkness before he shoves the wooden end of the knife inside me and fucks me with it.

Chapter Three
Cade

"I should have listened to my gut when you asked to meet at your home instead of my office. You don't even look like a Carl. You do look like a sick twisted fuck though; you won't get away with this." The fear in the man's voice causes eagerness to jolt down my spine.

I can smell his near death in the freezing air. It's a desirable high like no other.

"Sick and twisted, damn straight I am. Carl, I'm not. That was my dad's name, so unless you want me to carve your lips off your face, I'd shut the fuck up. Gotta hand it to you though, didn't think you looked like a murderer either, but you are. Isn't that right?" Watching the man's face go pale, a speckled expression of remorse streaming across his features before it's gone as quickly as it came sends my chaotic mind into a frenzy.

Clay Irvine is the first victim on my road to vengeance. He's trapped on his hands and knees, naked as the day he was born on a wooden table in the middle of a room in an old run down decrepit house. The only occupants that have lived here for years are the spiders that have laced their webs around the cracked spindles of the stairs and dead rodents that have dropped their smelly shit everywhere. The windows are busted out, segments of ceiling hang lifeless in the moldy air. Pieces of faded drywall lie over a damp raised coupled hardwood floor. The cold wind and snow filter through the rotten and blistered window frames. It's the perfect place to put a match too. Dry and coated with dust. It won't take minutes for it to go up in flames.

I stay hidden in the shadows to let Nick have his fun before I make an appearance that's sure to give the squirrelly balding friend of my brother's a heart attack before I test his ability to pain.

At the moment he has no idea where he is or who clocked him in the temple. Then cloaked his head with a black hood after he stepped out of his car where he thought he was meeting a prospective client looking to get a divorce. The idiot made our job easy by showing up to a multi-million dollar home that's been on the market for years. Gives the cops good reason to investigate elsewhere. Don't give a fuck if the bastard who owns the place goes down for a crime he didn't commit. It ain't my problem.

"I don't know what you are going on about. I've never killed anyone. You need to let me go before someone finds out I'm missing." His shoulders shudder, skin breaking out in goosebumps. And not the pleasurable kind either. His body starts to twist and thrash about on the table. Bastard might want to look down to where his dick is within an inch of being caught in a trap we designed and rigged to slice it off. Dumb fuck.

"Keep struggling, and soon those chains are going to squeeze all the air out of your lungs, and the contraption around your shriveling dick is going to cause you all kinds of pain. You're trapped, motherfucker. Every move you make pulls those chains a little tighter which causes the clamps to shut. Might want to believe me when I say they are sharp. Take a look, man, they are less than a few inches from your balls. Hate to break it down to you this way, only one who will realize you're gone are the men you're in business with. Believe your partner's name is Drew, correct? The cops, man, they don't give a shit about you. Not to worry though, will make sure they find you. Sorry. Not sorry that you'll be fried to a crisp by the time the firemen get here. You'll be a cold case left unsolved. Just like the people you killed."

Shock. He doesn't wear it as well as he did the expensive suit we stripped him out of.

I smile. I can smell his fear before he tilts his head down to take a look.

My twitchy trigger finger is aching to put a bullet through his skull. Yet the need for vengeance embedded in my skin holds me back just a little longer.

"Jesus Fucking Christ. What the hell? Fuck, you crazy son of a bitch. I'll die before I admit a damn thing to you." His body starts to shake. Muscles are working overtime to keep him upright. Won't be long until the freezing air has him shivering so bad he'll be whimpering.

"Cool with me, man. Either way, you're about to die."

There's my cue. The word die.

As revolting and warped as the scene before me is, the word die is one of my favorite words. That and, hope. Because even a man like me, whose blacked out soul doesn't stand a chance to live a normal life, has hope swelling inside of me. Hope that Ivy didn't betray me the way these heartless fucks did.

I haven't been back to their house in several days. I drank my birthday away and barely slept knowing tonight was drawing closer. Still, the desire to see her up close mulls on my mind. I tried with every fiber in me to forget her. Not sure if I can't because she's the only good thing left of the man I used to be or if it's because the hate I've tried convincing myself I have for her is actually love. Don't really know what to think anymore except I have this bad vibe in my gut that tells me something isn't right with that marriage, and I'm not resting until I find out what.

Whatever is happening with her, I'll deal with later. Right now, I've waited for a long time to kill this slimeball.

Placing my pipe in my mouth, lighting it up, and taking a long sip. I walk out slowly to allow the fragrance to reel in his senses. The smell of this particular nicotine is rare; it's my dad's personal blend. Rich fire roasted Cavendish mixed with undertones of vanilla.

I puff, inhale and exhale. The wind carrying the smell directly to him. He sniffs several times before his mouth drops open and recognition hits. Closing my eyes, I inhale again, filter the toxins through my body and blow the smoke as I lower myself so he can see my face.

"Don't cough, Clay. Your tiny little weenie will be gone before I have my fun."

He sputters. Face turning red. One shocked gaze he gives me before dropping his head between his slumping shoulders. "Fuck. This cannot be happening. I should have known." I'd chuckle at his choice of words if I had a sense of humor. Can't recall the last time a genuine smile lifted my mouth. Suppose I could, but thoughts of Ivy are diminished for the time being.

"Admitting it won't save your life. You will tell me which one of you raped and shot Rachel before shooting my parents, then torching my house." As much as I tried to forget the visuals of someone doing that to her, they still wake me in the dead of night. At the time, I was too shaken up to recall which one of them made a comment about how tight she was, how she fought and called out my name before he gagged her and fucked her virginal body. Not anymore though. I remember his voice as clear as crystal and the sound of it now is like gasoline being poured over the fire that's been smoldering in me for years. It roars through my veins. Igniting.

More shock, this time it's turned him as white as the freezing snow. Eyes widening, he inhales before lifting his head to glare fearfully into my dark eyes. His entire body rattling the chains.

"Cade. Shit, I always wondered if you made it out alive. I... Please man, it wasn't me. I didn't touch Rachel. I didn't want to do it. Your brother, he forced us. Swear to God he did." The high volume in his tone lifts a corner of my mouth. Fury pulses through my veins. I don't care who forced who to do what. All I care about is extracting every last one of the men involved from this earth.

"Keep moving, and you'll be bleeding out. Rats will be sniffing. Ain't no telling what they'll do to your dick and balls. A dick you raped my sister with before you shot her. The last thought she had was of you violating her with your dick. Consider yourself lucky I don't chop it off and stuff it in your mouth."

I back-hand him across the face and began to pace. Seconds pass as I fall further insane, yanking on my hair as his pleading echoes.

I need to kill him in a hurry; it's the only way to stop the unleashed raging beast that has been waiting to get this started.

"You see me, Clay? Do I look like a man who gives a fuck whose idea it was? Over the years I've been taught a lot of things. One of them is when people lie. I've been waiting a long time for this. Your death is going to hurt like a bitch. Might want to hold still, Clay. That clamp is about to pinch your balls." I take a puff of my pipe, the sweet burning sensation curling down my throat and lungs. The smell piercing its way to my head.

Sweet fucking torture.

It ain't easy standing next to this piece of shit, look him in the eye and recall how my brain bounced back and forth with each laugh, each word they said as I laid low in the grass. My stomach churning, mouth-filling with bile. How the pain of what my sister must have felt scorched through my skin and took away every feeling of safety she ever had. She trusted them. Hung out with them as much as I did and they killed her spirit before she took her last breath.

Faster than a speeding bullet, I pull two knives from my back pockets, stab it through the back of each one of his hands, lodging them into the wood.

One for each filthy paw that touched her.

His shriek of pain, gasping and choking, the gears in his head trying to tame down his shaking is an adrenaline shot straight into my brain.

A goddamn motherfucking buzzing bleeding high.

Blood gushes out of his hands.

I crave the sight of it.

"You are c-c-crazy. Drew always promised us there wasn't a chance you got out. He doused your door with gasoline himself. Look, I ca-can't bring your family back, but I can give you half of the life insurance. It's yours, Cade. Take it, and I'll disappear. Swear it." He stutters. Teeth are chattering and lips turning blue.

"I'm not my brother, motherfucker. I don't want the money. I want you dead. You can beg and plead all you want. Bet it sounds familiar doesn't it? Did Rachel beg you to stop when you tore through her body? See that's the kind of crazy that's eaten away at me all these years. Wondering how it felt for my family to watch their son and his friends they treated like their own hurt them. Ever wonder what inhaling smoke does to the body? How about the smell of flesh burning, ever smelled it? I have, and it is the worst smell. It stinks like fucking bullshit."

It takes mere seconds for Clay's body to tremble into uncontrollable shudders, his body locking up, his face contorting in pain as the clamp squeezes the fuck out of his balls and the sharp blade slices off his placid dick.

I've never seen so much blood ooze out of a person in my entire life. It's pouring out of him like water from a broken hydrant. Squirting in every direction. My stomach nearly lurches up and out of my throat, his loud, shrilling screams ring in my ears until Chaz walks over, stuffs a rag in his mouth to stifle them.

"You raped my sister, asshole. Now you suffer." I'm done talking to him for now. As Nick said, his confession wouldn't save his sorry ass regardless. I move around the room. Taunting and teasing as I waft the last of the nicotine into the air. I want that and his smell of fear to be the last thing he inhales before the smoke suffocates and collapses his lungs.

His eyes bulge when I lift a couple of cans of oil from under the table and kneel on the floor in front of him. "You'll probably die before the fire reaches you. Then again, maybe not. Once the flames hit your oily skin, you'll sizzle and fry," I say with no empathy, no emotion at all.

"How does it feel to be tortured? To know you have no control over the people who have you trapped?" His answer is a whimper.

His body continues to shake as I pour the oil over his skin.

"Goddamn, you're fighting to be free of these restraints. Your skin is going to itch here in a minute, muscles will cramp, and your arms and knees will give. I'll be seeing you again, Clay. In hell where we'll do this all over again."

I don't look back as I make my way to the rickety door where Chaz and Nick stand waiting. I bend, flick my lighter and watch the gasoline we previously poured make its way around the room.

His pained yells fade the farther I walk away.

I can only hope the screaming I never heard from Rachel will do the same.

Chapter Four
Ivy

"You bitch. You really think I'll let you sleep naked next to me." I'm woken to a smack to my head, blinding light from Drew's phone in my face, the smell of whiskey breath and a half hard dick trying to glide between my legs.

My fingers dig into the sheets as my fists squeeze in a silent plea to hold Drew's weight. I can't catch my breath. My chest throbs, my lungs catch and release. My everything hurts.

The throb between my legs is brutal. Disgustingly raw.

Despite the beat down he gave me, I found sleeping on my stomach is much more comfortable than any other position. For some odd reason, it's alleviated a little pressure from the aches and pains.

"Of course not." I swallow. I've been down this long lonely road with him many times. I was hoping after what occurred a few hours ago he'd leave me be when he came home. Proves how stupid I am. Proves even more how a crazy man can flip his switches.

Years ago, when he first started coming home drunk and mumbling shit about his opposing counsel. I'd think I was being punished for them pissing him off. Like maybe they angered him so much that his mind closed off, and when it re-opened, to him I was someone else. Typically, I'd discarded those thoughts out of my head just as quickly as they appeared because to Drew, I was his punching bag no matter what kind of mood he was in.

However, tonight as I fight against my aching ribs I'm beginning to believe he hates me for not loving him, or he hates himself for wanting a woman who loathes the sight of him.

The reason why he does this shouldn't matter. What matters is how long I'd lived in hell and how much I hate myself for letting it continue.

I laid on my stomach the entire night thinking about my father before I dosed in a fitful sleep. How seeing me this way would have killed him before the lasting effects of his stroke did. He might not have been able to communicate with words after the stroke, but he could with his eyes, he could with a nod of his head or a weak squeeze of his hand. He would have understood. He would have been proud that I stood up and not continued to be a victim.

I can't do it anymore. I'm lost and angry. On the verge of giving up on life. Because if this is how I'm going to spend the rest of it, I'd rather die at my own hand then give Drew the satisfaction of killing me himself. I should just do it. The next time I walk out the door by myself. I should drive straight to one of the many bridges in this city, get out and jump.

Then again, that's what he wants. He wants to break me until I'm left with no options. I need to find a way to escape. Disappear without a trace and start over, or else find the courage to kill him.

I'm twenty-eight years old, and I've wasted my life out of fear. I'm a shattered, weak and pathetic excuse for a woman. Allowing him to control me has only made me even weaker when I'd believed being a survivor of rape, domestic and verbal abuse had made me strong.

I tense when he gets on his haunches, spreads my legs and glides his hands up to palm my ass.

"The client's wife was a gorgeous bitch. She reminded me of you. Wonder if she lost her sex drive the way you did. I need to fuck my wife. Get in the middle of the bed, Ivy."

Maybe she hates him as much as I do you.

I hate how he says my name. Hate how he demands me to do what he wants. Most of all, I hate how I bend to him. I'm not doing it anymore. If he wants to fuck his wife, he'll have to do it after he's beaten me unconscious.

"You're drunk, Drew."

I squeeze my eyes shut. The tightly wound ball of hatred I hold tightly to singes my mind. I want to kill him.

"I'm not drunk enough, sweetheart. Wouldn't matter if I was. You don't ever deny me what's mine." He chuckles. I hold in my flinch and vomit when his fingertips trace from my jaw to my temple. "Things could have been different for you and me if you would forget about a man who can't love you back. In the beginning, I gave you everything. I took care of your father instead of killing him. The man was half dead, and I let him live, for you. That wasn't enough for you, was it, Ivy. This home, your car, clothes. Freedom to roam the city. None of it was enough to make you forget him and love me, was it?"

It could have been if you weren't some deranged monster.

Anger crawls out from under my skin.

"Fuck you. I would have killed you if you had hurt my dad. Whatever game you're trying to play isn't working. I hate you. I've hated everything about you for years, Drew. I hate the way you smell. I hate the way you look, dress, eat. I hate myself for not trying to run into that fire to save the man I love. You will never compare to him."

The possibility that I'll never be able to escape him has me wanting to land on death's doorstep. I'm over this. All I've been doing is laying down when I should be standing tall. Making a life for myself while forgetting the mistake I made by marrying him. I'm going to push him until he snaps faster than normal, and I know he will. He's going to attack me with his fists again. But, I'm going to survive, and somehow I'm going to get away from him.

"You don't scare me, you know? You hate me for not loving you. You hate me for Cade living in my heart and not you. Isn't that right? You are so possessed with me that you've taken it upon yourself to choose my destiny. You don't get to choose for me anymore. Either kill me, or when I get the chance, I'm going to kill you and believe me, there's going to come a day when I'll have one."

At that, he starts to laugh malevolently like the crazy man he is. I push upward with my hands, my legs shaking, muscles yelling to lay back down as they stretch and moan in agony. I'm playing with a fire that's bound to destroy me, and I know it. My hand flies up, and I grab a handful of his hair. He flops down beside me with that condescending, smug look on his face. It pisses me off so much that I slap him across his face as hard as I can.

I have nowhere to go when he grabs my arms, twists my body plastering my back to his front. "Fuck you Drew St. James. Fuck you straight to hell."

"You tried once and didn't succeed. You're too weak to try again. Why would I be living in hell when putting your mind, body, and soul through it is the one thing I live for. I'm in heaven, darling. Fucking heaven watching you suffer. Let me tell you something else. Don't take me for a drunken fool, Ivy. Being drunk doesn't mean I don't know my wife. You're plotting. Wheels are spinning in that pretty head of yours. Think twice about leaving, think twice about wanting to die. Let's see how much more your body can endure for that stupid as fuck move you just made. I'm going to make you pay dearly for that. I'm done having you test my patience. You will never hit me again."

I've been with him long enough to know he's going to do whatever he wants no matter what. So, I continue on with my goading because if this is my destiny, then I want it to end right here.

"You are so much different from your brother in every possible way, Drew. Cade would never call this love. He would call it for what it is. A sick man who nobody gives a shit about. A creature which everyone uses for his looks and money. You think those women I know you fuck, want you? They don't see the real you. You seek comfort from them out of desperation when you fuck them. You want someone to give a shit for just a little while. Only they don't. They all hope you'll leave your wife for them because they want your money. They don't want you, Drew. No one does. And here I thought I was the pathetic one for staying with you as long as I did. You're the pathetic one. That's what I see when I look at you. That's what I see when I drive my fancy car. That's what I see when I pull into this monstrosity of a tomb. Pathetic."

His fist comes down on my back, knocking the air out of my lungs. I claw at the sheets trying to get away, but he's quick to latch onto them with one hand. I hear the metal clang of his buckle coming undone, the hiss of the leather flinging through the air. I kick and scream, fight with all I have in me to get him off, to try and stop him from weaving his belt around my hands, but it's a wasted effort with his size and my banged up body.

"Drew, stop, please." My voice quavers around the salty taste of my tears.

"Just remember when we go to BURN tomorrow night, and you can barely move, you asked for it. And you will move, Ivy. You'll shake your sweet ass for my guests and me." His words aren't a request. They never are. How he expects me to sit there and pretend he didn't violate and beat me proves how crazy he is.

I suck in a sharp breath when he plunges inside of me. My body obvious only to me I'm not ready to take him. I rarely am. I'm on all fours, my head on the comforter while he takes from me. Plunging his dick in and out with brutal pounds against my dryness and wounds. I'm so sore down there I wish I were dead.

I whimper around his heavy, thrusting weight. More tears leak from the corner of my eyes as he pushes in hard and deep. "He's not the one fucking you, is he? He's not the one who's going to come inside of you? He's not the one you smell like. You want to die, you stupid woman. You'll die after you give me what I want."

Please God, don't ever let me get pregnant by this man. I won't survive if I do.

He molds his front to my back, fingers digging into the bruises on my sides. Each thrust of his cock burns and blends into the darkness I've come to live in. I reach for my memories of Cade, longing for his face to cloak me in comfort, but Drew's grunts in my ear keep me in reality.

"Christ," he roars. His dirty release spilling inside of me. Tears continue to fall down my cheeks, each drop a reminder that I might never get away to find myself.

"That was a reminder of who you belong to. What's coming next is because you brought up his name. I think you do want to die, don't you?" I remain speechless as he continues to rant, grabbing me by my hair and throwing my naked, injured body onto the floor.

He stumbles, chuckles, shakes his head and lands a fist into my back.

I cough and wheeze.

It doesn't matter to him that he'd kicked me hours ago. It doesn't matter to him that there will be bruises over bruises. This is what he does, this is what he loves, and this is his way of marking me when he just raped me.

"Who has the control here, Ivy?" He grabs my face and wrenches it, so I'm staring into his face.

"WHO. HAS. THE. CONTROL?" he yells in my face.

His whiskey mixes with desperation.

Well, fuck him. I'm not answering.

"Oh, so now you have nothing to say, huh? No sentimental words about love and my brother? Am I scaring you now? You should be scared. It didn't have to come to this, but you leave me no choice. Fuck me or beat me? Kill me or don't? Escape or stay? Those thoughts are what's running through your head, aren't they? Let me do the honors by making up your mind for you."

Something snaps in me. I turned wild, kicking and screaming and yelling. "Stop. You do not get to tell me what to do or who to be. I hate you. Do you hear me, you vile, disgusting human? I hate you."

Whatever fate has in store for me, this time. This time, I'm fighting back.

Tears fall down my face. But I keep on fighting. Clawing and scratching my nails anywhere I can connect with his skin. I hate this man more than I want to die. More than I want my freedom that after tonight I'll surely never get.

"You'll do as I say or I'll take away someone you love. You aren't going to be able to walk for a week for drawing my blood." He stands above me, his legs caging me in on either side of my head.

There are only two people in this world I care about. My best friend Casey and her daughter.

"You wouldn't." I wheeze through heavy breathing. I've exerted myself. Just another long list of things I'm going to pay for.

"I would. I'll take your best friend's little girl and sell her."

I believe he means what he says. I cave. Give in to the monster standing above me.

Maybe, just maybe if I close my eyes so I don't have to see him, it will shut him out of my head, to close myself off from the fact that he is about to do God knows what, but I can't. All I see is him and the feral way he is looking down at me.

Either I'll survive this, or I'll die.

I've withstood this man many times before. However, when his fist connects brutally with my mouth, his rage more severe, his kicks more untamed. It's before I black out that I see something hidden in his glassed over eyes.

To my blurry vision, it looks a lot like fear.

Chapter Five
Drew

I remember the smell of burning flesh. All those years ago, the rancid smell had my buddies and me fleeing the house. As I sit in the dark with a drink in my hands, the reminder causes the muscles in my stomach to tighten. It smelled worse than the smoke.

Didn't smell as nice as all that cash sifting through my hands, that's for sure.

"Here's to you, old buddy. Dumb ass went and got yourself caught." Tipping my head back, I raise my glass, knock back the Glenlivet Clay bought me after we won our last big case.

Lowering my head, not out of fear of what I might see if I strain my tired eyes toward my wife sleeping in our bed, but because I know if I move, the chains binding me down will squeeze harder against my chest, and I'll take out the death of my friend on her even more.

Ivy didn't deserve the last thing I did to her. Couldn't seem to help myself. Someone had to pay for the disturbing phone call I received while trying to convince my client that his ex-wife didn't deserve any more child support than he was paying. Never understand why a man has to support a kid he didn't want in the first place.

I glance up at Ivy wondering why the fuck she hasn't given me a child yet. Preferably a son.

"She hates you, Drew."

"Shut the fuck up Rachel. You are dead. Get out of my head." I groan, my throat dry and in desperate need of water. It seems she only comes out to toy with me on his birthday, hers, or the anniversary of their deaths.

"Or when shit isn't your business." This is a fucking joke. The little pest is gone, and here I sit letting her invade my thoughts. "I blame you, Clay. Your murder triggered shit deep in my mind that I've buried."

Yet I knew there would come a time when Cade would strike.

Suppose I should move my ass and do something about it. Make sure I'm protected a little more. Guard my wife with every man's life I can find.

"He's coming for you soon, Drew." For shit's sake, our parents can't even shut you up from the grave.

"If you were here Rachel, I'd kill you all over again. Cut your tongue out of your whiny mouth."

Memories flood. My chest heaves and the chains pull tight. I count back slowly from ten to control my breathing.

He might be coming for me, but rest assured, I'll be waiting when he does.

Chapter Six
Cade

"What the hell are you thinking? Fuck! This isn't like you. Pull it together asshole." Dragging a hand through my hair, I curse the man staring back at me in the mirror while the steam from the shower spreads across the glass, slowly fading the image along with the man away.

I need to get myself under control before I lose my goddamn mind. After years of hard work, I sure as hell can't allow my head to get tangled in wondering why the hell a woman who doesn't belong to me hasn't been seen in days.

For the first time since I've killed, my nerves are on edge. It has nothing to do with worrying about the cops; we didn't leave a trace. It's my suspicion Drew knows it was me and he's somehow slipped her past me. Meaning, she's in hiding, or worse.

The possibility he would hurt her has never crossed my mind. What if he has? What if she didn't know what he's done and now that Clay is dead, she's somehow found out what they did. Ivy would never allow him to get away with it. She'd go to the police. And I can't have her going to the police. I've planned these killings to perfection. But I'm no fool to know that even the best thought out plan can change.

"Goddamnit." If he's hurt her in any way, I'm not sure what I'll do.

My heart spreads open inside my chest as if it needs more blood to survive. The thought of him doing anything to hurt her tests my patience more than the waiting I've endured to begin Drew's execution.

"Son of a bitch." My head and heart duel in a bloody war.

I breathe in and out through my nose to quiet my tempered muscles, the rage bubbling in my veins ready to explode any minute.

Stepping into the shower, I hiss when the scalding water pounds across my back, steam hitting my senses, increasing the buzz from the bottles of Jack swimming through my bloodstream I've consumed since my birthday a week ago.

Instead of working in the office of the gym, Nick, Chaz, and I own like I usually do during the day; today I decided to work out some of my angered aggression.

We needed something legit after we got out of the army. Deciding on a gym seemed the best route to go since we spent most of our down time in the desert pumping iron.

That's how we met Roan Diamond. The man had a warehouse he was looking to rent out. We needed a cover to protect our names. So we offered him a deal. Our services for him to put the gym in his name and us as silent partners. We shook hands, gave our words and invested our savings in getting the gym up and running. It took us six months to start turning a profit. From that day forward, Roan Diamond and his family have had our backs as much as we've had his.

I tilt my head back, the water soaking my hair and face.

I knew I was taking the risk of Ivy seeing me by stepping out of my office this week. Pacing a hole in the hallway floor while I waited for her to show. She's been coming to our gym for over a year. Her days are sporadic. Some weeks she's not there at all. I can't say why her not showing this time is bothering me more than before.

When she is here, she stretches with her ass in the air before running four miles on the treadmill. Her tight ass and toned legs hidden in a pair of skin-tight work out pants. Then she hits the weights. Flexing her chest with the machines in a sports bra that enhances her handfuls of tits. So fucking beautiful it physically hurts my chest to look at her.

Every damn time she works her legs, spreading those thighs, stomach down, ass in the air, extending those long, long legs I become hard. Painfully hard. Balls like a rock and dick like granite. Truthfully, it doesn't matter what machine she's on; her curvy body has me sitting behind my desk stroking my dick.

The woman has filled out in all the right places. Curves for days. Handfuls of lush skin that left me with no choice but to find a willing body to sink into.

Only none of them have ever felt like her. None of them will be her. She's irreplaceable.

Worst of all, she isn't mine.

Several times I wanted to kick every motherfucker out of there. Lock the doors and creep out of the shadows. I wanted to fuck her pussy, her ass, her mouth on those machines without her even knowing who I was. The thrill of it is filthy and repulsive even for a man like me.

Don't know how the three of us have managed to avoid her whenever she comes in with that loof of a bodyguard. Sure the hell isn't luck. If I had any, she'd still be mine and my family would be alive.

Something feels off about her not being here this week. In fact, she hasn't left her house.

Something ain't right.

"Where the hell are you, Ivy?"

My voice vibrates thick with lust. I glance down at my long hard cock jutting straight ahead. My balls heavy and in need of dumping my load.

"Fuck, I'm a damn fool for wanting her."

Leaning my forehead against the tiles, I shut my eyes, curl my hand around my shaft and stroke from base to tip. My balls tighten, nearing a painful state. They remember how fucking blissful her cunt feels. My hand will always be a sorry excuse compared to being inside her body.

Memories take me back to the first time I slid my finger inside Ivy's tight pussy. Fuck, that warmth spreading all over my finger had me hard.

"Feel good?" I asked, nibbling on her neck as I picked up the pace, finger fucking her until I damn near blew my load. Couldn't stop my hips from dry humping her thigh. I needed to get off as bad as I wanted to get her off.

"Yeah, let me take care of you too." Her breathing was choppy. Hips thrusting into my hand.

"Fuck yes, please, I'm in misery here." I added another finger while she fumbled her tiny little hands trying to unsnap my jeans and lower my zipper. We'd done some fooling around, but this was the first time she was actually going to touch my dick.

My hips jerked when she wrapped her hand around him, her

*eyes glazed, teeth nibbling on her bottom lip as she started to
stroke like she'd done it a hundred times before. "Damn babe, keep
doing that, and I'm gonna come before you. Always want to get
you off first." I pressed my mouth to hers, didn't want to talk
anymore. Just wanted to feel this girl who was quickly filling up
every waking moment of my thoughts. Hell, she'd been creeping
into my dreams too. Slipping her sweet self right in the spot that I
knew belonged to her. I was falling so hard, so fast.*

This beautiful girl and me are right for each other.

*"Cade, I think you need to take out one finger. It hurts." Pulling
my mouth off hers, as well as slipping out a finger.*

Christ. I never wanted to cause her any pain. She was too sweet.

Too tempting.

*"I'm sorry. Don't ever want to hurt you. You want me to stop?"
Please say no. I want to see you come so goddamn bad.*

"No."

*"Good. You're a gift, you know that right? A gift I'm going to
wear on my sleeve. Literally."*

*She didn't respond with her feisty little-wicked tongue. She
nodded, eyes rolling in the back of her head.*

Untainted. Unmarked and gorgeous.

*Even though her hand felt a hell of a lot better than mine, it
wasn't enough. All I could fathom was how good it was going to
feel to have her pussy wrapped tight around my cock. I wanted
those toned thighs hooked around my neck as I ate her out. I
wanted to be balls deep inside of her. Her hands clenching the
sheets while she screamed for me to thrust harder. Deeper.*

*I slid my hand up her side, the pad of my thumb caressing her
cheek. "You drive me so fucking crazy." From that day forward I
did my best to hold her face in my hands when I kissed her.*

Never wanted to part with such a precious gift.

Keeping my eyes closed. Those memories of how her face
flushed, her mouth opening, her hand matching the push and
pull of my finger inside of her undid me that day. I watched the
beauty come for the first time for me. I couldn't stop watching
her, couldn't pull my finger out until she did it again. Her face
glowed, the girl looking like an angel I wanted to dirty up.

Pure and innocent. And mine. Every part of her belonged to

me.

I wasn't a fool to think we would last forever. All I had was hope that we would. Hope that she'd want to live her life with a man like me. If she did, I'd make her happy. I'd treat her right, and I'd watch her come as often as I could. Nice and wet. Tight and mine.

I'd give her everything. But not anymore. She doesn't belong to me and yet here I am, getting myself off like so many other times before to her.

Goddamn *her*.

My eyes pop open. The pleasure in my balls jarring another memory as my orgasm tears through my cock and lands on the tiles.

"You can sleep naked, or you can wear my shirt to bed." I slipped out of her bed, quickly got dressed while never taking my eyes off of her.

Steam is billowing out of my ears. Surprised she hasn't seen it yet. I am pissed. Livid is more like it.

"What? Why are you leaving? Did I do something wrong?" Fuck no you didn't. You just came all over my face and then my dick.

I didn't want to tell her what I swear to God I just saw. The thing was, Ivy and me, we didn't have secrets. We told each other the truth whether it hurts or not. I wasn't sure she could handle the truth, so I lied.

"No, you did everything right, Ivy. You always do. Especially with that mouth." I might have been a testosterone filled teenager, but I was in love with this girl, and I needed to make sure the everyone knew it. Including the person who was just peeking in her window.

I lifted my phone out of my pocket. First time I was grateful my little sister had sent me a half dozen texts a bit ago I didn't open.

"Rachel's been texting me for the past hour. She said Mom was going to come over here and drag my ass home if I didn't get my chores done." Goddamn lie. Rachel was freaking out over Clay again. The guy was always creeping up in her shit. Sitting in the middle of her bed when she came out of her bathroom wrapped in nothing but a towel. Sending her texts. Peeking his ugly mug in her windows.

At first, Drew and I laughed it off. Told her Clay was family. He was messing around. Besides, he knew better than to be wanting in her pants. For one, she was too young. Two, she was our little sister, and we'd kick his ass. Because it was Rachel, I told him to knock it off. He didn't like me telling him what to do. We ended up wrestling around on the ground until Drew broke us up, took over and laid Clay out. And, now, after seeing my brother creeping on the two of us I know he doesn't give a shit that our sister was always freaking out about Clay. Peeping Tom is just like him. What I should do is bring it up to my dad and let him handle it. But I won't. I might be a lot of things, a tattle-tale I'm not.

"Okay, but don't you think your mom is going to know what's going on if you show up without a shirt?" She giggled, pulled my shirt over her head and settled back in bed.

"I'll start mowing the yard. She'll never know." I leaned down and kissed her. Took off to find my brother who had his face plastered against her window watching me as I finger fucker Ivy.

"What the fuck was that?" I grabbed him by his throat and threw him up against the side of the house.

"Nothing. It was a dare. Same thing Clay's been doing to Rachel. Chill out, man; I had no idea you were fucking her. All I was supposed to do was scare the two of you."

"You're a liar, Drew. What else have you and your buddies been doing? Huh? If I wasn't certain I could kick your ass, I'd tell Dad. He arrests assholes like you."

"Right. Pretty boy little brother. The one Dad sucks up to because you want to be a cop." I drop my hands from his throat. Take a step back. Lately, he's been carrying on about this shit. I don't know what the hell has gotten into him.

"You starting this shit again? Grow the fuck up, Drew. We're brothers. Blood. You have no right to be jealous of me. I want what's best for you. Don't turn me into a competition like you and your friends do to each other." Can't stomach any of his friends. Adam being the worst. Asshole is always rolling up here in some fancy new car. Pushing Drew's buttons about how someday he'll have everything he wants once he becomes a lawyer. How money really does buy happiness, because happiness is having pussy, cars, and possessions. Crock of spoiled rich boy shit.

I pounded his face in that night. Told him to stay the fuck away from her. He was done shoveling their snow. Done mowing and done looking at her. We fought until our knuckles were raw.

We never spoke to each other again.

One week later, the sick son of a bitch killed my family.

Chapter Seven
Ivy

Somewhere in the last week since Drew put yet another crack in my soul, I've lost count of my days. They've all bled together. Sucking what little bit of life I have left out of me.

There were times when I'd wake not knowing or caring if it was morning or night. I preferred it that way. There was less of a gamble of me getting my hopes up of a better life if all the nothingness I had to live for blended together.

It didn't matter to me I'd slept through Thanksgiving. It wasn't like Drew has given me a reason to be thankful for a damn thing.

My heart lurches with an unshakable fear as I step into the club. It pounds against my ribs a thousand times harder than when I stepped out of the limo moments ago.

Awareness settles in my soul with every painful step I take. Someone in here is prying me open with their eyes, and it scares the hell out of me.

An avalanche of rippled pain scrapes down my sides. I wince when Drew grabs my elbow, spins me toward him glaring cunningly.

"The only person you dance with is Casey. Don't make me angry tonight, Ivy. This meeting was postponed once. Just remember I fucking own you, and I'll own her too if you push me," Drew enunciates in my ear, his eyes icy. "You look good enough to fuck by the way," He flexes his hips, his hard cock pressing into my stomach. Jaw tense, eyes boring into mine. I cringe, rebounding quickly as the gun he has tucked into the waistband of his suit pants hits the still healing bruises on my stomach.

Why in the hell is he carrying a gun?

"I know." I stare hard into his eyes, ignoring the need to cradle my stomach. To do whatever it takes to distress the flare of pain shooting through my ribs.

I slide my hands around his neck just like I've been programmed to do when I'm in public, crushing his lips against mine, his tongue coercing itself into my mouth. I'd love to vomit down his throat and embarrass the hell out of him. Instead, I surrender, whimpering as if I would miss him while he conducts business. I won't be missing him at all.

It's pathetic really when I think that coming to his club is a reprieve for me. It's the only time I let my guard down and have fun with my friend regardless if the fun I'm having is at my own expense. For Drew, it's a demand he takes seriously, it's a show for the men he sucks up to in the VIP area. The happy, sexy wife out having a good time while her husband celebrates a victory. He treats his clients better than he does me. I used to care; now I don't give a shit if he bends over so they can fuck him in the ass. I hurt so badly that dancing is the last thing I want to do, but I know better than to bring it up to him.

He had to reschedule this get-together that should have been last week because of the brutal murder of one of his partners. My head is still reeling from Clay's death that has suddenly forced my husband into a state of panic the likes I've never seen before.

I guess that would explain the gun.

Every man and woman in his firm has double-crossed dozens of people, and yet the police haven't a clue who killed Clay. At first, they suspected the people who owned the house where they found Clay's car. When they had solid alibis, it's left them at square one. I've given up paying attention because I really don't care. Clay was a disgusting pig. Every time he looked at me he made me want to crawl out of my skin. I only wish whoever did it would have killed my husband instead.

Truthfully, even though I couldn't stand the man, no one deserves to die the way he did. His charred body was found with chains wrapped around him in an abandoned house.

His death has left my husband more possessive than before. Tonight is the second time he's allowed me out of our house since he degraded and beat me. After what he did to me, it wasn't like I was able to leave our home anyway.

My stomach and sides feel like someone is poking me with a burning, sharp stick. It's extensive. I hurt everywhere. It won't be long before I'm feeling the pain ten times over. Makes me wish I'd put more in my mouth than ibuprofen. Like always, I suck back the pain. Being weaned off drugs as a newborn can have many effects throughout life. An addictive personality is one of them. I might allow my husband to do things to me, but I refuse to be out of my head while I heal.

He would never admit that Clay's death was why he attacked me when he came home from his dinner meeting. Yet it was. Instead of a husband seeking comfort over the death of his partner, mine took it out on me with his fists and a brutal fuck that's left me raw and bleeding. After all this time, I'm beginning to think Drew really is crazy. A psychopath who is on the verge of losing all control. The man has come home many times after being drunk, but not once has he beaten me when he can't get it up. It's usually the next morning when he remembers that sets his rage aflame.

Dua Lipa thumps through the speakers as I swing my hips and make my way to my best friend Casey at our usual table. The one no one is allowed to sit at but her and me. Reserved right in front of the dance floor where Drew can keep his eyes on me from his lurking perch above.

"Hey, I just called Ryan. Molly talked him into building a fort in the living room. Which means, she'll be spending the night, so I'm getting drunk. Sure wish you drank." In spite of hurting, I slide into the booth, plaster on the smile I've perfected so damn well that even my best friend doesn't have a clue what my home life is like. I place my clutch on the table, my dress hitching higher up my thighs than it already is.

Well, at least Molly is safe for the night. Ryan would kill someone if they tried to hurt her in any way.

A shiver rolls across my flesh, whoever is checking me out was doing it with so much intensity I feel the pull from here. It's like a lightning bolt has zapped through the throngs of people and sparked parts of my body to life. I suck in a breath, reach for the water that as always is waiting for me when I arrive and take a long cool sip.

God, I wish I could turn around and scan the bar to find out who it is.

I shudder.

"I know. There are days I wish I drank too. Trust me. It's a good thing Ryan was available tonight with the change of plans. I've missed you. Sorry I haven't returned your calls this week. It's been crazy. Between the funeral yesterday and trying to decorate the house for the upcoming holidays, I've been busy." I lie so bad I stink from it. I haven't decorated. I've been lying in bed trying to breathe air into my lungs from what I'm sure are a few broken or badly bruised ribs and more. And let's not forget I've worried about her and Molly on top of making sure my husband doesn't fuck me. Although, after me fighting back, he's barely said a word. I've also been trying to figure out a way to escape. I haven't one. Bastard has doubled his security since Clay died. Making me feel more like a captive than before.

The idea that whoever is out there is seeking revenge against Drew's firm has my tongue growing thick, leaving me at a loss for words. The piece of shit's death couldn't have come at a better time. Maybe Drew will be into this investigation that he will leave me alone.

"I've missed you too. Ryan and Molly get along so good. He loves her as much as she does him. I just wish he wasn't so worried about me all the time. Clay's death sure was a shocker. How are you holding up?"

I'm not. I'm worried about you too, about Molly and I thought about killing myself, but if I do, Drew wins.

The alarm that Drew has threatened her and Ryan is doing its job as her brother cripples my thoughts.

"It was shocking, to say the least. I'm doing okay. Drew's taking it hard. Why is Ryan worried? Did something happen you're not telling me about?"

Casey was at the funeral yesterday, more out of respect for Drew and me than anything else, but I didn't have the chance to talk to her. She left to go pick up her daughter Molly from pre-school right after the service. We spoke briefly about her brother, Ryan, babysitting tonight earlier in the week and that's the last time we spoke. Usually, we talk every day whether I'm laid up in bed after getting my ass beat or not.

"No, nothing's happening with me. My life is boring. He's overprotective. Sometimes too much." She waves it off, takes a sip of her drink and briefly glances at the top level. She can look up there all she wants. I won't until I'm forced to.

A panic attack comes out of nowhere. The walls close in making me feel claustrophobic. I feel dirty and weak, my insides coiling tight over what Drew is soon going to make me do. I hate that man with a fierceness that if given a chance I could lose control. Tear him to pieces so I could become whole.

With shaky hands, I grab my glass of water and take a ladylike sip when what I really want to do is fill my mouth, spit the expensive shit all over the floor and wipe the excess off my lips with the back of my hand. Anything to act like a normal human instead of the weak robotic woman he's trained me to be.

We sit for a while, chatting about the holidays and how excited Molly is. Her little girl was nothing short of innocent and curious joy. The cutest little dark-haired, dark-eyed girl I've ever seen. Completely opposite of Casey's blonde hair and blue eyes.

Sometimes when I see the two of them together, jealousy plucks a chord in my chest. I love them both dearly, but it hurts my heart when being a mother is one of the things I always wanted to be. I want to feel that unconditional love. The kind that nothing could touch or break. A rare kind of love that can only be felt between a mother and a child.

"Her father still isn't coming around?" I ask. I've never met Molly's dad. I know Casey is still hung up on him. If she wasn't, she'd be here talking about taking someone home with her instead of getting drunk.

"No."

"I'm sorry. Let's go dance. I'm sweating just thinking about it." I fan myself, force a smile. Dizziness making the room sway.

I glance up to see Drew leaning over the edge of the wall. For a beat, he glances back and forth between me and Casey. When our eyes lock, we play the game of a happily married couple. Only I know that stare of his isn't a game tonight. He wants to fuck me. My stomach contracts violently. Let's hope he gets piss ass drunk and catches his usual case of whiskey dick. With him, it's a real thing.

I stare at a set of darkening glossy eyes that are telling me to get on the dance floor so the men he's with can watch his wife. I take several more sips until it's gone. Place the glass back down and prepare myself for the show.

Desire twists his lips when I stand, my black heels hitting the floor, my long legs are bare for everyone to see. The dark purple dress that doesn't leave a thing to the imagination begins to suffocate me. "Let's have some fun." I shimmy my dress down, wait for Casey, and wobble on my feet. I'm slightly dizzy, but my body burns with a desire to be fucked.

"Are you okay?" she asks, concern in her tone.

"Yes. I think I stood too fast." My sex clenches and I nearly gasp. My psyche fires off the what the hell question before I quickly straighten. It's been years since I've felt any pleasurable sensation down there. Years since I've had a release that wasn't from my fingers.

Sliding my hand down to grasp hers, we hit the dance floor ignoring the hungry predator's eyes from above. It's a sick, twisted diversion Drew loves to play. He'll pump these men full of expensive scotch while he has their eyes gravitating to my ass, my exposed back, and my thick long hair that has his prospective clients telling him how lucky he is as they talk business and eventually sign on permanently with his firm. All of it makes me want to catch this damn place on fire with him in it.

"Let's get you hot and sweaty before that handsome husband of yours decides it's time to leave." God, if she only knew how her words make me want to run out into the freezing night and get hit by a car.

Shivers run throughout me, and my vision blurs, they don't have a thing to do with what Casey just said. I feel high. Cold and clammy. Completely different than I've ever felt before. One I can't explain.

Something is off with me.

That awareness of being watched hits me again like a violent stampede. My pulse quickens, chest thumps and heart bangs its own tune loud in my ears.

The longer we dance, the sweatier I get. My head suddenly feels foggy, and there's an ache between my legs like I've never felt before. It's as if I need to get fucked.

I try ignoring it and dance until my feet ache. Belting out every song, and fantasizing the way I always do when I dance. I pretend I'm dancing for a man who loves me. One with dark hair and a deep set of eyes that sees into my soul while he makes his way toward me, and once he's near, he spins me around, takes hold of my hips and grinds his throbbing cock into the crook of my ass before rotating me, slamming me to his chest and taking hold of my face. Telling me how he can't wait to taste me on his tongue, make me come over and over before he fucks me until I beg him to stop. Satisfying each other the only thing on our minds.

Cade used to be that man.

Always, always touching my face.

Thinking about him increases the intensity between my thighs. It's worse than I've ever craved before. The desire races through my blood, claws at my muscles and pounds every part of my sex.

"You look pale, Ivy. Are you sure you're okay?" No, I need someone to fuck my brains out. I'd take my dirty rotten husband at this point. That's how bad I need it.

"Yes, why?" I lie again. If I don't relieve this ache; I might just die. I've never wanted to be thoroughly fucked in all my life.

I'm losing control of my mind as well as my body.

It feels good and bad, and oh so deliciously dirty.

"You're clutching your stomach and squeezing your legs together." I glance down, and sure as shit, I am. The truth sits on the edge of my tongue.

How could I want sex when I'm still sore. Right now though, I don't feel the pain.

I feel the desire. The urge to be fucked so hard I'm screaming for it.

With Drew watching me, I strum up a lie. It's not like she'd recognize one from the truth anyway. I've been lying to her for years.

"Cramps. It's that time of the month. I'm going to the bathroom, be right back." I leave her standing there yelling my name. The room spinning and taking me with it.

The smell of tempting sex fills the air. The dirty, mingling, sweat pouring out of bodies as they grind against each other on the dance floor in tempting foreplay that will likely lead to a night of filthy gratifying sex has my fingers inching up my thighs. God, I want to jump in the middle of them and grind out this release.

I can feel Drew's eyes on me with every step I take toward the hallway. They never once leave my face. "I'm going to the restroom to wipe off this sweat," I mouth, wondering if he can read my mind through the look of desperation I've no doubt is written all over my face.

He shakes his head, sets down his drink and starts toward the stairs continuing to look at me like a piece of meat he wants to pound until it's tender. I don't want him to fuck me. I want Cade. Always Cade.

My pussy quivers. The ache to be touch strumming so loud in my ears I can't think straight. Everything is noisy around me. People are squeezing me in.

I'm falling, falling, falling.

Tumbling into a black hole consumed by lust.

I swerve around when someone calls my name. There's a man walking toward me, a man I surely must not be seeing. "Cade?" It can't be. I shriek and back away, my gaze drifting back to my husband. Fear plummets down my spine.

"Cade, Is that really you?" Those words rush out of my mouth separating the truth from reality. Leaving me frazzled and unsteady.

Placing one hand on the railing leading upstairs, I slip my free hand under my dress, my clit hard and swollen. "Yes," I hiss, plunging two fingers inside me and glare at the man I think is Cade to hurry. God, to have him inside of me would be sheer utter bliss. I would roll over and let him fuck me for days in front of Drew no less.

Drew's eyes are crazed, or maybe they aren't his eyes at all. Maybe he's Cade. Maybe I'm crazy. Maybe I'm having a nightmare. A terrifying hallucination.

My head volleys back and forth. One brother in front of me, pushing his way through the people to get down the stairs with wild anger on his face, eyes glowing with shock, and the other walking toward me with worry on his.

There's something else in both their expressions. Something

more potent. More dangerous.

"What's happening to me?" My legs buckle when they both yell for me to come to them.

"No, you're not real." Even through my delirious desire, I know I'm hallucinating that Cade is there.

Knees trembling, I glance at Drew, place my hand on the banister and scream when the lights go out and a hand clamps over my mouth. The loud music replaced with screams and thumping feet.

I try and fight in a state of panic against whoever has hold of me when suddenly my legs are lifted off the floor.

Everything became fuzzy. My realization floating through a dark space filled with static.

The throb between my legs multiplies until I'm consumed in darkness.

Chapter Eight
Cade

"No. Don't strap me down. Not again. I'll give it to you any way you want. Don't force yourself on me, please, Drew. Please. God, don't do this."

"Jesus Fucking Christ," I grumble, slug the remainder of my glass of whiskey down and watch Ivy struggle. Her back arched, muscles in her neck fluttering like the delicate bird she is.

A gift Drew's been breaking with an unimaginable string of defilements continuing to fly from her mouth. When I track him down, he'll be sorry, but for now, I'm letting her agony soak beneath my ink.

"Please. I need to be fucked. Cade, where are you?"

"Goddamnit." I can't take this. It's breaking my eardrums hearing her ask to be fucked. Can't quite decide if hearing her beg for it, or the tiny whimpers she makes when she thrashes her head and my name leaks out of that fuckable mouth have me clenching the glass in my shaky hands.

There's so much pain scrunched on her face that even a man with a lost soul like me can barely handle.

After seeing her tan skin peppered with cuts, welts, and bruises. Faint fingerprint marks hidden underneath her makeup. Tiny scars that look like she's been cut with the tip of a knife on her upper thighs. I don't know whether to sit here any longer or say fuck the suffering I want Drew to feel and blow his sick and twisted brain out.

"Damn it; she won't stay still. You're going to have to press down on her shoulders Chaz; I can't get the needle in her arm." Doctor Hanson, who lives a few floors below me struggles, the veins in his old man arms ripple as he tries to hold her down.

"Cade. God, where are you? I need you to fuck me. Just touch me, you'll see I'm wet and ready."

Motherfucking shit.

"Make sure you give her enough to knock her out. She's going to rip that IV out of her arm if you don't." I repeat. I've already informed the Doctor about her fear of drugs. Her getting them will just be another thing on her angry list once she finds out I'm alive.

I turn my attention to Chaz, taking him in. The guy is doing a job I should be doing. Stroking her hair, whispering calming words, and wiping the sweat from her forehead.

I can't fucking breathe, let alone move far enough to touch her. Not after the guilt and shame bleeding right through my skin.

"Goddamn, she's strong." Hearing Chaz's words are more than I can take. She sure the hell is strong, and not in the way he means. Any woman who endures what's written all over her perfect body is stronger than any goddamn thing I've ever seen or done.

I feel myself slipping into dangerous territory. One with visions of her laying there and taking what Drew's been violently doing. I can almost hear the crack across her skin, see her ripping open and blood oozing out of her flesh.

By his hand.

My own brother couldn't stop at killing our family. He had to maim and mutilate the last person who means everything to me. If I didn't suspect he knew I was alive before. I sure the fuck do now.

Didn't have a clue what to expect when we stripped her out of that sexy dress, and her eyes popped open lazily gazing into mine before they rolled into the back of her head. Sure as shit wasn't prepared for her to scream out my name, face turning as white as a ghost. The ghost her drugged mind told her she was seeing. She gasped, fell back on my pillow and give me a view of her body.

What I saw dropped me to my knees.

Flawless skin painted black and blue. It gripped me tight enough in the chest that, for the first time since the death of my family, I felt tears prick my eyes. Why in the fuck would he do this to her? He always treated her with gentle hands when we were growing up. Half the time he beat me to mowing their yard, shoveling the snow. At the time, I didn't think a thing about it. Figured as long as he was doing it, it gave me more time to be with her.

Just like everything else when it comes to my brother, I thought wrong.

The sick fuck did it for selfish reasons. He wanted her to think he was good when deep down he had planned all along to kill and sweep in and make her his.

I don't want to set his flesh on fire anymore. I want to destroy it with my bare hands. Rip it off his bones and then watch it go up in flames.

After this, I'll kill him any way I can.

I kidnapped her because I couldn't help watching her fight against her pain anymore. Didn't fucking matter that for years I swayed back and forth on the line of possibly killing her. The minute she stepped into the club, unknowingly giving me a shot of those mesmerizing eyes, I knew she wasn't an accomplice. She looked scared to death. On the verge of petrified.

I definitely know after seeing the shit show go down a few hours ago in front of me. About lost my mind when she stood there with her fingers between her legs. Eyes wild and fierce to relieve herself in public no less.

The room goes quiet. Her breathing slows, and her body relaxes. Christ, how I want to lay by her and make sure she's breathing. Can't force my guilt-ridden ass to move. Can't risk the chance she'll wake up and realize I wasn't a figment of the drugs. That I'm as real as her and breathing the same enclosed air.

"I'm not sure what she was given until I run a blood test. My guess is a sex enhancer. I'm going to check her blood for everything. She should sleep peacefully for several hours. Give me a call if you need me. Ellie will be here in the morning; I'll have her tend to Ivy's personal needs. Be prepared for a confused woman with a lot of questions when she wakes." I nod, pull out a wad of cash and clamp my fist in thanks around his.

Doesn't take a genius to understand what he means about needs. It ain't like we didn't see the fresh cuts and bruises on her upper thighs and across her swollen pussy. "There's extra. Appreciate you doing this."

Please check her blood for sexually transmitted diseases and anything else you can think of.

My eyes search his, pleading for him to grasp on to what I'm asking. The thought of saying it out loud thins my blood.

"Of course." He knows not to ask questions. The way he treated her with gentle words and calm hands as she scratched and clawed at him, I'm pretty certain he knows what's she's been through. I sure as fuck do and it has me struggling to slow my ragged breaths that jet from my lungs.

Self-control and wrath glow a bright red stream through my veins. I know who beat her, tortured her, and did things I never suspected, it's finding out if he or someone else drugged her. And, if it wasn't Drew, the person who did adds onto the pile of vengeance.

Fuck, I hope she isn't broken beyond being fixed.

I'm going to need something ten times stronger to drink if I have to sit in this chair and watch her sleep naked in my bed. Her long arms and legs are strapped down to stop her from hurting, escaping and touching herself if she were to wake. Any other time I'd be stroking my cock while she played with her pussy, my mouth watering to be buried between her legs. She'd be begging in her right state of mind full of desire to come all over my face and beard. Not this time. Not when someone has fucked her up and warped her beautiful mind.

The doctor wrapped her chest and stomach tight to protect her broken and battered body. And her mind is closed off by the drugs dripping through an IV. Unlike her husband, I'm not letting her go untreated. Sweating out her misery or taking the chance of a rib poking and collapsing a lung.

Tonight we were supposed to sit back in the shadows and scope out the place. Our next course of action was to burn it down. And now, years' worth of planning are down the shitter because my brother has shocked me yet again.

Our inside contact cost us a pretty penny when he called to tell us Drew and Ivy would be at the club tonight. I had to see her, had to look hard into her eyes to see if she was part of my nightmare. I couldn't go one second longer without seeing her up close. I was beginning to think the sly bastard beat me and killed her.

She has no damn idea what the man she's lived with has done.

Not a fucking clue. This knowledge, plus seeing her like this, has me drawing an entirely new set of plans to massacre Drew.

I knew something was off with her the minute she walked in; nothing tamed my anger as I saw her wince when she walked. Then dance like she wasn't in pain at all. She had been drugged. With what I didn't know until she opened her eyes on the dance floor. They were hazed over in hunger. A need shined out of them, one I've seen and dreamed about many times. She wanted to be fucked.

I bolted out of my seat, only to be jerked back down by Chaz. Not once did I take my eyes off of her as I listened to his plan.

When she left her friend, I made my move. Didn't give a fuck if anyone saw me, I had to get her the hell out of there before whoever drugged her got a hold of her.

Doubt she'll remember seeing me, but the look of sheer utter shock on her panic-stricken face when she did will stay with me forever.

Drew, he's an entirely different story. He saw me the second I came out of the darkened hallway. If Ivy wasn't on the verge of stripping out of her clothes and finger fucking herself in front of everyone, I wouldn't have allowed either one of them to see me. Lack of control took over, and I called out her name. My own a mere whisper out of her mouth.

I snatched her right out from underneath him. Hated not to shoot my brother before I tied her up, put tape over her mouth and listened to her thrash around in the back of my Suburban. The only good thing besides getting her away from him is the raping, beating prick is probably shitting his pants about now knowing I have her.

Goddamn victory it would've been if she'd come to me the same woman as I left her.

Watching Ivy dominate the dance floor tonight has left a permanent branding of angered images that will never leave my brain. Her sinful body moved as it used to. Screaming seduction and sex. Her face though, it wasn't glowing with sunshine, it was pinched in agony and screaming in a violent storm.

Not only did that leave swelling ridges to kill trailing down my spine, it was also the way she commanded the attention of every man in there. All of them were caught up in her elegance. I'd like to break the hands of every rotten motherfucker who probably went home and spit, gripped, jerked their dicks with her tight ass, sculpted legs and dreaming of the scent of her pussy on their fucked up minds.

I sat there with my twitchy trigger finger begging for a release about as badly as my cock did. I wanted to shoot every one of those cocksuckers while they watched me fuck her sweet little cunt. At first, the sick fuck that I am wanted to be the man to relieve her. I might be a killer, a rapist I'm not.

By the looks and sounds of it, my brother is. And that is a whole other set of torture. For him and me.

It grinds my ass to remain rooted to this chair over it. I could tell she didn't like being a bullseye one bit. She was living in her own little world while my brother flaunted her beauty from high above. Sick fuck was playing her, and for whatever reason, she was going along with it. All of this made me regret what I was going to do to her.

My eyes glide up her elegant neck, landing on her mouth. Christ Almighty is she stunning. All grown up with curves and tits my cock wants to slide between. My palms itch to trace every inch, dip into those valleys, right before I slide my dick inside her pussy and my finger in her ass.

I want to grab her face and kiss her mouth.

"You wanted to see her up close, well there she is. Shame you might have to kill her."

"Not gonna happen, Nick, she doesn't have a clue what he did. You saw her body; he beats the hell out of her. There isn't a chance in hell she knows."

Adrenaline kick starts my system, amping my pulse until it damn near thumps out of my veins in my neck. I should have never left her. Should have gone to the police instead of letting the beast claim my senses. If I did, she wouldn't have been living in a darkened corner of hell.

"I know, man. Needed to make sure what we saw doesn't screw with your head. You need to keep it straight, man. You're human, Cade, you might have acted like you hated her, might even believe you aren't capable of love, but like Chaz and me, you are. Our love is just all kinds of fucked up."

True goddamn story. I never once said I didn't love her. Always claimed I loved to hate her when truthfully it was the other way around.

That was then; this is now. I'm not the same man I used to be. True love doesn't exist in my world full of violence and hate. It's a goddamn shame I can't keep her. Can do her one better than being with a man like me. I can get her mind and body healed, and set her lively spirit free.

By killing the man who dared to touch her.

By letting her go.

Guilt leeches onto my black heart. She shouldn't have gone through the hell she did. There was always the part in the back of my mind wondering if whether she stayed with Drew for the benefit of her father. Guess I should have figured she did before dropping to my knees after seeing the bruises, the marks, and the way her body tightened like a string ready to snap when she kissed Drew.

I cracked when her lips touched his. About busted my fingers from clenching my hands tight.

 Slow torture dragging up my arms.

"I let her slip from my hands right into his. Every mark, every strike from his hand is there because of me. There's no undoing that kind of wrong, Nick."

I've never felt guiltier for leaving her than I do now.

"I can smell the bullshit from here. No one can dig and bury the bad out of anyone's head unless they try. You want to help her, then you remind yourself why you walked away. Talk to her. You owe her the right to let her know her suffering was worth it. I guarantee in time Ivy will understand. Bet my balls she'll want him dead. Hell, she might want to kill him herself," Chaz adds from his spot beside her on my bed.

The spot that should be mine.

I harden my features. She isn't going anywhere near Drew again. "Since when did you get all sentimental and shit?"

"Don't have a sentimental bone in my body. I call it as I see it and you, my friend, did what needed to be done. What happened to Ivy isn't your doing. It's his. You want her, then be the man you are, one a fuck ton better than him and make up for it. That's all I'm saying."

My gut clenches. His words drive another nail in my coffin. I want her so bad I'll ache until I draw my last breath. "Wouldn't know where to begin to make up for this or lost time. I'm not the man she remembers." Sure as I'm sitting here, I ain't going back to that man either. Not when killing people controls every cell in my body. I get a rush from it. Right or wrong it's who I am. Doubt this perfect woman could handle it. Then again, she's a hell of a lot tougher than I can begin to understand.

"Ivy isn't the same woman either." Nick's right, she isn't. Guess time will tell. At the moment I want her physically healed. I'll deal with the rest when I think she can handle it.

"First things first. We need to check every person who works in the bar. I want her friend checked out too. Might have to dig around and find out who those men were with my brother."

"We have a wide range of people it could be. You know as well as I do, her display out there wasn't the first time." Nick's right again.

Might not be. It was her last. That I can stamp with a bullet that will shatter Drew's skull.

Chapter Nine
Ivy

Dread.

It coils through me. Tightening my chest, and restricting my breathing.

Suffocation swallows me whole.

My eyes spring open. Their stinging and burning like the rest of me. On instinct, I go to shoot up when the worst pain I've ever felt punches through my arms and legs.

I can't move.

It feels like my lungs are in my throat. My brain feels dead. If I wasn't breathing, I'd believe I was.

Terror lashes through my being when I take a deep breath, my chest constricting. It's then I realize I'm wrapped in bandages of some sort.

"What did you do to me, Drew? I'd rather be dead than to be at your mercy this way any longer." I cry out. Panic crawls across my flesh. I can feel scratchy tape on the top of my hand, the prickly twinge of an IV. "No. Take this out of me." My entire body fires off in uncontainable tremors. I can't stop shaking.

"Oh, my God. That smell. You're trying to drive me insane."

Wherever I am, it's not a hospital. Hospital's do not have the familiar smell of Cade mixed with vanilla.

My brain races in a fret of fright trying to remember what happened. Am I dreaming all of this? Did he hurt me more?

I can't recall a thing after walking into BURN. Nothing. My body shakes as I fight with the restraints that have me strapped down, and my mouth goes desert dry. Tongue thick and heavy. Pain and fury clash in my veins. It builds until I release a blood-curdling scream.

Terror. I nearly laugh at it when I thrash trying to get this IV out. Of all the things he could do to me, this is the worst.

"Did you have your way with me again? Beat me until you broke every one of my ribs, and now you're going to pump me full of drugs. Why not just kill me, you son of a bitch."

The pain grows like a weed gone wild, spreading from my

toes to my teeth. There's a dull ache between my legs.

"Oh, God, did you rape me again? You sick animal."

Clarity moves through the depths of my brain, poking and prodding in the darkest depths of my mind, ripping wide open every wound the man has ever conflicted on me. All the bits and pieces of scattered agony of the life I've lived have destroyed the woman I used to be.

I want her back and I'll be damned if he breaks the little bit of me I have left.

"If you didn't have me strapped down, I would run this time, Drew. Run and make sure you never find me. I won't let you win. You will not break me. I'm stronger than you think. So much stronger."

Nausea churns in my stomach without any notice. My head swims in a vacant pool of nothingness. My heart feels weighty as if the blood pumping through my veins becomes too thick to help give it a steady beat.

"Get this out of me," I scream until my throat burns. "Are you happy now that I'm begging? God, I hate you. Hate you so badly that if I ever were to be free, I'd kill you."

My mind reels back to that frightful night when I lost who I was. The one who stood on the sidewalk, shaking, terrified as she watched the home of the man she loved go up in flames, knowing he was trapped inside and Drew nor I could do a thing to save him.

"We have to save them, Drew. Please?"

"I tried to save them. He's gone, sweetheart. All of them are gone. I've got you. Everything will be alright."

Everything was never alright.

Confusion consumes me.

I'm lost in my frozen mind.

Unease winds through me, and I swear my throat is closing tight from anxiety. The air around me thins, and a sob burst from the depths of my stomach.

My sobs swallow me whole, raw from the inside, so very real on the outside. I've been robbed of everything. That despicable man stole not only my life, but my soul, a part of me no other person except Cade has ever seen.

Cade. Why does he always enter my mind in the most troublesome moments? He's gone. Has been for years, and yet like the tiny sliver of hope I've carried with me to be free, his face and name are a constant dangle in the air.

If I could only pluck him out of it so he could be with me.

I blink. Chaos and disorder dot my vision when a ray of light streams across my legs. It's in that moment when I tilt my head that I realize I have no idea where I am.

I'm not alone either.

"Changing your sick game on me now? You can't have your way with me strapped down like this, what did I do wrong? You married a piece of shit, that's what? I can hear you breathing, Drew. Don't pretend like you aren't there."

I haven't a clue where I am, but the view from the windows that run from the ceiling to the floor is one of absolute magnificent beauty.

What I see, takes my breath away. The sky is a hazy slate of gray. In the mist of the dusky sky are millions of lights. They twinkle like somebody has taken handfuls of gold and silver glitter and tossed it in the air. It's a view I've seen several times when my dad and I first moved here. We were both so hypnotized by the bright lights of New York that we spent many nights exploring. Banking in our memories of how every skyscraper glistened and glowed.

The morning light slowly filters in. The snow is falling heavily. I draw in the deepest breath and lose myself to everything outside running wild and free.

"I've made a mess out of my life, Dad. I know you don't want to hear this, but I'd go through it all over again just to have you here. I miss you so much it hurts." My lips tremble, and the sobs wrack out of me like a raging river ready to drop and crash into an angry waterfall.

Nothing but jagged rocks below.

Cutting me deep.

The lights across the city flicker, bringing memories that do the same.

Raw and real and rage.

My father taking his last breath. Drew beating me. Debasing

my inner self until there was nothing left of my spirit. Clay being murdered and the way my evil husband went on a tangent to double security.

A recollection. It flashes through my brain like lightning.

Awareness.

Wide and heavy.

Someone was watching me at the club. Maybe he has me and not Drew. "I can feel you. I don't know what you want, but if your plans are to torture me and send me back to my husband you've failed. There isn't anything you could do to me he hasn't done. It's obvious I'm ruined so, by all means, do your worse."

"You're wrong about that. My worse would be to kill you."

I tense, gasping. Eyes widening and focusing on the deep, yet tired and slurred rough voice coming from the corner of the room.

Drew is here, and he's drunk.

Oh, God. Please let me die.

"Don't you dare look at me, Ivy. If you do, I won't take out the IV. You understand?"

Fear and confusion slam through my tattered nerves. Every one I've ever had buried deep surfaces and slithers across my skin like a harsh warning.

Insanity has stolen my mind like an unhinged thief. It has my mind muddled.

"What's dripping in my veins, Drew? Something is clogging up my mind. You need to take it out."

"It's not coming out. You hear me?"

I should disobey him and turn my head. Tell him to end my suffering now.

"Yes." I gulp down my fear. It's an easy thing to feel when the man who embedded it in you thrives on it.

The smell of vanilla hits my senses again. Either I've really lost my mind, or he's trying to make me. There are only two men that smelled like that, and both are dead.

Silence hangs in the air. An empty void with unspoken promises I can't decipher. I choke down a laugh. The only thing he ever promised me was something to fulfill his sick gratification.

"What do you want, Drew?"

I've no doubt tensing against the shaking of my limbs isn't good for what lies beneath these bandages. On impulse, I do it anyway.

I'm hit with more silence. More confusion.

"You already have me right where you want me? Taking what you want. Beating and raping me. Making me stand by your side when I'd rather stand in hell. Where are we and what kind of game are you playing? Did I refuse to suck you off, not dance the right way for your perverted clients, so you beat me again? Did you torture me like you've done plenty of times by fucking me with the handle of Cade's knife? Why won't you just kill me? I don't want to be owned by you anymore. I want my freedom."

"Fuck!" he roars so loud I swear the floor underneath me shakes. "That's enough. You'll get your freedom as soon as I know you're safe. Right now I'd appreciate you staying still. You're hurt, Ivy." He hisses out words he's never spoken before as if he's the one in pain.

Something's off with him. It blares like a foghorn in my head.

His heavy words linger in the air, pushing piercing spikes through my insides and slicing me with the burn of a dull blade. Why does his voice sound the same, yet different? Deeper even?

"Since when do you care if I'm safe or stay still. What the hell is going on with you?"

My chest caves, my heart dropping. So much turmoil is racing through me that I can't rationalize anything until I get some answers.

"How long have I been here and where is here? Where's Casey? Do you know who killed Clay?"

He laughs. A mockery of sorts that pisses me off.

"Answer me. You bring me to what, a hotel? Fix me up, which, you've never done before and do God knows what to my body. You have an IV in my arm, and it's filling my veins with poison, and you don't have the decency to shed some light on what's going on." Of course, he doesn't. There isn't a decent bone in his body.

"I didn't kidnap you. I saved you. You were drugged, a sex enhancer. You weren't acting like yourself. All you need to know is you needed pain medicine. Enough with the questions, Ivy."

Drugged? This sick man is giving me more questions than answers. Stirring my thoughts until I don't know which way is up or down. The more I mull it around in my brain, the more it spins.

"Who drugged me, and what did you do that we've had to disappear?"

Hopelessness wraps around me. I'm already living in hell. A cruel, merciless life so why would someone want to drug me? The only person who would do such a thing is him. But why? He takes any time he feels like it, and he would never get me sexed up enough to share me. No, it's someone else. Someone who has him running.

Pain clutches my stomach when I let the idea of what could have happened slip into my mind. Fog swoops in and skirts a hazy mist in my being.

"I don't trust you. You could be lying."

"I could be. That's for you to decide. You've been here for over twenty-four hours. That's enough information. Process it and when you're ready, I'll tell you more. I'll have someone come help you shower, get you something to eat. The IV stays in until I say otherwise, and you will not be leaving this room until I say."

Chapter Ten
Cade

"You going to tell me what that bullshit was that went down in there a few days ago or you still think that whiskey is going to make this all go away? Because it sure sounded like you were pretending to be your brother." Chaz is angry. Good. That makes two of us. Three if you include Nick who, after days of trying to find out who drugged Ivy is coming up with nothing. Ironic as hell that the one night someone dares to harm her, the security cameras at BURN had been disabled. Every fucking one of them.

I knew I should have gotten out of the chair and had him go in there when she started to stir, and like the torturer I am, I sat there listening to every pain laced word filter out of her mouth. Her words slamming deep into my soul, ripping me apart. Since then, I've been stewing in my own misery. All kinds of guilt and anger weighing me down.

I went along with her thinking I was him while listening to the hell he put her through all over again. Nearly jumped out of the chair to let her see me, begging to be her savior when she made a comment about my knife. Her suffering became its own ghost that will plague me the rest of my life.

Guilt cutting me so deep it had my insides spiraling with a crazy out of control need to remind Ivy what we had. The problem is, was, always will be I'm to fucked up. A man full of evil when everything about her is good.

"She's not ready to see me yet," I exhale. Been pacing the floor outside my bedroom, refusing the urge to go into my study and watch her yet again on my security cameras while Doctor Hanson's daughter, Ellie, takes care of an irate Ivy. The woman screaming and hollering my brother's name, asking her if she's one of his whores all the while mixing it in with demanding answers. Answers I can't quite give her yet. Not until I rein my shit in.

"I know. You could have at least let me talk to her. Took a big risk by doing that."

Right, and miss having to hear only what I'm sure was a touch on all the shit Drew did. Can't choke any of it down.

"Yeah, well, I've been taking risks ever since the first bullet I shot off splattered brains all over the place. On top of her not knowing I'm alive, I had to see how brainwashed he has her. She didn't even move her head when I told her not to look at me. Part of it was due to the fact she hates him; other was she does what he says. Scared to death of the man. I would never have guessed the woman I used to know would surrender that easily. She was feisty, full of life. A willingly submissive woman she was not." Not my girl. Everything she did was done because she wanted to do it.

I heard and felt the spice she used to shake around whenever she was angry wanting to pour out of her. Pretty sure the remaining drugs, the confusion of where she is and why held most of it back. That, plus, she's frightened.

Hearing her speak the way she did. Expecting to be tortured, made to do things forcefully alienated me. Left me reeling about what needed to be done. Made up my mind the second I walked through that bedroom door closing her cries behind me it was time to make a call I never intended to make.

I've hardly left that room. Been sitting there the entire time slugging back whiskey and watching her sleep. So beautiful, so not the woman I knew at all, but I saw her in there hiding when she woke up. Saw her wanting to soar and be free. Angers me to no end, her freedom and my vengeance is going to come with a price. A price that's bound to be my death, because in the end. I'm going to have to let her go, and after seeing her, hearing her speak while trying to be strong, I don't know if I can exist in this world without her. Before, I didn't give a fuck if I lived or died. Vengeance was all I needed.

Now my mind is focused on her. Intoxicated by her presence. A need to fix her, make her right before I send her away. This whole nightmare has left me struggling to breathe.

My cock stirs, and my chest constricts. Emotions that fuck with my head, coming out of nowhere.

That's a damn lie. They've been hiding in a black space. The pieces of me only she could claim. The only woman I've ever loved. The one I wanted but was ruthlessly taken away.

The one I left behind.

"You sure about this, Ivy?"

"Yes, please don't make me beg," I chuckled. Loved it when she begged. Especially when she did it by thrusting those sexy as fuck hips farther in my face whenever I was between her legs. Licking and eating every part of her pussy. I was always starving to taste her. Always wanting my tongue in that tight cunt. Couldn't wait to bury my cock inside her.

"Tell me if it's too much." I never wanted to hurt her, not in any way. This girl deserves the world to be laid at her feet. She deserves to be loved, but shit I need inside her. Needed to let her wild side run free all over me.

Slowly I sunk into her warmth. Dick straining as she wrapped me in her tight little body. Stopping when I hit that barrier separating her from forever being mine. I paused long enough for her to catch her breath, pushed forward and gave as good as I took.

After that night. We couldn't get enough of each other. My dick stirs again thinking how she was the one who mostly initiated sex. Wanting to please me, wanting to take my cock in her mouth and suck me dry.

I clench my teeth and force myself to shove the past where it belongs. Deep into the void where I've buried it, only letting it surface when I have the urge to conflict pain on myself.

"When was the last time you took a risk with your heart, man? Your loyalty to vengeance means everything, and I get that. Fuck all knows I do. Vengeance isn't going to have your back for the rest of your life. That woman in there will. What about loyalty to yourself, or finding happiness at the end of it all? If you think you aren't capable of giving Ivy what she needs, then you didn't hear the same thing coming out of her mouth that I did. In a drugged up haze, that woman was calling out to you. A man she thinks is dead. Stew on that shit for a while. See how rotten and bitter it's going to taste, because I'm here to tell you, Ivy might want to beat your ass at first, but she's a woman who would seek vengeance by your side all the while showing you what you'd be missing if you let her go."

His brows shoot up, head tilts, studying me. Sure as shit

wasn't expecting him to say all that.

I'm not in the mood to have a heart to heart. Fucker knows mine's dead. "I need to make a call. You do know this changes things, right? I won't leave her alone." Not that I'm worried Drew will find her. It's for my own piece of mind.

"Go ahead and sit in denial all by yourself, you stubborn fuck. We got your back, Cade. Ivy's too. One of us will be with her at all times. Far as getting vengeance, think you've waited long enough that you could finish it off in your sleep. Nothing needs to change there. You have your work cut out for you. I'm gonna call it a night, get some sleep. When I wake, I'll move on finalizing things for your next kill. Don't wait long to tell her, Cade. She deserves to know. Once she realizes you're alive, you're bound to see an entirely different woman. Pull your head out of your ass. Never know, with some luck, you'll see I'm right." For shit's sake, it's going to take him ten minutes just to catch his breath after spewing shit out he knows nothing about.

Luck ain't ever been on my motherfucking side. If it was, her dreams, her life wouldn't have been destroyed, and she'd be mine.

I grit my teeth. Grind them until my jaw clenches.

"Need a few days with her. Give me that, and I'll be ready."

Killing is what I need right now. Not sitting here letting something that will never happen eat up space in my head.

My guts twist. What he said nor the need to kill isn't what has a hitch rising furiously into the cavity of my chest. It's what I'm about to do that does.

Moving from my spot after he shuts the door to one of my spare bedrooms, I take a quick shower, check on Ivy, who is sound to sleep. So damn gorgeous, so irresistible lying there in my bed. The spot next to her calling my name. Fuck, how I want to crawl into bed with her, take her in my arms and tell her I'll keep her safe. The thing about that, I haven't slept in a bed all night with a woman since her. I fucked them down and dirty, got what I needed and sent them on their way. It wasn't that a scent of a woman on my sheets didn't calm me, it did. They just weren't her. Now here she is, taking up a huge part of that space I only let vengeance take.

I've had plenty of women try their best to wind me into their clutches. The fantasy of a bad boy. A man with the mystery behind his face. None of them are real. All as fake as their tits. All out for a good time. Ain't a one of them a keeper. Not by standards. Ivy set that bar high years ago, and there isn't anyone who could jump high enough to touch it.

She's a wet dream in a middle of a goddamn nightmare.

Looking at her gives me the calmness I need to make this call. Silence meets me on the other end of my phone as I take a seat on my couch. Fucks me up just a little more when both our breathing increases. I can feel the hatred at both ends of the line.

"Been waiting a long time for you to call me, little brother. How's life in hell? I see you aren't all that little anymore. All muscle no brain."

A smile quirks my lips. He knew I was alive all along. Good for him. Asshole sure didn't share his knowledge with Clay. Has me wondering if he did with the others.

I hesitate before draping my arm over the back of the couch and flexing. Kind of funny how the man decked out in an Armani suit that's price tag could have fed our entire family for months notices my muscle.

He's intimidated. Pussy should be.

"You fucked my woman with my knife." It was more a statement than a question. Bastard inhales, then lets out a demonic laugh that burns my ears.

"That's the first thing you say after all these years. I'm disappointed. Wish I could break it to you gently all the different ways I fucked Ivy, just don't have it in me. Sure you know already that wasn't the only thing I fucked her tight little pussy with. I don't know how she still has the tightest pussy I've ever felt after I've pounded it thousands of times. So tight she milks every drop out of my dick. Shot more cum in her tight little hole than you've dreamed of. Balls fucking deep. Fucked that ass, mouth. Goddamn her mouth, brother, it might be my favorite hole in her body."

Bile collects in my throat, and every muscle in my body stiffens. Tightening with resentment that fumes from the bottom of my gut. Figured he was going to goad me, push those buttons.

I guess for a man who thought he'd prepared himself for the day I'd hear his voice again; I didn't prepare myself fully because the vile man is crazier than I thought.

Of course, how the hell can a man prepare himself for the ambush of unspeakable things he'd seen with his own eyes. He can't. Just like I wasn't prepared to find out my brother, my flesh, and blood. The man I talked to more than anyone about how much I wanted to give that girl everything. How she deserved the whole fucking world and every good thing in it could rape and hurt her.

Maybe that's why I took her from BURN because I could feel she was holding in something bottomless and shameful. A dark existence that no one else could see. The same as me. Searching for freedom and the only way to get it is for something to set it free.

"What's the matter, little brother, did her pussy catch your tongue already. Did you taste me, cause I marked her good for you? Knew there'd come a day you'd be back. Knew you were alive. Did a lot more than that to her, Cade."

I can hear him cracking a manic grin. One I'm going to carve off his face.

"I'm not going to go all in with the game you're playing, Drew. Ivy is in my bed where she should have been all along. You went after her to get back at me. You knew I'd be coming for you. Should have shot you when I had the chance. Believe me; I've had plenty of them. When I do kill you, it'll be face to face. Brother versus brother. Will see just how much of a man you aren't when I've strung you up by your balls, drain all the blood from your body and watch you die. I mean, I think it's only fair I watch the last member of my family die, don't you?"

My trigger finger twitches. Gonna have to tame it down. Killing might be in my blood, but so is Ivy and her well-being, safety, and healing are what's important right now.

"Let's get one thing straight before I take back what's mine. You left her behind. As far as I'm concerned that made her free to be with whoever she wanted. She chose me. She isn't your woman anymore, she's my wife, and if she isn't home within twenty-four hours, I'm filing a missing person report. Cops will be crawling all over your war-zone ass."

Christ, that pinches my ink covered skin hearing him call her his wife. Thousands of pokes draining the air right out of me.

I close my eyes, trying not to shout out like I want to. Not about to take my chances on waking Ivy. Not sure what Ellie told her to convince her to keep the IV in for a few more days. Doesn't really matter, all that does is in an instant the drugs leave her sleeping for hours. She needs to rest. Regardless, when I let her see me, Drew won't be a part of it. He's taken too much already. Not about to let him steal the little bit of good I'm going to have with her.

"She's a woman who would seek vengeance by your side all the while showing you what you'd be missing if you let her go."

"You won't file shit, Drew. You know why and so do I. Keep searching brother. While you're spending money trying to find her, the money you wouldn't have if you hadn't killed to get it, you might want to think about how my war-zone ass is going to find you when you least expect it. You didn't expect me to be in your club the other night where you left Ivy out in the open, on fucking drugs. Did you give her the enhancer so she'd sleep with you willingly? She isn't coming back to you. Not fucking ever. I'm going to kill you, Drew. Slice you right down the middle. Starting from that brain you used to concoct the death of our family, to those balls you claim to have, and when I'm done, I'm taking Ivy anywhere she wants to go. Gonna set her free from you. You get what I'm saying, brother?"

A sharp hiss flies from his mouth. I can feel the sting from the whip of my words slicing him open. Goddamn, revenge is a beautiful thing. Fucked up knowing it came with the price of torture conflicted on Ivy.

"Someone else gave her whatever the hell she was on. Whoever it was, paid one of my employees who no longer has arms to work with to cut my security feed. You're putting my wife in danger by not bringing her home. I'd re-think what you're doing, Cade. Not sure what you've been doing since you got out of the military. You sure as shit haven't been making connections in this town. I'd know if you did." He hasn't a clue about the connections I have. One call and I could have his head blown off.

No questions asked. Besides, my connections think he's a piece of scum they'd scrape off the bottom if I asked them to.

I toss my head back and laugh. Might be the first real one in years. Danger, my goddamn ass. She's safer with me than anyone.

"If you didn't drug her, then one of your connections did. I'm going to find them. Just have to decide which one of you I want to kill first. Let's talk about the night you let someone rape our sister, torched the house, and murdered our family. On second thought, I'd rather do that face to face. Brother to motherfucking brother. Vengeance, Drew, it's coming for you. I'm coming for you. There isn't a connection in this whole city who will stop me from getting it. Mom, Dad, Rachel, Ivy. I'm going to take a piece of you for every one of them. It's my turn to tell you to get something straight. You killed *my* family. Innocent people who loved you. You placed your hands on a woman in a way no woman should be touched. You're going to pay for that, Drew."

Hanging up, I scrub my hands down my face, pull my hair back and squeeze the sides of my head. I'm better off placing the barrel of my gun to my temple and pulling the trigger than I am to swallow down anything when it comes to what my brother will do to find her. He'll tear this town apart, and I know better than anyone how nothing will get in your way once you want something.

Vengeance comes with a price.

A price that not only cost Ivy years of abuse. If he finds her, I've no doubt it'll cost her with her life.

Chapter Eleven
Ivy

The chilly air stung my nose and sent a numbing cold across my skin. Gray and threatening clouds flowed freely across the sky, promising the first signs of snow. The freezing temps and snow never bothered me; I was used to it. I loved it really. The holidays. Cade's birthday. Christmas break from school.

Most of all, I loved the way the sun glistened across the smooth blankets of white while I woke up on Christmas morning with my dad already waiting for me to open gifts. Him telling me how he loved wrapping presents and waiting for me to go to bed before he put them under the tree. A tradition. It seemed the older I got, the earlier he rose. Clanging the pots and pans as loud as he could to wake me.

I slumbered downstairs, thumping my head against my dad's chest and groaning that it was five in the morning.

"Humor your old man, would ya? It won't be long before my baby girl leaves me to experience college life. Won't be long after that when you are teaching kids with special needs. So proud of you sweetheart. I have to set some traditions to make you want to come back home during the holidays, don't I? Waking up to her favorite breakfast, your old man giving you the things you deserve, and seeing those happy eyes."

"Cade and I will always come home, Daddy. Besides, I'm only going to college in the city. It's not like I'm flying to bum-fuck-Idaho. And, it's going to take four years, plus student teaching. Don't age me yet."

"I love you sweet girl, but language."

"I love you too. I'll go do my choir while you make breakfast. Then we can open presents."

"Right. Maybe this time you'll beat Drew."

Rolling my eyes, zipping my jacket, and putting on my gloves, I grabbed the shovel off the porch and started shoveling the sidewalk when a familiar voice called out my name as he made his way to me from across the street. I mentally fist pumped because I did beat him out here. Drew had been beating me to shoveling the past two years; today was Christmas, he didn't need to be over here like he was every day.

I wanted to get it done before eight too. That's when Cade and his dad were due home. His mom invited Dad and me over to open gifts and enjoy the day with them. I hadn't seen my boyfriend since yesterday morning when he left to go on a ride-along with his dad. The past six months he'd been talking a lot about following in his footsteps and becoming a cop. His dark eyes lighting up whenever he talked about it. He was accepted into the academy a few weeks ago on his birthday. He went on and on about how lucky he was to receive the two gifts he wanted. His acceptance and the knife I gave him.

"Drew, you need to get in there and help your mom and Rachel. We both know the surprise your dad has for your mom, she deserves this vacation. Now go help her so she can enjoy herself for once. Besides, every time you do this, my dad finds some other chore for me to do. Like cleaning the toilets."

"They have everything in the oven. Give me the shovel, Ivy. Gorgeous girl like you doesn't need to be shoveling snow."

I giggled, scooped up a pile of snow, took a step back to toss it onto the pile, and slipped on the ice, catching myself from face planting by falling on my hands and knees.

"Shit, you okay?"

"Yes." I lie, taking hold of his hand and wince when I stand. My knees are going to be black and blue.

"Thank you."

"Welcome, that right there is another thing you shouldn't be doing."

"What, slipping on the ice?" I brush off the snow, wobble carefully to the steps to grab the bucket of salt.

"No, being on your hands and knees. You're a princess, Ivy. Make sure my brother treats you like one."

"Don't you worry about me. I'll never drop to my knees for any man unless I want to."

My body trembles with the urge to cry. It seems I always have that dream around the holiday season. It plagues me, drains me until I want to curl up and die. "You dropped to your knees against your will with the first bitch-slap to your face." Stupid,

stupid woman.

A round of laughter flies out of my mouth, followed by angry sobs I fight to hide from the pretty blonde who's been helping me the last week. The woman always looks at me like she wants to tell me everything is going to be okay. When in truth, nothing will ever be okay for me again.

Ellie. She's late this morning. The sweet young little chatterbox is always here before I wake. Her tender smile is always plastered so wide on her face I felt the jealousy trickle down my spine before I'm completely awake.

The first couple days I yelled, screamed, and fought. Told her to go find Drew and leave me the hell alone. She insisted she wasn't sleeping with him. It'd be right up his alley to pay someone to help me, then turn around and pay her to fuck him. I don't think she is though; she seems too smart to get tangled up with a man like him.

The woman loves to talk. Always carrying on about how excited she is to be finishing nursing school, wanting to follow in her father's footsteps by working in the medical field. I don't care what she's doing with her life; I've wanted to punch her in the face ever since she told me she was ordered to make sure I kept my IV in and to ask me how I was feeling down below.

I just stared at her until she got the hint I wasn't telling her how raw and uncomfortable I was between my legs.

I've all but physically attacked her, and she still walks in here like it's a privilege to take care of me. Promising me the medicine was to help me rest when I broke down in tears over it. Promising me what they were giving me was not addictive. I don't believe a word she says, but what choice do I have. All I've been doing is sleeping away the day or staring at the view outside. All of this hidden secrecy shit is driving me absolutely mad.

Last night I faked a smile, chatted with her a bit. Tried pressing her for answers as to where I was and why Drew hadn't been back to tell me what the hell was going on. She told me he was busy trying to find out who drugged me. I call bullshit. All of this is out of character for the man who has never given a shit before, nor has he slept next to me once since I've been here. Not that I really give a rat's ass. It's been a blessing not having him flip me over and slide his dick inside me to wake me up.

Today though, I'm volatile. I woke to the IV out of my arm, the restraints are gone and no one to tell me what the hell is going on.

The hot blood running through my veins has me seeing red in this room that smells of danger. Danger in a different way than I've felt before. Like it's a safe place to hide with some kind of damage to my heart on the other side of the door. Like it wants to consume my every thought. Tear open my heart and stab me a million times in the chest. Rip me wide open and expose every malicious thing that has ever happened to me.

It has me in a bewildering state of turmoil. None of what I'm feeling makes sense.

Warm air circulates throughout the room, blending in with the angry heat rolling off my skin. There's something about this place that makes me feel safe too. I don't know why, but I do. I just wish I knew why I was here and what Drew has planned. And, why here happens to be someone else's home? I know this because I've snooped. There are clothes in the dresser drawers and closet. All of them mostly black. All of them a man's, and none of them are Drew's size or smell.

They all smell like vanilla.

"What in the hell do you want from me, Drew? Why does everything smell like Cade and your dad?" An angry, pain-filled sob passes through my lips when not a sound comes from the other side of the door. "Bastard," I mutter, pulling the long silk robe Ellie gave me tighter across my stomach and struggle to breathe as I climb out of bed. The pain is severe, but I refuse to take anything more for it. I want out of here, want answers, and I'm going to get them today one way or the other.

Pausing right before my feet hit the floor, I sit back on the bed and pick up the t-shirt I took out of the drawer and press it to my nose. The smell so intoxicating I slept in the thing. Part of me wanted to give Drew a dose of his own medicine in hopes he'd come in here and find it on me. He didn't. He just left me in a room that smells like my dead boyfriend another night to crack a little more.

This is a sick and vulgar joke at the expense of me losing my goddamn mind.

Slowly making my way across the room, the mesmerizing view of the city below is a stark white of fluff that calls out to me. I'd love nothing more than to be outside walking the streets. Filling my lungs with the crisp air and my heart with jealousy as I watch families, couples, and friends smile and have a great time.

I miss Molly and Casey too. The worry she must be feeling about not being able to reach me. Knowing Drew, he's strummed up another one of his lies.

Guilt flows, it trickles nice and steady. "What if he hurt them. What if he took Molly. Oh, God. I have to know their safe."

Heart pounding like a swinging hammer against my ribs, I place my head and hands on the window. I can barely make out the cars below. "What building are we in, Drew?"

"The Diamond building. Top floor." I spin around. My hand flying to my chest. Goosebumps zigzagging down my spine when I see a strange man standing in the doorway, rubbing the back of his neck, and holding a pink bag in his hand.

"Who are you and where's Ellie?" I cross my arms over my chest, suddenly feeling underdressed in front of a man I don't know. The pounding in my chest hits my ears. My brain rattles with unanswered questions and fear. Is he going to hurt me? Did Drew finally say fuck it and hire someone to kill me? One thing is for sure, the man is huge, arms as wide as my waist. Extremely tall. Dark blonde hair that hangs pasts his shoulders, a short neatly trimmed beard and eyes the color of acorns.

He's beautiful.

"The Diamond building? Isn't that, this is owned by Roan Diamond, as in the mafia?" I think my heart just crashed to the ground below. I'm as good as dead if Drew has himself mixed up with the mob. They must be holding me hostage. I won't tell them anything because I don't know anything.

"The one and only. This building is one of the safest places for you to be, Ivy. I'm not here to hurt you. Name's Chaz. I brought you some clothes. Well, technically Ellie bought them. There's more being delivered later today. We sent Ellie home. It's time you got out of this room, don't you think? Get dressed." He smiles. Dimples and all. A handsome man like him is one of those you never see coming until they grab you by the throat and squeeze the life out of you.

Just like Drew.

He tosses the bag on the bed, turns to leave while I'm standing here with thoughts of how they'll torture me running through my head.

"We? Safest place? I don't think so. Are you part of them, the mob? Did Drew do something like not pay a debt, or is he working for you guys now?"

God, what if he sold me.

I remember several years ago when Drew and Clay were working night and day on a case. Apparently, it was the men being accused a second arrest of sex-slave trafficking. Kidnapping women and selling them to the highest bidder. The first time the charges were dropped before the trial even began. These men were some bigwigs in the mob or a gang. I can't really remember now. I remember very well when Drew came home to me watching the news. I flipped out about how dangerous it was, they could have killed him, and I wouldn't have shed a tear, but I was worried sick about my dad if Drew screwed up. As usual, I didn't have time to react before he slammed his fist in my stomach, knocking the air out of my lungs. I dropped to my knees. He fisted my hair, pulled out his dick, told me to open my mouth and mind my own business. That if he wanted me dead, I'd be dead and if he wants to sell me, he would. I never brought it up again, not even when they lost the case.

"You want answers then get dressed. The door is unlocked, come out when you're done."

Chapter Twelve
Cade

Hell wasn't for people who told white lies. It wasn't for the child who stole a pack of gum. Hell was for men like me. Like Drew. A spot already waiting for those who knew their actions were wrong and carried them out without a sliver of remorse. Repeatedly. Those of us who enjoy the ruining of others and taking the life of someone else when it wasn't yours to take. Beating on your wife, cheating, making her prance around like some goddamn stripper in your own club, and not giving a shit about her in any way, shape, or form until someone came along who did.

Living in hell doesn't always mean you're dead. Not when it takes up space in your mind. Closing it off while it spins its black magic to destroy the good. When it cracks open, the web is spun, the victim is caught, and you set your plan into action bringing them to the gates of Hell, and pulling them inside. You choose to inflict your own kind of pain, or you let their own take over their mind while you leave them with no choice but to burn inside the circle of fire you've pissed around them.

It wasn't me who brought Ivy into the circle. Both of us were drawn into the abyss by the same man. The same man who shoved us both into hell.

Since hanging up with him, I've lifted my arms out wide. Let the fire burn my skin until the flames materialized into an inferno. Drank until I passed out in front of the computer screen watching her sleep. Catching glimpses of her naked body, her lush tits, her ass, her pussy I want to claim as my own and those scars that made her life a living hell.

I want to lick, kiss, tease those scars until all she remembers when she looks at them is me. All she feels when she touches them are my lips and teeth and tongue.

A few hours ago I watched her wake. Those eyes wide with shock when she wasn't restrained. Her beautiful mind calling out for me to save her.

Rubbing my hand over my beard, I remind myself I don't give a shit if keeping her here is the right thing to do or not. It's my way of making things right for her.

I lift my head when I hear her tentative footsteps coming down the hall. Swear my black heart beats for the first time in ten years as her shadow comes into view. That beautiful heart of hers is beating so loud I can hear it. Can also hear those wheels turning in her frightened mind.

She's scared to death. Suppose I am too. Except my fear is caged in. Need it to be to make her understand, and it needs to stay locked inside my hell. Because for me there's no getting out. Not with the shit I've done.

"No. You are not Cade. No, you're not. They've, you've poisoned my mind into believing. This entire place smells like him. What the hell is going on with me? Why would you do this? Why?" That whispered last word coming off her tongue holds a lot of meaning.

I can't fucking breathe.

Can't contain the memories of the man she remembers me to be. They slaughter me. Her shock covers her skin in dark red blotches that I feel on my own. Her mouth hangs open. All I want to do is cover it with mine. I can't help but notice how tiny and vulnerable she looks. The woman was never very tall. She just had a face like an angel, a mind she used wisely, and a body made for me. My cock jerks at the sight of her.

"Goddamn you, Drew St. James. I hate you. I want you to die. How dare you pretend to be Cade."

There she is. That feisty anger, it flares like a firework shooting up into the darkened sky. She's a gorgeous vision as her tiny hands grip the back of my couch to steady her shaky frame. Her hair is a tousled mess of curls, making my fingers itch to wrap it around my wrist and devour her neck while she rides me. Her eyes are swollen, worn, worried, and filling with tears. Face free of makeup, and so beautiful she has no clue that even at the core of her despair, she sucks me straight into her orbit. Those lips I want to kiss are trembling. Her skin shines, making my fingers itch to run my calloused blood stained hands over every inch. To tell her I could give a fuck about the scars my brother has lashed across her soul, her skin. Because with Ivy, there's so much to her that I can see past them. I see into her soul that needs to be set free, and I see it's wings wanting to take the first step to fly.

She's stunning.

It's in the moment when her shock filled eyes notice my tattoos that she realizes I'm not Drew.

"Oh, my God. It is you. You're alive?"

Yeah, baby, it's me. I'm about to tell you I don't want you when I damn well do.

Not sure if she's asking or if it's a statement. Don't matter; I see the signs she realizes it's me falling off her like wilted petals.

Disbelief stares me down. Those lips quiver for all of a minute until they form a straight line and that mouth of hers fills with questions. I knew she'd be pissed and hurt. Has every right to be. When you add confusion to the mix, it makes those questions hard as fuck to answer.

She stands there moving one hand over her chest, the other on her stomach. Eyes scanning my entire face. Swear to Christ, I see her flinch when she squints enough to make out the word written across my knuckles.

My chest growls. Blistering anger is imprinting me more than my ink she scans from turbulent eyes.

She has no fucking idea how much I want to draw the lost woman buried deep inside her by covering her mouth with mine and sucking it out of her. Sweep away the years of pain I've caused her.

"You. I watched your house burn. You were in bed. You took me from the club. Got me away from that monster who broke me, but you couldn't take me back then?"

For years I couldn't stop the nightmares of seeing her screaming in the aftermath. Her fragile body shaking in her father's arms. Those years of falling into the blackness that settled into my bones, that took over and kicked my heart out of my body. Left it lying at her feet.

She was the part of what I left behind I regret the most.

"Yes. I took you from him. Someone drugged you, Ivy. Whoever it was, was going to have their way with you or God forbid, kill you. Fuck, I have answers to everything, I just don't know where to begin. Tell me you're feeling better. There's something on the sofa for you." I've never been a man at a loss for words. Don't intend to be now.

I hesitantly watch her move around to take a seat, her velvet lashes blinking, the small gasp escaping from her sensual mouth when she eyes my gun resting on the table next to me, and the tears that flow down her face as she shakily picks up the purple tulip and brings it to her nose. My mind clouds with the fact she's so close yet a million miles away.

"Wasn't sure if those were still your favorite flower or not."

I intended to kill this woman if she participated in stealing my life from me. Make her think I wanted her, fuck her and then blow her apart. That's a question I hope she never asks. Lying to her again isn't an option for me. The only thing that should be is taking away every single bit of her pain, regardless of whether it kills me.

It's a whole lot of fucked up when all I can think about is running my twitchy trigger finger over her exposed bare shoulder. Slide my hands into all that hair and hold her. Be who I used to be. Ellie did a damn fine job in picking out her clothes. Skintight workout leggings, off the shoulder gray sweatshirt.

Fuck. Me.

"They are. I just haven't seen one in years. If you're not planning on using that gun on me, then I suggest you start talking, or I'm walking out that door. I've been held captive for years, Cade. I won't let anyone hold me hostage, again. Where have you been and why are you here?"

The way she says captive and hostage pisses me off. Those words don't belong coming out of her mouth. Burns my ass thinking he kept her under his thumb.

And I'm doing the same.

"Not going to hurt you." Not in the way you think. "You aren't going anywhere. Not until I know you're safe and strong enough to take care of yourself. When I think you are, that door will be open. Until then, you're stuck here."

She blinks a few times, blocking out her tears. It feels like emotional suicide watching her pull her eyes off of me to gaze out the windows behind me, those broken wheels in her head just spinning.

"What are you going to do then, beat me with it, place more scars on my heart. Shoot me and bury my body somewhere? Isn't that what the mob does? You have no right to demand a thing from me. You're the man who let me think he was dead for ten years. Do you have any idea what I've been through? Of course, you do. You probably know everything about me, or you think you do? Goddamn you, Cade. A part of me hates you for being alive. The other wants to kill you and make sure you stay dead."

That makes two of us, sweetheart.

"Last time I'm going to tell you. I'm not going to hurt you, Ivy. The Diamonds don't have a thing to do with you and me. I happen to live in their building. That's the end of it." Fuck. I wasn't going to lie to her. That part of my life she isn't ready to hear. Don't know what's she's ready for. It fucks me right off wondering how screwed up Drew has her. Is she timid, afraid to be touched?

Her attention darts to the tattoos on my forearms, her brows furrow, breath catching before she diverts down to her flower, kicks her head back up and she takes in the room. It's as black as my bedroom. Not a splash of color. Color left my world right along with the man I used to be.

"You didn't answer me, Ivy. Are you feeling okay?"

"I don't know how to answer you, Cade. God, saying your name, seeing how much you've changed, yet haven't. It has me numb from the inside out. Right now, I'm coming to grips with the most shocking, truthful realism in my life. I take that back. I don't know what's more shocking. The first time I found out what kind of a monster your brother is or the fact you didn't love me enough to take me with you."

I did love you. Still do. Always will.

Her face crumples like a bulldozed structure crumbling to dust, sturdy one moment, a pile of ash and rubble the next. She's hurting, and I haven't even begun to tell her everything.

I'll sit here and take her wrath, but when she's done, that's the end of it. She's going to sit there and hear my side of the story, or I'll strap her down myself. I have to believe the woman is a hell of a lot stronger than what she should be.

"I'm sorry about giving you drugs. The doctor I had look you over said you needed them. I wasn't going to watch you hurt, Ivy. No matter what. From now on if you want something to cure your pain; then you're looking at him. I mean all of your pain. Every last bit. And I don't know everything about you. If I did, I would have taken you the minute I found out what Drew was doing to you. What I do know is the night I saw you at the club, you were hurting. Didn't quite know how much until I saw what he'd done. How long has it been going on?"

She swallows. It's her turn to hold me prisoner. When her pain and humiliation become visible, it's all I see. "You're beautiful. Every part of you is Ivy. So damn strong you're swimming in strength."

"Strength? You want to talk about strength. I haven't any. I'm wiped out. Dead on the inside. He's done..." she pauses, wipes away tears and closes her eyes. Fuck me; I'm not sure I have the strength to hear this again. "It started shortly after we were married. I'm not going to tell you everything he's done. I'm sure you saw the bruises, my scars. Let's just say I could go the rest of my life without having a man touch me."

She's lying. I'd bet if I touched her right now, she'd melt into me the same way I would her.

This woman deserves to have a man's touch. My touch. My hands should be caressing every exotic curvy inch. Her body is like a worship temple. But that's not what this is about. It's about a strong woman standing tall against a man who did all he could to destroy her.

"Now you know. So the hell what. Everything you're saying is a crock of shit. If I was strong, I wouldn't have let him touch me. I wouldn't have fallen for his charm. Him telling me you'd be happy that he was the one taking care of me. I don't want you to help me with my pain. I don't want anything except to be free from both of you. I want to disappear and never be found."

Shit, her wanting to be free of me stings when it shouldn't. Wish I had the strength not to care, but I do, and that's a big goddamn problem. "I do want you happy. I always have."

"Really? Then why did you leave me behind? What do you

want from me, Cade? I walk out here expecting to see members of the mob or my husband only to find the man I've never stopped loving, the man I thought I lost sitting here in a room that smells like vanilla and danger. I want to know why you told me you were protecting me? I want to know why you pretended to be Drew? Do you know who drugged me, because I remember nothing past walking in BURN and seeing my friend."

All I want is you.

After all this time she still loves me. I knew she did. Dear God, I need to get the hell out of here before I do something neither one of us are ready for.

Probably a good thing she doesn't remember the club too.

"Told you I took you to protect you from him and whoever drugged you. I happened to be at the club that night. Damn good thing I was. I don't know who gave it to you yet. I'm working on it. Fairly certain it was in your water. There's a reason I left without telling you, Ivy. Give me a minute and I'll tell you. As far as your friend goes, she seems to be fine. I have a feeling Drew beat me to her. Otherwise, I've no doubt your face would already be plastered all over the television." Either that or, this Casey is the one who drugged Ivy.

"Give you a minute? I've given you years. Drew, he probably told her to keep her mouth shut. He'll hurt them, I know he will. Are you sure she's alright?" I grit my teeth as I sit here and listen to her choking down her sobs telling me about how Drew held her dad's health over her head, then flipping to her friend and kid.

I can't comprehend what life must have been like for her. All this time worrying about her dad, going home to a man who drained her dry.

"She's fine, Ivy. Working, taking her daughter to school. She's not hurt."

For a second, while she studies me. I hold my breath wondering if she's going to push the issue on why I left her. She's not, at least not at the moment. She's working around making sure I'm telling the truth.

"You had no intentions of coming back for me, did you? How long have you known about Drew and me? Did you hear from some source, some spy the despicable things he did? Is that why you came back. Guilt sparked a little inside of you. Such bullshit that you want to take it away because it's your fault I have it in the first place."

Fuck, ever since I hung up with him, I've tried not to let my mind go there. Kind of hard when it's left bloodstained ink on your soul.

The pain in her voice pierces me instead of bringing calm to my raging storm. Her chest rises and falls. I have a feeling she's only beginning to lash out. After all, she probably couldn't speak up to defend herself. If she did, she knew what would happen. I saw that in the way she stiffened the few times she slipped up while she thought I was Drew.

I sit there like the betrayer I am. She has never been more wrong and right than now.

"I gave up on saving myself. I had two weeks, two weeks to grieve after my dad died before Drew got his hands on me again. The man I married put my body and heart through a shredder, ripped it to pieces and destroyed me. He has beaten and taken me by force more times than I can count. I'm full of pain, Cade. How in the hell do you think you can erase the last ten years of my miserable life?"

Jesus motherfucking Christ. I can't sit here and listen to what he did much longer. I need to get gone. Lock my mind down over the misery he put her through.

"Your dad was a good man, Ivy. What you did shows how strong you are. Now, if you'll let me talk, I can answer the rest of your questions. The night of the fire, I tried to save my family. The flames were too strong. I jumped out the window. Couldn't think of anything except my whole family was burning inside the one place they should have been safe." My blood runs cold as I sit here and rehash the worst night of my life.

Her sobs rip me in half while the creases of agony on her face about do me in. I recognize the moment the truth of what I can't say pushes its way into her mind, choking the space between us with a vile of ugly vengeance.

Reaching for my pipe, I light it, take a drag to calm me down before I tell her more. The last thing I want to do is hurt her more than she's already been hurt. Ivy doesn't deserve the shit my brother has done to her. Fuck, neither do I. She's owed the truth whether it makes her hate me or not.

"Drew set the house on fire. He planned it out. He wasn't alone in his planning, Ivy. Clay and a few others were in on it. I left, roamed around for a few days and enlisted in the army. I sealed my life in revenge. I killed Clay. I'm going to kill the rest, and find out who drugged you and then set you free. But Ivy, there's something you should know. I would have killed you if you had been involved."

I promised I wouldn't hurt her.

The look on her face proves me a certifiable liar.

Chapter Thirteen
Ivy

Shock. Surprise. A good old punch in the heart confines me where I sit. The dangerous man in front of me is real. Him being alive has my mind twisting around my skull. It wants to combust into a million pieces, the same way my heart does.

It's *him*. The him who isn't the same. The him who looks at me like he wants to devour me, yet he's made it perfectly clear he doesn't. The him who wants to hold me prisoner to keep me safe, or so he says.

The power of Cade's presence cast a shadow of anger on everything around him. The rolled up sleeves of his black button up expose arms full of tattoos. Not just any either. Poison ivy and tulips.

I run the pad of my fingers up and down the silky pedal of my favorite flower. Drew would never put tulips in our yard. Everything had to be neat, red and trimmed.

Perfection.

These stunning flowers bring back happy thoughts. I first fell in love with them as a little girl. Dad and I drove to a town in Michigan where they had this big tulip festival. Every color imaginable lined the streets. He bought me one from a street vendor. It was purple. They've been my favorite since.

I feel as if I've been rutted up in a tornado that has me wishing it would drop me down on my head. It won't stop spinning.

As my world flips in violent directions I'm not sure I want to follow, I stare the man down. Dark hair, tattered jeans, black boots. A clean-cut beard across his clean-cut jaw, and perfect lips that I've missed the taste of. He really is dangerously handsome. So much so that parts of me come alive that haven't in years.

It explains the scent. The way I clung to that shirt as if it were saving me.

His eyes turn hard and unforgiving as they drill holes in my head. Nothing about the way he looks at me now is the same. Not a trace of the man he used to be is staring back at me. He's closed himself off. Obliterated the nice guy and in front of me is the man he wants people to see.

A monster.

But the monster, nor the man hiding behind him can hide from the sexual tension darting back and forth between us. Raw, sexual power in a carnal way. It has me clenching my legs together. Arousal making my panties wet.

It makes me want to follow it around the room like a bitch in heat.

An ache in my core which lifts a purr from my stomach. Dangling to release from my throat.

It's thick. It's heavy. It's frightening. It's also something I'm going to ignore.

It's black sexual energy.

A part of me wants to drop into that oblivion again. The one where I see and feel and hear nothing. Demand he gives me more medication and let it take me away. And the other part, the one beating hard in my chest. Begs to stay alert so I can watch his chest rise and fall.

He's alive.

And, just like his deranged brother, he's played me for a fool.

"I'm sorry. I didn't know. If I did, I would never have gotten involved with him. I would have turned him into the police. I would have fought with everything I had to make them pay."

I feel utterly sick. Dirtier than I've felt in my life.

"Know that, Ivy. I can't let them get away with it. They took innocent people lives. My family's lives. My own fucking brother did that shit, and to this day, I don't even know why." The rage in his voice and on his face over what Drew did should frighten me. It doesn't. It makes me angry at myself.

I knew Drew was a horrible man.

Abuser.

Rapist.

But a murderer?

God.

"I'm so sorry."

"I know."

Oh, no. He is not going to hide from me. This man owes me more than just a damn `I know.`

"That's all you have to say is 'I know?' You have tattoos of poison ivy on your arms, Cade. Why?" I shouldn't be angry, shouldn't be raising my voice when he just spilled his agony all over the place. He may have answered some of my questions, but I have plenty more. Ones he better answer truthfully, or I'm going to rip years worth of tape off my mouth and speak my mind whether he stomps on the breaking pieces of my heart and crunches them beyond repair or not.

"What else do you want me to tell you, the gruesome details about them dying? How my heart turned pitch black? How the idea of you being with my brother made me go insane? The tattoos are a reminder that you belong to someone else when you should belong to me."

He has no idea how untrue that is. I've always belonged to him. Even from his grave.

"I don't want details. It was bad enough talking to the police when they asked me about suspects. I can't believe the murderer stood next to me and my dad the entire time."

A sharp pang of sorrow hits me in the gut. Drew. Every damn thing comes back to him. "Do you really believe I'm innocent, Cade, or am I a ploy to get back at Drew and once you have what you want, you're going to kill me?" It wasn't but weeks, days, even hours ago I would have welcomed death. Now I don't know what I want. Except, to kill Drew for every bit of pain he caused.

Damage him.

Destroy him.

Death.

"I don't blame you. I blame me. I blame him. When I heard about you and Drew, I was at war busting my ass for this country, plotting my revenge while making sure I kept my own ass alive so when I got out, I could put my plan in motion. Didn't know what to think at first. I felt betrayed the same as you do now. Once it sunk in, I did everything I could to convince myself you were a part of it. I marked myself because I wanted to reach out to you many times. These reminded me you weren't mine anymore. You were his. Over the years, I had you followed, took pictures, studied your face, but I could never get close enough to look in your eyes. The night I took you was when I knew you were innocent."

I'm not quite sure what to say. I know I'm a lot stronger than I give myself credit for. Otherwise, I'd let loose and cry. I've let weakness lead me long enough. I don't know how I'll ever get over the unmentionable things Drew has done.

"I married him. There's nothing I can do to change that. I needed him. I thought he needed me too. How wrong I was. I'd do it again for one more day with my dad."

His eyes pinch closed. When they re-open, they are clouded with so much pain that makes me want to rush across the room and hold him.

Years planning his vengeance has detached parts of him from his body, and what a body he has. He's all those dreams I've had about him come to life. I want to lick him everywhere and come back for seconds.

Of course, I'm not the same either. Perhaps that makes us one in the same. Pretending when deep down you are dying slowly every single day. Both of us begging to be set free. That's not the case with him though. He's sealed his freedom tight.

Seeing him through his eyes makes my heart hurt. He's gone all this time living with the pain of being betrayed by his flesh and blood in a way I can't begin to comprehend.

My heart aches to see him broken beyond repair. I miss the young boy in him, his laugh, his love, his touch. Cade St. James will never be that young boy again. The man sitting before me, smoking a pipe similar to the one his father used is a man full of hate.

"I can't believe I thought about killing you." That makes two of us.

Vicious tremors agitate my muscles. I can tell he means it by the way he's shut down those eyes of his that minutes ago couldn't believe I was sitting across from him. He restrained me. Knocked me out. Had a doctor look me over. Sent in Ellie. And none of it was to hurt me. It was to heal me. He took me to protect me from God knows who and the thought he could have taken what was left of my heart and stop it from beating furies me to the point I want to curl into a ball and cry.

Grief spills from my pried open veins, bleeding out guilt, and shame. It drowns me in revulsion. Seconds pass before I breathe in air. My heaving sickly breaths rush out and choke me. I gag. Bile rises, only to be pushed back down when I scream and cry for the deaths of people I cared about, the last ten years Cade has suffered. Everything he's told me and for my father. A lot of that blood money went to keep him alive. I feel dirty and used more than any time Drew has touched me.

Our gazes lock and load emotions running wild inside of me while his features show absolutely nothing. The man I used to know would never have let me sit here and cry.

I hate Drew for turning Cade into this man. I want him to die. I want them all to die for changing a beautiful soul into one I don't recognize.

There are many questions still left unanswered. I open my mouth, close it again, wipe my tears, The smell of vanilla, his hardened glare. Everything suddenly has my ears popping. My brain is firing off like a malfunctioned firework in a deadly direction.

I want answers. I want him to hold me, to touch his skin, feel his lips, smell him.

I want everything I was supposed to have.

"What do you want to know, Ivy. I'll tell you anything. Do anything to make you feel safe, to get you back to the woman you were. Except I won't give you the one thing I see in your eyes."

He won't give me *him*.

"Why?"

Harsh eyes meet mine. Ruthlessness and regret and things I don't even want to try to pick apart fire from his eyes.

"My life is dedicated to vengeance. There's no room for you, Ivy."

Disorder and anger ricochet off the walls, rippling more confusion through my veins. All of this causes shivers to roll across my aching flesh.

Gone is the man full of desire for me. All that remains is a hollow soul. The marks of his past leaving no room to see his true self anymore. But I do. I see him in the way his finger twitches. A habit he developed when he wanted something. Never settling until he got it. I don't have to wonder what it is he wants now.

He wants *me.*

He's pretending not to care. He was doing a damn fine job of it until he exposed his finger.

"How long were you in the military?"

There wasn't a day gone by I didn't miss him. My dreams featured him, and my nightmares filled with his brother. I'd agonized over what it would be like to be touched by his fingers that caressed instead of marked. My body revisited his time and time again whether it bled me raw all over again or not.

"Eight years. Those years taught me how to kill without looking back. Going in a shattered man, coming out with an impenetrable shell. I don't have a heart to give anymore. These hands are stained with things I've done that I can't erase. I have no shame in my head for any of it. You though, I won't tarnish you with my past. I can't touch you the way I used to. But I can teach you how to defend yourself if anyone puts theirs on you in a way you don't want. That's all I can give you Ivy. I can give you your freedom to do whatever you want. You just won't be doing it with me."

He should have just slapped me instead of blankly tossing the last part in my face.

His dark eyes snare mine. So dark I feel like I'm looking at an endless midnight sky. His body projects forceful power. One hand clenching the arm of the chair, the other curled around a pipe.

His strong jaw ticks as I study him. Masculine, strong and defined, his features molded from granite.

My lips tingle, remembering the way he used to kiss me. Tender at first, hands cupping my face. A tease before it turned fiery, erotic, and demanding.

"Don't let your mind go there, Ivy. That boy you fell for is gone. I don't kiss, don't touch, don't fuck the way I used too. He died that night and in his place became a man out for vengeance. I kill people, Ivy. That's who you'll find if you look hard enough."

This time, I feel the hard slap from his words. They strike me between my breasts.

How could I forget? Cade killed Clay. He's the one who chained him up and lit him on fire.

"What do you mean by kill people? Have you murdered more people besides Clay?"

His chest rises and falls. I risk a glance at his fingers on the chair. The index one is twitching badly. Seeing it move turns my insides to frost and with it comes a heavy freezing drip of just how dangerous he is.

"It means I was a sniper. It means I killed people who dared take away something that didn't belong to them. Diamond Gym, I'm partial owner of it. I'll take you there at night after it closes. I'll show you how to use those muscles you've been working on. I'll take you to a friend's gun range and teach you how to shoot. Don't ask for anything more from me. I need to leave. Chaz will be here if you need anything. You're still not healed. Go back to bed, Ivy."

The anger I'd kept hidden for years empties from where I'd left it. I want to lash out and kick his ass because he's hiding more from me. So much more.

"No. You're not just going to leave me here with a stranger. You might be keeping me safe, but you will not come back into my life after leaving and making me believe you were dead and then locking me away in a room. I deserve better than this. How dare you do this to me. You selfish son of a bitch. I loved you. I loved you so much I wanted to die along with you. You hurt me. Damn you. You hurt me!"

"I told you my reason. Deal with it, Ivy. No one tells me what to do. Especially the wife of my brother."

I never realized how bad it hurt being Drew's wife until he just threw it in my face.

I hurt everywhere. My heart, soul, mind, body. All of me cries out in the deepest kind of agony.

I remain where I am as he picks up a bag, walks by me and slams the door, leaving me on his couch.

In his home.

Without him.

His smell suffocates me while I brace to ride out the violent blizzard inside of me that whipped up out of nowhere.

Chapter Fourteen
Cade

"Hey, you Sam? I'm Nick. Like I said on the phone, my buddy and I are looking to do some hunting. He's just finishing up a few things in the truck."

"Well, you've come to the right place then."

We sure have, you rotten scumbag.

My hands curl into fists, my twitchy finger half tempting to pull the trigger.

"Ain't that the truth. We've been planning this trip for quite a while." Nick speaks to the man, though his eyes remain on me, no doubt checking to make sure my mind is where it should be one more time. I've made it clear at least five times in the past twenty-four hours that I am.

I'll be even better once we get this done.

Be ten times better if Nick can find out who drugged Ivy.

I left my place the other day and went to Nick's. Told myself if I couldn't do what I wanted to Ivy, I'd help him gather suspects. Helping distract my mind, it didn't do a damn thing for my craving.

I wanted to touch Ivy.

I wanted to kiss her.

I wanted to fuck her.

I craved to get close to those widened eyes of hers that trailed over every inch of me.

I craved to shake the way her face turned from shock to rage when I told her she wasn't going anywhere until I said. The way her spine straightened. The way she mouthed off.

I craved everything about her.

It's all fucked me up.

I had to put an end to those thoughts, so I turned into an asshole. Filled her head with lies in hopes she'd quit analyzing me, quit trying to dig under my skin in search of the man she remembered me to be.

As I pointed out to her, she doesn't belong to me anymore. Still, I felt what was meant to frighten her backfire in my face when her breath caught; her lips parted shadowed by a chaotic mix of revulsion, disgust, and desire.

It made me hate myself more. I had to get out of there before I fucked shit up and asked her to forgive me for being an asshole. Get down on my knees and tell her we might have been apart for a long time, but my goddamn coal black heart needs her light to set me free.

Or, worse yet, tell her that I not only killed Clay, that I've killed over two dozen people in the past two years while they slept. I've killed fathers, brothers, sons. If I had a conscience, then I'd give a fuck about killing people. But I don't. Besides, all of them deserve to die. Same way my brother does. All I care about is freeing her, making her see she's isn't as weak as what he tried to make her. Given time, she'll see it on her own. I wanted to lay everything about my life at her feet and leave her with the decision to pick it up and hold onto it in her hands. Wrap it tight and never let me go.

Just watching her rest and heal she got under my skin a little farther. So I bolted, left her in Ellie and Chaz's care.

"This trip? When you called, I thought you wanted a tour of the place. We're booked for the remainder of deer season."

Sam Fredrick. Victim number two in my need for vengeance, prideful tone brings me back to what I should be focusing on. He took his portion of the money and invested in acres of vacant land he bought at auction. Over the years he's bought more and turned it into one of the largest Hunt Clubs in the states. Scoundrel makes a mint off it. Two grand per person, per day. Another hundred a day for food and lodging. Deer, elk, duck, geese. The majority of wildlife can be hunted in his fancy fenced in land.

He leans back on his worn cowboy boots, takes a sharp look at Nick's bow slung over his shoulder, and the arrows he holds in hand. Two is all I need to kill this maggot. The rest is to play with him a bit before I put one right through each of his eyes.

Not sure if he's the one who was watching for Ivy the night my family died. My gut tells me he was. Over the years my gut told me if she would have tried sneaking over, she wouldn't have made it past the porch before he did the same thing to her that

Clay did to Rachel. The creep was always looking at her. Always making comments about how lucky I was. Told me once if she ever dumped me he'd be more than willing to tap her ass. That caught him a right hook to his jaw. Didn't care much for him after that.

"Well fuck, I thought my friend booked it. You sure we can't pay for one day? I'm in the mood to do some chasing. Will sort this out as soon as my friend gets out here. In the meantime, do you ever wonder what's going through the prey's mind when they think they're about to die? Imagine you're just standing around waiting for someone to show up, then out of nowhere someone starts chasing you. Your first instinct is to run, right? You run as fast as you can, but your predator is faster. He finally catches you, he either toys with you a little bit. Taunting and teasing before he stabs you repeatedly. Or shoots you in the head or breaks your spine. Kind of creepy, right? I don't know, guess I always wondered about that." I chuckle. Chaz sure has a way with words.

"Uh, no never thought about that and sorry, man, I can show you around. Get you booked for next year if it's deer you're looking to hunt." Sam tilts his head, brows creasing as he places his hands on his silver belt buckle, and peers up at Nick from under his brown faded cowboy hat.

Idiot is trying to intimidate. Makes this hunter all the hungrier.

We drove the eleven-hour hike down to the hills of Gatlinburg, Tennessee. Stayed in a shitty motel several hours from here last night, then drove to where we hid my truck, grabbed the stolen one Chaz set up for us and hauled ass to meet this stupid fuck whose about to become our prey.

With the word die mixed in with that bullshit the dumb fuck didn't catch onto, I grab my rifle, push open the passenger door, sling it over my shoulder and stalk up the drive. I watch Sam's eyes shift to mine; they flutter shut, his arms falling to his sides. "Fuck, fuck. Goddamnit. Jesus."

"Yeah, shit. That's what you're going to be doing in about five seconds. Grab his phone and keys, Nick. We don't need him making a phone call or using his keys to slip through a gate. Get to running, Sam, or I'll burn this place down. If I do, there won't be anything left for your wife and sons. I'm giving you a minute head start, motherfucker. That's more than you gave my family."

"You know, I wondered why your brother acted like he had no idea who would torture Clay. I never expected it to be you. Drew did though, didn't he? We all went our separate ways after that night. All promised to get the fuck gone. Except him and Clay. Drew wanted to stay for Ivy. He was always obsessing over that girl, and well, we all know Clay loved city pussy. It isn't going to do me any good to beg, is it? Probably shouldn't even run. Difference between you and me, I know this land like the back of my hand."

He needs to shut his fucking mouth. I need his blood draining out of him to cleanse another piece of my soul.

His face breaks into a frenzied grin.

I feel a little more of my insanity crawl under my skin. Slithering, coiling tight like a snake ready to strike.

"Not here to talk about why my brother didn't share I was alive. Think he already shared enough with you." I refuse to let him get to me with his instigating about Rachel and Ivy.

Whipping my handgun out, I pull the trigger, the bullets landing next to his feet. He's not so intimidating now as he dances the goddamn jig.

Bastard takes off running. Gravel and dust trailing behind him.

"Whose idea was it to chase this asshole?" Nick asks about an hour later, his question failing to draw my attention from the deer stand where I saw movement a second ago through my scope.

Both of us are drenched in sweat from running through the woods. Woods we've studied. We might not know it as well as Sam, but we know where every deer blind is, every restroom, every trail. Every gate in and out of this place.

"Sure as shit wasn't going to catch fire to this land. He'll be dead that's all I care about." Placing my scope in the side pocket of my camo's, I turn to see his lips forming a smile. If the man hadn't saved my ass a time or two in the desert, I'd blow that smile off his face. "Don't start your smartass shit again about me having a conscience. Ivy's an entirely different story than burning thousands of acres of land and killing all these animals."

Don't matter to me if these animals are free to roam or not. They are still trapped. Still sitting ducks for people to hunt down. I shake my head. Here I'm worried about animals when I'm holding a woman hostage in my apartment. That's all kinds of fucked up.

"Not starting anything, Cade. I'm stating a fact. You pretend like you don't care about her when you do. Claim you want to make her stronger, then when she puts you on the spot, you leave. Shit's bad enough we had to change up and leave Chaz behind to keep an eye on her. This revenge can wait. She can't."

Revulsion reels through me.

"I've got plenty of time to deal with her. Let's get this done." What happens between Ivy and me isn't anyone's business.

"Sam," I yell with a deep southern drawl built up from the hatred I have for him sifting through my throat. "You up there shitting yourself yet? You scared?" I taunt while slipping on a pair of gloves. "It's been a long time since I've hunted in the light of day. You didn't make it easy on me Sam."

Of course, he doesn't answer me. The man is probably gasping for air. "You should be. Think it's only fair for me to kill you on the land my parents paid for, don't you? With all the hunts you've been on, I'm sure you know how this goes down. It seems we have it backward though. I should be sitting up there, and you should be down here."

Pushing myself up, I take the arrows from Nick, make my way out of the weeds and stand at the bottom of the ladder leading to the stand. "Gotta say even these deer stands are nice. You did well for yourself with the blood money, Sam. To bad your fortune has come to an end. From what I understand, neither one of your boys are into hunting. I might have to pay your wife a visit after she's done grieving. Or, maybe I'll change my mind and burn it down. Either way, your wife is going to be a rich single woman. She's going to become some sick fucker's prey. She's beautiful, Sam. Might have to get to know her so I can tap her ass." I have no intentions on paying her a visit. Lucky for her she thinks he inherited the land from his dead parents. If she's smart, she'll sell it and let her kids do what they want.

Leaving Nick to stand guard, I pull out my knife in case the sneaky shit is quicker when he's cornered than he was while being chased. Dude is definitely out of shape.

I lift my boot on the first step, taking two at a time until I reach the platform landing me at the open door of the blind. I wasn't kidding when I said these things are fancy. All of them look like tiny log cabins. Each one has a bathroom with a shitter, sink, and two twin beds.

"You're cowering in the corner? Is that what you did when you were watching for Ivy?" I toss my head back and laugh. He's tucked up in a ball. Pussy is shaking like a leaf.

"Just shoot me, alright. Get it over with. Just leave my family alone."

"You aren't in a position to demand anything from me. Just know you'll be dying not knowing whether I fucked your wife or not. You didn't leave my family alone. Why should I leave yours? Stand up Sam. Now!"

I want him to bleed the fuck out through his eye sockets, feel the pressure in his blood flow bursting his eardrums from beating so goddamn hard in his ears that his brain explodes.

What's left of the color on his face drains away like a poof of smoke when I fling my knife through the air, and it lands within an inch of his dick.

"I'll show your family the same mercy you gave mine. None." I pull out an arrow, set it in place, position my bow and draw it back. An arrow landing within a half inch from the top of his head. I repeat until I have at least a dozen arrows around his head. His body locking up more with each one, his mouth pissing out drool while a pool of urine saturates the floor under his ass.

He's a quivering mess. A pile of wasted air who won't get up off the floor.

"Please stop. Killing all of us isn't going to bring your family back. I'm s...sorry, Cade. So fucking sorry. Been praying for forgiveness ever since I met my wife," he sputters through his Tennessee twang.

"No it isn't, but it gives me the vengeance I need, Sam. I'm going to make damn sure there isn't a part of your body that doesn't feel pain so deep you'll wish you never agreed to help. I find it ironic you would speak about family considering mine thought of you as theirs, you filthy cockroach," I roar. My hands begin to shake uncontrollably, and before I realize what I'm doing, I've dropped my bow and cut the distance between us. My hands circling the base of his throat. I watch him intensely as I squeeze. His perfect life he thinks he had flashed before my very eyes. "It's also funny how my brother never told you he knew I was alive. Some fucking friend huh? But hey, no big deal to you since you ran off with a million dollars." Christ, I could easily crush his Adam's apple the way it's bobbing up and down; those nerves of his closing in behind it have to make his throat burn.

"Gotta be going now Sam. Need to check out how sweet Raeanne's ass is. Might take pity on her being a widow and take her for a ride on my cock."

I release him. He coughs and sputters. Swear to Christ I can smell his shit blending in with his piss.

"You're going to rot in hell," he mumbles.

"I'm sure I am. Be seeing you down there too." I pick up my knife, slice through his femoral artery as his scream rings in my ears. He'll be dead in less than a few minutes, but not before I nail his head to the wall.

I take several steps back until I hit the open doorway. Pick up my bow, grab an arrow and shoot. It lands right in the middle of his steel blue iris. Nailing his head to the wooden beam. His screaming growing loud enough to chase away a flock of chirping birds. Lifting the last arrow, I do the same to the other eye. Tears of blood drip from his eyes.

The dead man took his last breath ten seconds later. I left with the smell of his shit lingering in the air.

Chapter Fifteen
Drew

The first time I struck my wife, I startled her.

Her face crumbled. Sturdy and strong in one moment, a ruined weeping petal in the next. As angry as I was, as much as I loved her, as many times as I struck her, and took everything I could without asking, there was always a pang of sorrow somewhere in my chest. I despised myself for hurting her. For not taking care of her as she deserved, but it didn't stop me from trying to break the stubborn stem on her that refused to snap in half until she could no longer sprout those gorgeous petals.

They returned every damn time.

As time went on, I didn't care how much she was hurting over the deteriorating health of her father. I didn't care how hard I'd pulled on the rope I had around her neck. It forced her to drop to her knees, straighten her spine, and pull back her shoulders. It required her to light her stunning face with a smile that to everyone else appeared real. But to me, it meant I held power. It meant I trained her to do what I told her. I didn't care about anything except to ruin her the same way she ruined me when she fell for my brother instead of me.

In the beginning, there were times she dared to cross me and I let her. I drew the line when she refused to spread her legs like a good little girl. I had to show her who owned her. Who made the choices in our relationship. It sure the fuck wasn't her. Mostly, my violent streaks came when I'd see her drifting off into space, thinking about someone she shouldn't have.

The tenth, the hundredth, and so on, time I beat her down she regained her footing. This last time though, she didn't. I had finally pushed her over the edge. The edge she had been clinging to for years.

And now, right when I thought I had her where I wanted, someone else besides Cade wants to take her from me. Whoever drugged her wants to kill her. I can feel it in my bones. On top of trying to find where Cade has her, I've been on the hunt trying to find out who dared try and hurt my wife. I'm the only one who can hurt her. She's mine to do what I damn well please.

I knew she was off the minute she stood to dance at BURN. I stood like a statue, clenching my drink in my hand while watching her. At first, I thought maybe she stumbled because she was in pain. The pain I caused. The pain I relished in while watching her lay in bed moaning how much she hated me in one breath, and how she wished my brother were alive in the next. But nope. She was high. Out of her head and doing shit she knew not to be doing.

I'm empty handed on who would come after a woman who hasn't hurt anyone but me in her life. I've made sure her circle was small. I've made sure no man comes near her. No woman except Casey and there isn't a chance she slipped Ivy something.

"Where the hell is my wife, Cade? I want to tear your eyes out for looking at her in my club. I want to rip your tongue out at how arrogant you sounded on the phone. I'm more than angry at you. I'm livid. I'm enraged."

A goddamn beast.

Ivy would have never had to claw her way through life if she would have forgotten about a man she had no clue was still alive. No, she could have had it all. Could have celebrated my victory of finally ruling a kingdom of my own. Of finally being something other than the outcast of a family who in spite of them loving me, I didn't feel a part of. To this day I've never quite understood why. I mean, my parents were good people. Encouragers. They always treated us the same. They did for one; they did for the rest. Still, I didn't feel equal.

Maybe I wanted to kill them because I wanted more than what we had. Maybe it was the way my mother always doted on my sister. Praising her innocence and telling her to never give up on her dreams. Maybe it was because my brother became the shadow of our father. The one who was so much like him it made me sick. I wonder how it makes him feel knowing he isn't like him now.

I wanted Ivy too. So goddamn much it destroyed every brain cell I had. Whenever she was near me, my cock grew with a ferocity that begged to fuck her. It begged until I became possessed to watch her while my brother buried himself inside of her. I watched the two of them fuck with my dick in my hands. I watched the way her face glowed when she came. I wanted what was mine, and no matter what I had to do, I was going to have her.

Every time I saw them together I wanted to take her sweet smelling flowery form in my hands and crush her until she couldn't stand. I wanted her to pay for choosing him over me. I craved to wipe her friendly smile she sent my way off her gorgeous face. And gorgeous she was. The woman with a backbone as strong as indestructible steel, still is.

A plan to get Ivy dropped in my lap. One I started formulating thanks to my father always sharing his stories with us. There was one particular story that ruled my mind. I perfected it. At least I thought I did until the one mistake that's still alive surfaced and stole my wife.

The plan I ended up hatching wasn't one I thought of. I copycatted a killer. As obsessed as I was with Ivy, it was the one I knew I would take and twist to my advantage. The mere idea of millions of dollars was an added bonus if Ivy became mine. I wanted it all, so I decided to kill my entire family. It was the easiest thing I've ever done.

"Even our parents and Rachel's blood is on your hands, Cade. Not mine. You forced my hands by taking something I wanted. Something I craved. The only blood on mine is Ivy's, and that's your fault too."

God, the sight of her face when she would get on her knees made me go crazy with the need to hurt her, watch her beg me with those eyes just to stop. I couldn't. She deserved to pay for loving him. Deserved to bleed on the inside.

She belongs to me. She should have always belonged to me and not him. It was never about how I saw her first, and he stole her from me. But the truth is, he did.

From the first moment I saw her, I was obsessed. She became a desperate infatuation I had to have. And now, she's in his hands.

I killed my family for her. A family I never think about and now here I am on a plane traveling to help an innocent woman and her two sons bury a man who gained as much money from those murders as I did.

The only time I think about my family or what I did is when Rachel's ghost decides it's time to taunt me. Bitch better stay out of my head from here on out.

I rarely spoke to Sam anymore. The man changed when he met Raeanne. Not that I can blame him for wanting to make sure she never found out. I didn't blame him at all. I envied him. That woman doted on him the way a wife should her husband.

I forgot all about my family until Clay was murdered. All except Cade. I buried them with no remorse.

I held Ivy's hand through the funeral. Felt her tits pressing against my chest when she cried. Her pussy pressing against my dick. It was damn hard trying to tame a raging hard-on while she stood there and bawled her eyes out.

I tamped it down. Held in my victory of becoming rich, for her. I had to pretend to grieve. It was the one way I could remain close to her. Pretending how heartbroken I was, how awful my life was going to be without any family around. I cried in her arms while telling her she was all I had left of my baby brother when in reality, I left my grief deep in the ground with what was left of the dead bodies.

"Wonder what you'll think when he tells you I killed them? Wonder what you'll think when you find out he isn't any better than me? Will he harden you up for me to have to train you all over again, or will the years of me beating and fucking you into submission have worked? Doesn't matter, I'm going to get you back."

I've done everything for her, and it wasn't enough for her to forget about him.

"Can I get you another whiskey, Mr. St. James?" I snap my head up to the flight attendant staring down at me. Her eyes don't match her question. She wants a repeat performance.

My kind of woman. One eager to please.

The last couple of times I've flown in the company jet, she was all over my dick. I had her several times right here in this chair. Now, the idea of fucking someone who isn't Ivy is the farthest thing from my mind.

Pity too because pussy is constantly up in my face. Kind of hard for a man to deny it when it's easy to take.

For one brief moment, my stomach flips. Ivy and her mouth the night she decided to fight back. I couldn't have cared less that she kicked and slapped me. What had me lose control worse than I ever have was the way she threw my words back in my face about me not having anyone who loved me.

The truth hurt, therefore, I had to hurt her back. No one speaks to me that way and gets away with it. But then she shocked the shit out of me when a week later she was up in the shower getting ready for the club.

The club. My sanctuary. The one place I enjoy watching her be the woman she used to be, the one place my brother took her from.

"No thanks, will be landing soon." I bow my head, dismissing her. When she's out of sight and earshot, I unhook my seat belt, lean down and pull the file I've kept with me everywhere I've gone in the past ten years out of my briefcase.

"I knew you'd come back for her. Your so-called gift will never escape me, Cade. You surprise me though. I didn't think you had it in you to become a monster like me. But, you are? You were right about the military training you. You're good. You have something that belongs to me, and I want it back." He's days past the twenty-four hours I gave him. I knew as well as he did, he wouldn't return her. The only way I'm going to get her back is to kill him. And, that is something I've been looking forward to since the day my father's attorney told me Cade was alive.

I flip open the file.

"Damn, I'd almost forgotten how much you look like me. You sound like me too. It's too damn bad you aren't me. I've had ten years worth of fucking your gift. I'm sorry, she isn't polished and clean." I flip through the dozen or so pictures of him in his army fatigues. His fake death certificate. All of the heroic bullshit I had to bribe a judge for. A half million bucks to find out his whereabouts. Everything I could find on him for the first eight years after I murdered our family is in this file. How strange it is that I don't have a thing, not one scrap of where he's been in the last two.

The desperate part of me wishes the sly man my brother is would have died like he should have out there in the desert. If he had, I wouldn't have laid a finger on Ivy other than the way she deserved. But, I knew he would come back. I knew he would seek vengeance. So, my obsession to obtain her heart turned into a fixation to not only ruin her because she didn't love me the way I did her. I wanted her damaged and destroyed for him. I wanted her to die inside. To become unfixable.

"You aren't unfixable though are you, Ivy? You're right where you want to be, somewhere hiding with him. If he fucks you, touches you in a way he shouldn't, I'll be forced to kill you." I'll carve her heart out of her chest. A heart that she unwillingly held wide open for him. "You had no idea he was alive, and you still loved him. You just couldn't let go of him, could you?" Sweet naïve woman who stood by my side as if she had a device shoved up her ass, and I controlled the button that turned it on to switch her into pretending in public that she loved me. "But I could never control your heart, could I? I could never control your brain like I did the rest of you."

The clever man stole you from me once again. "I want you back, Ivy."

I internally laugh at his audacity to call me and accuse me of doing her harm when he's the one who damaged her more than any strike. Any time I fucked her without her permission could.

Goddamn though. I hated having to do that. In the beginning, sex with her was good. The woman knows how to fuck. Heavy breasts bouncing up and down. Head thrown back while she comes. The thing is, she wasn't thinking of me when my dick was inside of her. She was thinking of him. That's his fault too. All of it rests on his shoulders. By him being alive makes every wicked torture I put her through his fault.

"Where does he have you? Surely you don't know what kind of man he is. Then again, you didn't know what kind of man I was when I convinced you to give me a chance." I scoff. Anger surging. It pumps throughout me with enough force to yank on the panic chain I shut off shortly after I found out Clay was dead. Not that I really give a shit he died. The man was a first stage clinger. Always wanting to walk one step behind me. Always looking at my wife the way he looked at Rachel.

"You're coming for me. This I've known all along. You might have one-upped me by taking Ivy. I suppose I should thank you for it because otherwise, she could be with whoever drugged her. First, though, you'll kill Adam. Or at least you'll try. He's prepared now that you've killed the other two. Hell, I'm jealous he'll be the one to beat the shit out of you before me."

I need to find Ivy first. If I don't, I might never get her back before Cade dies.

"Goddamnit." I unclick my seatbelt, toss the file on the floor and pace. I should have blown his brains out. Should have tied him up and had him watch me fuck his precious Ivy.

I press my temples; I need something, anything besides alcohol to calm me down.

"Here, Mr. St. James." I spin around. The sweet little intruder to my thoughts bites her lip as she hands me a glass of whiskey.

"Thanks," I take it, drain it and drop the tumbler on the floor. My cock growing hard the longer she stands there.

"Take your clothes off and bend over."

Chapter Sixteen
Ivy

"I felt you out here." Fighting my shudder, I hold the towel wrapped around me in place as I step out of the bathroom and into the bedroom. I knew he was back the minute I climbed out of bed.

I rushed into the bathroom and started pacing back and forth. My nerves twisting and jumpy in my stomach. I don't want to see him. I'm a mess. I'm scared, angry. A mixed up woman who has been locked away, and even though I understand why. It still reminds me of Drew.

After realizing I couldn't stay in there forever, I took a shower. I felt him out here before I heard him rummaging around.

My heart pauses as his eyes travel up my legs. Stopping at my stomach long enough for them to flare before softening as they roam across the swell of my breasts, my neck, my mouth and lance onto my eyes.

It's been so long since my skin has spread heat from his caress across my flesh. I've been cold, withdrawn, tucked into my safe place after everything I've been forced to suffer through.

"Got back about an hour ago. Chaz and Ellie went home. I took a shower in the spare bath. Forgot to grab clean clothes. They said the doctor gave you the blood tests. I'm glad you're going to be okay, Ivy."

I don't know whether to laugh, cry, plaster myself against his wet naked chest in order to feel his heartbeat or melt into his skin with those muscular arms around me.

"He did. The idea of someone slipping me something scares me. I'm not around many people. Then again, you know this, right?" My mind stutters. Does he know the doctor ran all kinds of tests with my blood? Blood, the kind doctor apologized for taking without my permission. I told him I understood and appreciated what he did for me even if I couldn't remember. I sigh. I'm thankful, which, I've told him already. "Well, maybe you should grab your clothes and get out of here so I can get dressed. I'll be out in a minute."

Chaz wasn't kidding when he said Ellie bought me clothes. She bought more than that. Makeup, shampoo, everything I need to make me comfortable. If I could have walked around naked I would have, unfortunately, I can't, so I accepted what she gave me with gratitude, now that the man who paid for it is back, all I want to do is throw it in his face.

"I'll leave when I'm done talking. Nick is working on trying to find out who drugged you. There are several men he has to check out." He runs his fingers through his wet hair. Those eyes still trying to read me. "I don't know everything about you, not like I used to. Not like I want to either." Not like he wants to? What does he mean by that?

I don't ever want him to know everything. I wish he didn't know anything at all.

His inked covered chest expands with a deep breath. Lips I've missed curl into a crooked smile. He's staring me down, filling this room with thoughts of sweaty, earth-shattering sex, the kind that leaves me satisfied. All kinds of desiring thoughts are running through my head seeing him sitting on his bed only wrapped in a towel himself. The same bed I've been sleeping in as my mind drifted all over the place, my nerve endings fraying because I was in his bed wishing he was beside me.

A person's mind can race faster than anything else. It drums up the craziest things. It hopes. It deceives. It scares. It speaks lies and truths. It spins in a malicious circle until wondering gets the better of you. Over the past four days since he's been gone, I've learned how loyal it is too.

Cade might not have had his family with him, but he had friends. He had brothers who fought next to him all the while protecting his back.

I tried with everything in me to get Ellie and Chaz to open up and tell me more about Cade. Ellie gave me a look that spoke she didn't know a thing, and Chaz turned from the playful man he's been to a menacing one with the look of the devil.

On the outside, Chaz is the complete opposite of Cade. He's funny; he's loud, he watches sports. Yet underneath his soft exterior is a man similar to the one who left me on his couch with unanswered questions. Men who are hiding their pain behind brutality. Men who are hiding lies behind truths, and men who will take their last breath for one another.

I learned where and how these three dangerous men met. Nick, I haven't met yet. I have a feeling he was with Cade. Also, I'm pretty certain they killed either Adam or Sam. Those are the only other two friends of Drew's that hung around as much as I did back then.

I always wondered why Adam Chambers and Sam Fredrick left New York in the middle of their sophomore year in college. Now I know why. They didn't need an education to be rich. They already were.

I suppose if I wasn't so damn confused as to why Cade walked out and left me just when he gave himself back, I wouldn't be standing here in front of him after showering, happy he found people who stood by his side, so he wasn't alone. But the longer he gazes into my eyes like he wants to rip my towel off instead of talk, the more scared and angrier I get.

Cade is alive. He's been living and breathing the same air as me all these years. I don't know what hurts more, knowing he was alive and never told me, or him thinking I could ever hurt him, his family, or myself in an unbearable way.

From top to bottom I hurt almost as much as the day the loud boom that woke me up, forcing both Dad and me to rush out the door only to see the St. James house burning. Glass shattering, wood hissing.

Flames. They will forever haunt me.

I'll bet it's why Drew named the club BURN. Sick man who I want dead.

I've done a lot of thinking while he's been gone. A lot of searching inside my soul. Some people assume they have the right to do what they like no matter the consequences to others. To take without asking even if those actions end up taking a life. But, what does it mean when one person's actions affect the actions of another?

Drew killed his family for money, and for me. An obsession I knew he had. However, I didn't know just how obsessed he was. Those actions resolved in the man standing before me. His desire to kill, but there's more behind this man. More secrets and lies.

At the moment, Drew isn't part of this. It's me and a man who can deny all he wants that he doesn't have room for me. If it were true, someone forgot to tell the few parts of his betraying body. His eyes, his twitchy finger and his dick.

My heart freezes with an ache as my eyes scan his skin. Good God, the man is insanely buff. I guess owning a gym will do that to you. The gym I belong to.

What has me sliding to my left and using the wall to hold me up is the way the outline of his hard cock leaves little to the imagination. The one part of a man I never wanted to get on my knees again for. He's not Drew though; he's Cade. Dangerous Cade.

And I'm so, so scared that if he asked me to drop to my knees, I would. But I'd be doing it willingly. I'd be doing it for me as much as for him.

"You're a killer and a liar."

His mouth curls higher, the smirk should repulse me. It's devious, makes him look like Drew. For one brief moment, my instincts thinking it's the man who set out to destroy me scream for me not to speak another word.

"I am a killer. These hands killed Sam a few days ago. These hands are going to kill again. They are going to kill a man who took my life from me. They are going to kill a man who took you, a gift and hurt you when you should have been cherished. The one thing they would never do is hurt you."

I want to annihilate the cause of our pain myself. I want to be fearless of Drew and the things he's done to not only me but to Cade and his family. The things he's still capable of doing.

But I remain still. Like the way I was taught. A shadowless ghost I keep trying to convince myself I shouldn't be.

In his next breath, he's moving toward me. My legs wobble, my palms lay flat against the wall. The repulsive hate from the other night still hangs all around him, the veins in his neck strain to hide the angered pulse thrumming as wildly as my own.

Please touch me.

We watch one another. I see his jaw tic, his eyes dilate, his heart pounding in his chest.

"If I lie, it's for your own good, Ivy. It's to protect you, not hurt you."

I want to elaborate on that, but I'll leave it alone because the grown woman in me knows all too well how to lie to save hurting others.

"There are other ways to hurt me, Cade." I don't have to elaborate. Not when his face doesn't hide his guilt as easily as his heart and mind do.

"I know, Ivy. I shouldn't have left. Having you here. Knowing you were in pain from my brother's hands, it messed me up more. I'm not a good man. I'll never be again. I've planned this vengeance since the day I walked away from that fire. I told you I would have killed you, and I would have, Ivy, even if it killed me to do it. I've lived with guilt for not being able to save them. Lived with hatred for you marrying him when you should have been with me. Seeing you at the club in pain, feeling it in my gut that you were drugged and your life wasn't as perfect as I thought. It threw a wrench in my plans. I can't have distractions in my life. And you are a distraction. One I don't deserve. Not anymore. You can't fix me, but I can fix the mistake I made by leaving you."

Tears blur my vision as I drop my eyes to the carpet. I can't look at him anymore.

"You think I'm damaged. That's it isn't it? You think because of the things he did to me that I'm weak, that I can't handle what you're doing. I'm not going to try and stop you. He might have hurt me, but he didn't break me. Not like I thought he did."

Without warning, his hands come up and cradle my face. My God they feel good. Him touching me like this. It brings back the fondest memories of him telling me how holding my face was the best thing he ever held in his hands.

Slowly he lifts my head. My breaking heart pleas to pinch my eyes closed. I can't. Not after feeling his breath feather across my lips, the touch of his very much alive hands touching me.

I'm frightened. Terrified even. My legs are having a hard time keeping me upright. He's touching me. Oh, God. It feels so good when it shouldn't. I should be cowering and begging him to leave me be. I'm not ready for this. Not at all.

"You aren't damaged. You are the strongest, most beautiful

woman I will ever know. It's me; I'm damaged, Ivy. Goddamnit. I don't need this."

He must need this because before I catch my breath, his lips crash against mine.

"Open up, Ivy," he demands. Goosebumps scatter my skin from how close he is; they break out everywhere from his touch. My pulse quickens.

I open, proving I'm not strong at all.

This kiss is right in so many ways. Wrong in others. Ways I'm not going to dwell on for fear that what I'm feeling will slip away. And it will, as soon as my desperate mind realizes I'm not hallucinating and that Cade is actually with me, his hard cock pressing against my stomach.

I'm completely captivated. Enthralled and in tune with every ghostly touch of his across my face. His breath, his hands, his mouth, his tongue. They all steal my sense of reasoning. The way we both keep our eyes open as we capture a taste of each other.

He tastes like danger. Like tobacco, and a hint of the man I missed.

There's so much lingering in the air. So much that still needs to be said and yet here I am letting his tongue swipe every inch of my mouth.

I gasp when he removes his mouth from mine, his hand angles my head off to the side in order for him to kiss across my jaw, along my cheek, and inhale my scent before sliding his hand to wrap around my throat. I melt in his hands.

Desperately seeking to slip away with him just for a little while.

I whimper when I feel the growl rip from his chest and enter my mouth when his lips take over mine again. He's making me forget about everything that is my life and letting him take me to a place I frantically need to go. I've kept so much inside of me that I'm ready to unhinge. I need to stop bottling it up and storing my life's demons. I just don't know how.

I panic. Heart fluttering like a caged bird when the other hand glides down my side until it lands on my inner thigh. His fingers inching higher.

My momentary bliss fades when mistakingly I open my eyes,

and what flies out of his mouth throws those demons right back inside of me.

"How many times did Drew fuck you with my knife?"

Chapter Seventeen
Cade

What the fuck was I doing? I told myself I was going to ease her into opening up. I couldn't help myself. Couldn't stop from kissing her. Couldn't get my finger to stop that goddamn twitch. I needed to touch her. But I went about it all wrong.

I almost touched her in the one spot a man should never touch without permission. Even as fucked up as I am, I know better than to ever think of doing something like that. Especially when my purpose is to make her understand she isn't damaged. Christ Almighty how stupid can I get.

My heart races. Fury protecting her and fear of her state of mind drones on in my skull. Baking my brain with some godforsaken recipe I made up that's now burning through my veins.

I could feel her splintering down the middle the second her gaze landed on me. My gift. The woman I want to sink into for the rest of my life is fighting to be free, and here I come barging in here demanding her to tell me something that could crumble the both of us to our knees.

"I, I have to get out of here. Get out, get away from me!" Terror blazes in her eyes. Those holes to her soul I can't decide if I want to swim or drown in the minute she walked through the bathroom door. Standing there in just a damp towel. Hair wet, smooth skin, and smelling so good my cock came alive.

For one brief minute, I sunk. Nearly drowning in the strength she shields, her beauty, that gorgeous body, those lips that I know damn well have been shuttered to silence, caught me in a trance. The woman has no idea how badly I want to worship her like the gift she is.

I stayed away from her because I had no choice. I needed to pull my shit together before I came back here. Needed to figure out the right way to approach her. She's so damned lost, so confused, and I'd be more of a heartless monster than I am if I don't push her until she lets me fix what he's done.

If this stupid idea to get her to crack doesn't work, then all I can do is hope there's a God up there looking out for her, because there sure ain't one who gives a shit about me.

I have a few weeks to get Drew out of her head before I go after Adam. Little time after that to purge my brother from this world. That isn't very long to strip ten years worth of abuse away from anyone.

I had every intention of waiting for her to get out of the shower and come out of my room before speaking to her. As screwed up as it sounds, I knew catching her off guard, hoping I could get her to open up a bit would be the best way to start this form of healing I strummed up in my mixed up head. Still, don't know what the fuck I'm doing, but I'll be damned if I let her go before she's ready and I sure as hell won't let anyone else carry the weight of her burden. Not when what she went through falls on my shoulders.

"I'm not going anywhere until you answer me. The man stole two gifts from me, Ivy. I want them both back the way I left them. I'm going to cut his hands off with my knife for laying them on you, and when I do, I want him to see the gift that will always be my favorite isn't broken. That gift is you. If making you tell me what he did ends in you hating me then so be it. I'd rather you do; you should anyway. But I'll be damned to the very bottom of hell if I don't get you back to the strong, confident woman you were before I set you free."

I contain my grin as she pushes against my chest, trying to get out of my grasp. She's not going anywhere except back in time so I can find out how much damage he's done to her.

"Don't call me that again. Gift, my ass. I knew you were a liar. God, I want out of here. I'm not a prisoner. You have no right to keep me here. No right whatsoever to come back from the dead and demand anything from me. I don't want to do this. I can't. Goddamn you, I can't."

Right there is all the proof I need that what he's done is more messed up than I can comprehend.

The guilt of holding her like a hostage threatens to strike. I brush that shit away. I'm keeping her safe. It'll work like a well thought out plan if I can keep away from her.

I want her. And that want is only going to make my finger twitch worse the more I see bits and pieces of her feisty self-return. It's a tease to my cock.

A dagger straight to my beating heart.

Poison fucking Ivy.

Fuck me solid, I want to taste more of that poison on her wicked little tongue.

Frustration vibrates in my balls. The longer she stays here, the more my finger is going to twitch. I'm going to have to find something besides stroking my dick to occupy my time.

"Wrong. You are a gift, Ivy. Whether you want to believe it or not. You'll never make me believe otherwise. I'm not letting you go. I have every right to make you understand that what he did didn't damage you. Jesus, do you think any of this is easy for me? Do you think I wanted to see you bruised and beaten? Find out he used something that was precious to both you and me and hurt you with it. For shit's sake, Ivy, he could have killed you with my knife. Do you know how fucked up that is? I want to kill him ten times over for hurting you. Goddamnit, let me help you."

Ivy can yell and scream, Punch me. Kick me. Repeat until her throat is raw that she can't tell me. The cold-hearted son of a bitch in me is not giving her a choice. I heard her choice when she accused me of thinking she was damaged. She's been hollowed out. If this were anything other than making her feel good about herself, making her see she's worthy of herself, I'd turn her over my knee and brighten her ass.

"If you think you're protecting me then think again. I have you, Ivy." I center myself in her line of sight, running the pad of my thumb down her cheek. "Let me catch you. I'll protect you from anyone, including yourself."

The minute we drove away from Sam's, I lost control. Lost focus on everything else but what Drew did. I've no doubt I'll lose my shit when she tells me. And she will tell me everything. Right now, we're starting with my knife. The knife she gave me for my birthday.

Four and a half inch stainless steel bladed hunting knife with a leather handle wrapped around cherry wood. I had my eye on it for months. At the time, I wasn't into knives like I was guns.

For some reason though this one called out to me. Ivy talked her dad into buying it for me. I was in heaven holding that concealed weapon in my hands. Had no intentions of ever using it. Now I want it back so I can use it for what it was made for. To kill, to scalp Drew's skin off his head.

"You're just like him. A monster out to destroy me. I can't do this with you. Get away from me and don't ever touch me again."

Yeah, touching you is what I was born to do. But just like everything else my asshole of a brother stole from me, he's stripped me of those honors too.

"I might be a monster, but when it comes to you, I'm nothing like him. Tell me, Ivy. How many times did he use my knife?"

Taking my hand off her fluttering pulse is the last thing I want to do. Feeling her pulse underneath my fingers gives me a purpose for some screwed up reason. Let's me know she's alive. Let's me know he may have had her for years, but he'll never get the best of her.

Her beating heart.

The woman has no idea how bad I want to throw her on the bed and devour her. Worship the temple between her legs. Feast on her lush tits and mouth. Make her come so many times if only to erase every filthy thing he ever did to her.

I drop my hand, and back away when tears start streaming down her face. Taking with me my tormented conscience, which up till now I didn't know I had. Guess when it comes to her I've always had one, buried it deep like everything else when it came to her.

"You said you wanted to fix me. This isn't fixing me; this is torturing me. Is that what you're trying to do, you want me to suffer because I married him? Do you want to punish me? Ruin me until there's nothing left? H... he hurt me. How do you know about this anyway, have you talked to him?" Her gorgeous face tweaks in disgust as she crosses her arms over her chest with shaky hands, shoulders sagging in defeat. Christ, seeing her body tremor, her strength slipping away disengages me.

"Fuck no I don't want to torture you. Do you think this is easy for me to hear? Baby, you need help. The things he did to you." I can't even say it anymore. Every time I do it's carving away another piece of her beautiful soul. "I called him. I told him he's never getting you back. He isn't, Ivy. I'll die before I let that happen," I confess. I won't lie to her about this, if I do, it's only going to make it worse when she finds out just how dangerous of a man I am. It's the only option I've got right now. "He didn't tell me about the knife, you screamed it out the night I brought you here. You said a lot of things, Ivy. Things we need to talk about. Things you need to let out. Face them head-on. I'm not trying to hurt you. I'm trying to help you. I can't even look at myself in the mirror knowing he hurt you with that knife."

Every last fiber of my being is telling me I should walk away from her and give her the time she needs. I've walked away twice. One cost her years of cruelty. The other caused all this confusion I see beating against her head.

"He will find me. You don't know the kind of man he turned into. He won't stop until he gets me back. You stand here telling me you can't look at yourself. How do you think I feel when I look at me? God, what else did I say to you?"

"Wrong. I do know the kind of man he is. You need to get one thing straight. I will stop at nothing to keep you safe. Not a thing. I don't know what you see when you look at yourself. Obviously, not the same woman I do. That's a woman who is carrying the weight of the devil on her shoulders. It isn't going to be easy to talk, to forget, or to heal. You have so much strength in you Ivy. Let me help you build it up." I'll do anything within my power to make her smile and live again the way she wants to. Not the way some obsessed motherfucker who can't treat her right demands her to function.

The answers to the rest of her questions sway in the front of my mind; they've been there since she spoke my name in the throes of her drugged induced nightmare. Screaming my name, asking me to fuck her over and over in one breath, calling out for my brother to stop torturing, in the next. Both have gutted me until I can't think straight.

"Nothing as important at this." I shrug. It's a mute point that doesn't need to be repeated. Soon enough she isn't ever going to have to see either one of us again.

"You asshole. You expect me to tell you things. Things I've

blocked out when you won't share with me. How about this. I relied on your love for me to get through my hell. A love I'm finding hard to believe you ever had."

A smile wants to tug at my mouth because her feisty attitude is returning with a damn vengeance. I want her angry; she has every right to be. What I don't want, what I won't tolerate coming out of her mouth, a mouth I want to kiss again so fucking bad my tongue hurts is for her to doubt what we had was real. It still is. I can feel it simmering in the air.

"You really believe that shit coming out of your mouth. Christ, Ivy. I'm trying real hard here not to show you the man I am. Don't test me with childish bullshit."

"I don't know what to believe anymore. We could have disappeared together. My dad would have helped us. You didn't have to run off and become a murderer."

Fuck that stings. Another point is proven. She's not cut out to be with me. If she can't handle what and why I'm killing the people I know, she sure as hell can't handle me killing people I don't.

This hurts more than I thought it would. You think your mind is prepared for this when it's anything but. It's torture seeing her try and compact this on top of her abuse. It's a sharp whip that cracks across my black heart. Scars. So many of them they will never fade.

"Yeah, and you think you'd have been better off running with me? I don't think so. I'd still be the man I am. I'd still want my vengeance. I would have found a way, Ivy. Done told you I wouldn't let anyone or anything stand in my way. If I do anything right in my life again, it's to get you on track. I'm not fond of repeating myself. You staying here, letting me take care of you is more than I deserve. Don't twist this conversation around and make it about me."

All we do is stare at each other, drawing in one another's breaths. Her speaking to me at all is more than I could ask for in a moment so estranged, so full of enough sexual tautness it's going to be damn hard not to snap it in half and fuck her. There's confusion too, and a thing called murder that stole her away from me.

Makes me seem divided thinking about the families left behind of the men I kill. Guess today is full of points being proved. If I wasn't so sure I'd shoot myself in the head if I couldn't snuff out a life that needs to be gone, I'd think I was human instead of the monster I am.

I reach for her when she crumbles in a heap of wild hair and long, long legs to the floor. "Don't touch me!" She screams so loud it pierces my ears. The pain she's holding in flies out of her as hard as the snow falling from the sky.

She cries with more violence than any sandstorm I've seen.

I hate seeing her cry. Hated the fact she was the only one who could draw out the man I used to be. The man whose heart is rippling and raw. The man who will go back into hiding once she's beat these demons down. Not to hold her in my arms while she rides this out is killing me.

Point number goddamn nineteen. I'm not human after all if I can stand here and let the only woman who ever knew the real me, cry.

It's a damn good thing Chaz went back to his place because he'd knock me on my ass for this. She isn't rupturing quietly. She shakes and rocks before curling her legs up to her chin and cries while I stand there watching every molecule inside of her break in unison. Traumatized by what he did, devastated for allowing him to do it.

I honestly don't know how much more denial I can take. I want her badly. I want her to be mine again. I want to crawl inside her body. Sink so deep I can't find my way out.

Just when I think she's done, her cries turn to wracking sobs that I can barely listen to any longer. It guts me to the core, but she needs this. She needs to let the weakness she has drip out of her before I push her more. I know this better than anyone. All it takes is one violent push from someone, and that piece of you hanging by a thread will transform into a chain so strong no one will be able to break it.

"Let it out." I drop to my knees, scoop her in my arms as gently as I can and carry her to the bed where I tuck her shivering body under the covers.

It takes all I got left not to climb in and pull her to my chest.

The woman is a vision as her tiny frame lies curled up in a ball of emotions, her hair a disheveled mess, her eyes swollen and worn. Even in the midst of her despair, she takes my breath away.

Those lips I want to kiss again and again are quivering. Her shiny hair is irresistibly making my fingers itch to run them through it like I used to. I want to feel it. Smell it. I wish I could feel her in my arms, and take away her pain. Fill her life with nothing but happiness. The happiness she deserves. Think we both know that's not an option no matter how much we wish it to be.

I want to make all of this better for her and for her to see me. The real me. I want to get down on my hands and knees and tell her that no matter how much time has passed, I've not once, not one second stopped loving her. When it comes to Ivy, I just want. Want something I'm never going to have.

There was a time when I would hold her, wipe all those tears away, and now she's looking at me with the eyes of a stranger.

Brutally lost.

I can't blame her for that. I'm feeling the same way; only, I know who I am. My life will always be a war. I'll always fight some dirty battle to make someone else's life better. It's the way I'm programmed now.

She's every damn thing and more than I expected her to be if I were to see her again. She's stunning. A perfect individual who is reaching out for help without even asking. I won't move until she answers me. I'm not giving up, not when the rest of my plan will wait until I demolish this mental hurricane spinning out of control inside of her.

"Don't look at me like you don't know who I am. Like you don't know who you are. If you're going to look at me, then tell me what I want to hear."

"Nine times. He, he used it every year on your birthday." For fuck's sake. That means he used it a few weeks ago while I sat here by myself, drinking and thinking about her, my dream of following my dad, and my knife. Jesus H. Christ. Can this be any more sick and twisted?

I should have expected her answer.

What I don't expect are the silent tears that fall behind the lids of my eyes.

Chapter Eighteen
Ivy

I woke a bit ago to the grumbling of my stomach and a pounding headache.

Clarity and misperception of fears both past and present.

"I just want to get out of here." The suppressed feelings that have been buried and locked away for so many years have escaped their prison, running freely through my skull. Every lash, every name, every drive into my body by Drew is doing everything to try and terrorize me all over again.

An anxiety attack rises inside the calm of my storm. The blizzard conditions inside of me cause my brain to freeze and the air around me stills. If I let it, it will become so thick it will murk what I've dreamed of having.

Freedom.

Earlier when Cade was pushing was the first time I saw my life through someone else's eyes. It wasn't pretty. It was downright ugly. For reasons Drew kept tossing in my face, I came to a conclusion living with him was my destiny. Life in hell with freedom so far away and yet out of my reach that no matter how far I stretched, I couldn't clutch it firmly enough to hold on.

Physically, I might be healing, but mentally and emotionally, I'm far more messed up than I thought I was. I never realized just how much until Cade reached in with his bare hands and tore me open.

Such a strange thing to be done when the day I found out he was alive, I felt these walls trying to open me wide.

I was never blinded by the fact I was breaking a little more each day. I was too closed off to see it. I stapled my heart shut, closed off my mind like a lost woman at sea who'd given up on ever being rescued. I had intentions to save myself until Drew stripped those thoughts away.

"He's not here to take them your freedom away, Ivy." Will I ever feel truly safe? Will I ever be free and if I am, where in the hell am I supposed to go? I don't have my identification. I have no money. I have nothing. I'm dependent on a man once again, and I don't like it. A man I want with all that is within me.

Drew tried to rob me of the glue and tape necessary to put my soul back together. Apart from breaking me, and relishing every moment he could slip inside of me. His menacing eyes darting all over my face and body while he desperately filled his sickly desire by beating me and taking what should have been mine to give. He didn't break me beyond repair.

Sliding out of bed, I let the towel fall to the floor, look down at my healing bruises and ugly scars when an uneasy feeling settles around me.

That scent. Vanilla and him. Masculine.

I hate him.

I want him.

I need him.

Being here with him is going to break me if I don't prove to myself I'm strong enough to push the demons from our past out of both of us. I don't want him to stop his revenge. I want him to have it, but I want mine too. I want what was stolen from me. From us. The man is blinded and jaded by his past. He's ruthless and dominant, and I'm going to push him to prove he's wrong about who he thinks he is even if it shatters me.

Right or wrong I want to get to know him again, and I'll be damned if he makes that decision for me. He's a liar when it comes to matters of his heart. A coward not to grab onto something obviously still there. I'll be as devious as I can get to make him admit he wants me.

A wicked smirk lifts the corners of my mouth when my stomach knots, and pressure pounds against my core. Grabbing Cade's t-shirt I took off a few minutes ago. I slip it over my head, get back on the bed, fluff the pillows and lean my head back while I spread my legs and let his scent crash over me. I'm half-sobbing as an intense warmth rips through my body.

When I was snooping, I saw cameras in every corner of this room. I'll bet he's watching my every move. Well, he can watch what I've done many times to his face and memories.

Sliding my hand down my stomach, I palm my core. A shiver runs through me when I feel how wet I am. "Cade," I whisper. I begin to rub the shirt around my aching nipples. Sinking a finger inside my body, and wincing at the slight pressure of my finger. I ease past the pain, move in and out of me until my back arches. "More," I whisper, shifting my unsteady hand to my clit. I rub. I push. I pull. I expose myself for his viewing pleasure.

I feel Cade's eyes on me. His cock fisted in his hands. Smooth, firm, hard strokes over his shaft. I'm not scared to be touched by him. He's a man who would never hurt me. I see his face, feel his lips on my skin. It's always him. The man who always put my pleasure before his own.

I don't care if he's seeing my scars. I don't care that I'm walking on dangerous ground. He's getting an eyeful of what he does to me. My body may have been abused, but my mind and the way I'm responsive to memories of him aren't.

"Is this what you wanted? You want my cock, Ivy? You want it all; your greedy tight body wants to be fucked. I can't get enough of you either baby. I will never get enough. Every inch of this body belongs to me. No one else. No one will touch you, fuck you, or make love to you, only me. No one will taste this sweet cunt. Dip their tongue inside and make you squirm. I may be pounding my cock into your pussy, but Ivy, always know this, no matter how I take you, hard, fast, slow, I'm always loving you. I love you, Ivy. You are the best gift I'll ever be given. Now, tell me I'm the only one who will have this pussy. Tell me I own your heart. Say it!" He glides his hand up my stomach, pinching one of my nipples, tweaking it until I'm coming all over him while I scream his name. *"Say it, beautiful girl!"*

I whimper. My breast missing him the minute he releases it. I moan when he grips hold of my hair, pulling my head back and running his tongue up the side of my neck. *"Fucking say it, please."* His demanding tone has me screaming what he wants me to say. *"No one will have me but you. I'm yours."*

"I'm yours too, Ivy. Always."

Dizziness sweeps over me. I shoot upright as my intense orgasm surges right through me.

I gasp, a sob catching in my throat. That may have been for me, but all it did was remind me once again that it was my own hand bringing me pleasure instead of him.

Heaving a sigh, I set my feet on the floor. My tense body no longer strung tight. I hope he saw every exposed inch of me. I hope he heard me call his name. I don't care if I'm playing with danger. I've been living with it for years. I can handle a man who thinks I'm a broken girl. Let's see how well Mr. Know-It-All handles what I'll bet he just saw.

I feel confident as I push up and peddle my feet toward the walk-in closet where Ellie and I hung my clothes. I jerk down a pair of jeans and a sweatshirt off the hangers, grab a bra, socks and a pair of panties, I quickly dart into the bathroom to get dressed.

"God, you look awful," I mutter to my reflection. Dark cloudy circles hang under my dull green eyes. My hair dried wet last night, it's an out of control fizzy mess. And I really don't care. For years I had to adhere to perfection. I'm not doing it anymore. I drop the brush, gather my hair back and secure it in a ponytail.

My stomach growls again when my senses are hit with the smell of food. Not just any food either. It's bacon and chocolate pancakes. I don't know if I want to laugh, curl up in a ball, be angry he's cooking instead of watching me or let more frustrating emotions slip out of me.

I squeeze my eyes shut trying to push the smell, and the memories away. I can't. Not when the smell is so intense it gushes and swirls around me like a dream.

It isn't a dream though, it's real, and he's real.

I don't need him to fix me. I need him to admit he doesn't want to live without me any more than I do him. I want his protection. I want him to finish whatever plans he had of killing Drew, find who is after me and get to know each other again. Not necessarily in that order. I'm not going to continue to be a piñata filled with emotions for men to split open and scatter pieces of me until there's nothing left anymore. I've had enough.

"You can do this. Consider it a step toward healing. The quicker you do, the faster you can figure out what's going on in his head."

Sucking in a breath, I wrap my arms around my still tender stomach and make my way down the hall. My assumptions as to why he's making the breakfast my father used to, tenses with a verdict. He either wants a peace offering, or he wants to scoop out the remains of my hollowed soul. He's getting neither.

Cade's back is to me when I enter his kitchen. I can tell he senses me by the way his spine stiffens.

My heart pangs with anger from so many years lost that I can't help to let a tear slip free. My fingernails dig into my palms. I don't know how much time passes while he stands in front of his stove ignoring me. Watching him makes me happy and sad.

"I haven't made pancakes in years. Haven't done a lot of things. I'm not trying to cause you any more pain no matter what you think. I feel guilty about leaving you, I always did. I won't apologize for it, because at the time you had your dad and an entire life ahead of you. I told you I was sorry for the things that happen to you. It will haunt me long after you're gone. What I won't apologize for is the man I am. Now come and eat. I have questions that need to be answered."

I'm not going anywhere without you, so quit trying to shove me away.

"I have plenty of things to ask you too. I have quite a bit to say. For starters, quit bossing me around. After everything you've learned about me, that's the last thing I want from you or anyone. I'll do what I damn well please. Thank you very much." I want to elaborate and let all my questions tumble out on the floor at his feet.

His bare feet at that.

The man is standing in his kitchen, cooking in a pair of sweats. No shirt, muscles rippling.

Every inch of him is sharp and jagged. Muscles flexing in his back and shoulders. Ass tight, even his damn ankles scream out for me to take a bite. All of his body oozes sex. It's literally dripping off of him.

He's a riddle. A hidden treasure. A woman's fantasy. And I'm going to make him see what we had is worth chancing again.

When he turns around and flicks his eyes over my body, I combust. From them pulsates a force I can feel in my bones. The look hidden behind his darkened stare is far from polite. He saw me. This I'm one hundred percent sure of. His observation makes me want to shuffle forward and press against him. Feel those lips move in a ravenous kiss while his hands roam all over the curves of my body. Those eyes of his touch me everywhere, and I like it so, so much that I don't want to break away.

Well, if he wants to discuss my performance, he'll have to bring it up. Starting up another battle in our war isn't in my blood at the moment. Having a decent conversation while eating is. It's been so long since someone has done something nice for me without expecting something in return.

Putting the word nice with Cade has me chuckling under my breath. The two of them don't blend together anymore. I don't know what does with the man who has me hanging upside down with nowhere to go except to fall into a giant black hole.

He has the power to obliterate me.

Pulling out a chair, I take a seat. The aroma, the pancakes on my plate bring unwanted tears to my eyes.

"I'm bossy because you're stubborn." His tone is playful, but his appearance, his still explosive perusal screams foreplay. The intense fixation he has on my face quickens my pulse, my breath catches, and I can't help it when my stomach drops to the floor.

"You're bossy because that's who you are. There are some things about a person that will never change, Cade."

Silence flows thick and strong between us.

My body springs to life in a way I haven't felt in a long time when he answers back in the form of a devious wicked smile.

A heartfelt laugh juts from my mouth. "See. You didn't think I'd remember that little tit for tat we used to do, did you? I remember everything when it comes to you, Cade." I'll never tire of saying his name. It was blocked from my vocabulary for too long.

My laugh dies down; our gazes click and lock just like they used to. God, we used to just stare at each other until one of us couldn't take it anymore. It was usually him who lost. His need to touch my face and kiss me senseless was his reason.

I search for the boy I once knew. He may have smiled at me, but it's clear as a crystal snowflake he's hiding. In front of me is a man. A man who is full of secrets. Some of them he doesn't want me to know.

Lord, how I want to push him the way he did me. Poke and

prod until he gives in. The difference is I'm soft to all his hard, and I'd lose before I even got started.

I clear my throat.

"I remember you ate six of these the first time my dad made them for you." I wait for him to answer. Instead, he takes a seat next to me, all the while keeping his stare. I blink when he lifts a hand and tugs the hair tie from my hair.

My body lights on fire.

A wrench twists our attraction tight. I can't ignore it any more than he can. It's stripping us bare. Tighter and tighter it cranks and winds.

I'm the first to look away. I take a bite of the food I haven't had in a long time, wanting to savor every bite.

I can't. Not because of him. Because it's that good. A tiny moan escapes my throat at the feel of the gooey chocolate hitting my tongue.

"What?" I question through a mouth full of food when I notice he's standing behind his chair. Body tighter than a drum.

"Nothing. You got it wrong. I ate seven. I'll answer whatever questions you want, Ivy. Just not about how, or when I'm going to finish off Drew. I never liked it when you hid your curls. That's something about me that will never change." Tucking some of it behind my ear, he pins me in place with his stare. Only, he's not staring at me. He's staring at his hand glide down my cheek. I'm tranced when he touches the corner of my lip, shows me a drop of chocolate and slowly sucks it into his mouth.

Oh, my freaking God.

I lick my lips. An open invitation. I want his lips back on mine. I want his touch again. He didn't touch me to hurt me; he didn't kiss me earlier to take what wasn't his. All of me has been his since the day we met.

My numb mouth is immobilized and screaming for him to kiss me. Because that kiss earlier. That touch to my lips just now, they've branded me.

"Thank you," I mutter. I mean, what the hell else do I say to a man who looks and touches me like he wants to toss me on the floor and spread me wide.

The heat in his gaze breaks me out in a sweat.

It makes me wet.

Wakes me up.

Has me clenching my thighs.

"We need to talk about who might have drugged you. You need to think as far back as you can, Ivy. I need names. We're at a dead end here." He drops his hand, head angles to his plate and shovels in his food like he just didn't crank up the wrench even more.

All those feelings from moments ago vanish. They've been replaced with chills.

"Honestly, I don't know. Drew has many enemies. Whoever did it, has to be associated with him."

Silence settles over us once again for a few minutes. I haven't a clue who would do this to me. Not one.

"Tell me what happened at the club. How did you get me away from Drew?"

I turn to face him, taking in all of him.

He squeezes the edge of the table. His muscles in his arms and jaw are flexing as if he's fighting against something. Is it something I did? Something Drew said? I don't know, whatever it is, causes him to push out of his chair. Take our empty plates and toss them into the sink. They clank. Loud.

So does my heart.

"What happened?" The pained look on his face when he turns around has me sinking into my chair. I really don't think I want to know anymore. The answer terrifies me.

"I waited in the hallway. We made a plan to cut the lights so I could grab you. You started tripping on the drugs. Running toward Drew. You saw me on your way and freaked out. The lights went out, and I took you. That's it."

There's more. I know there is.

"What happened when we came here?" Tilting his head to the side, he studies my features. I know he sees the fear in my eyes. How could he not? It's written all over my body.

My mouth goes dry as my gaze slides straight to his cock. It's thick and hard. Suddenly, that ache is back again. The one that has only ever been brought on by him. It has me squirming in my chair.

Gravity wraps around us. A weightless force that had always been ours.

The man hisses as he gazes down at me with wild hungry eyes.

"You kept asking me to fuck you, Ivy."

Chapter Nineteen
Cade

Always tell the truth my dad said. It'll set you free. Crock of shit if you ask me.

The truth only hurt Ivy. And that truth came hours ago.

Hours after watching her finger fucked herself. Opening up that sweet pink pussy that had me jerking my cock until I came watching her please herself. The beauty was searching and finding what my cock should be giving her. Goddamn that was hot. Could watch her all day getting herself off. She knew I saw her too. Her cheeks turned pink when I skimmed down her body. There was no doubt she was remembering what she had done sprawled across my bed.

Haven't seen anything sexier than her showing me she isn't afraid to show me what she wants in my entire life.

I wanted to pounce on her. Fuck her with my fingers before sliding in with my cock.

My restraint is gone. The iron grip on my control snapped when I felt her body flush against mine. Christ, I wanted to yank that towel off her, lift her up and thrust my dick inside her body.

Swear after she sat there letting what I said sink in she turned cold as the outdoors. The woman didn't stop asking me about that night at the club. I told her everything she did. Right down to her touching herself with crazed eyes glued to mine. Embarrassment flooded her cheeks before she ran back to my room and hasn't come out since.

Closing the door to my office, I take a seat behind my desk. Papers from the gym are scattered all over. I've been working to get shit done, so I don't have to worry about anything but Ivy for the next several days.

I'm not fucking around anymore. The only thing Ivy isn't safe from is what she thinks she wants, and me. More me than her and that's a goddamn scary thought.

Enough is enough though. Either she pulls her shit together, gets her ass out of my room so we can hash out whatever the fuck is happening, or I'm going to fucking blow. My stress is erupting like lava seeping out of the black crevices of a volcano in my veins.

The first full day we've spent together, and it's a cluster-fuck of disasters. Making her breakdown in my room. Agreeing to answer questions. Then the minute she asks about the club, I go rock hard. Sick fuck that I am getting turned on when thinking about a woman asking me to fuck her when she was out of her head.

Not quite true, I'd been hard since she walked into that club looking like some angel that had fallen out of the sky. Testing my patience with her natural beauty. The minute I touched her I knew there'd be no letting her go. I was just too much of a chicken-shit to admit it. Still am.

This morning when she let out a sexy moan, it spoke to my instincts, pleading with me to do some very wicked things to that mouth. I wanted to stand, pull down my sweats, stroke my cock and coat her lips with my release.

I crave Ivy. I want her more than anything. I need her more than the monstrous, miserable life of blackness that looms on my doorstep once she's gone. The problem is, I don't think I can handle her being anywhere else than with me. And I am not going anywhere.

I rub my temples. Visuals are storming through my head. Stomping and telling me to wake the fuck up. I didn't think my heart could beat again until I saw her curled up in my bed this morning. Her eyes pleading for me to not ask anything more about the knife or what happened to her.

Still can't stomach it was two weeks ago when he last used it on her. I want to stab holes all over his body with it. Drain every last ounce of blood out of him. Killing him won't ever be enough for what he's done.

If I thought losing my family was hard, losing her again might be the end of me. Never did I think I'd see the light in my dark. The woman might be swimming in pain, but there sure as shit is light circling around her. Punching holes and seeping right in.

Years ago, I was drawn to her beauty. Now I'm drawn to her light. Her ability to walk out of my room, take a seat and laugh about knocked me on my ass. I crave her so much I don't know what the fuck to do anymore.

The way she looked at me at the table this morning. Her eyes darkening, her nipples like hard diamonds poking through her bra and sweatshirt. Her body trembling, eyes widening, lips parting when she saw how hard I was nearly distracted me. I fought the urge to toss her over my shoulder, strip her naked and spread her legs wide. My taste buds didn't taste my food at all. It was her I tasted, her I smelled, her I wanted to lick, eat, and fill with my cock.

"Tell me that these assholes are the ones who drugged her." I light up my pipe, inhaling deeply as I hand Roan a glass of scotch and wait for my answer. Him coming over is the distraction I need to calm my ass down or else I'd be in my room doing God knows what to a temptress that makes me weak in the knees.

A while back Roan started digging into helping Chaz find the missing piece of his past. We didn't have any idea Drew was involved with the notorious gang Chaz was linked to until we saw him standing next to the president of The Warriors during a press conference.

As their fucking attorney.

The Warriors are a dangerous gang in New York. Known for drugs, sex trafficking, and more. Any kind of date rape drug seems to be their drug of choice. Because of that, I had Roan dig a little deeper. I want no stone left unturned when it comes to finding the person who drugged Ivy.

"Let's just say they make you look like the Pope. They don't play nice. Always busting people up just because they think they can. Always trying to encroach on other's territories. I can't say for sure if they drugged her or not. What I can say is they left the courtroom unhappy after their men were found guilty. As far as we know there have been threats made here and there to your brother, nothing's come of them yet. But," he pauses, slides a photo across my desk, and shudders. "Look at that and burn it, shred it, turn it over. Don't care what you do with it. Just get it out of my face."

"Jesus Christ." I take one peek, flip the thing over when everything in my stomach threatens to come up. I've killed a lot in my life. Not sure if I've ever seen a bloodier massacre than that. What makes it worse, it's a woman. What's left of her anyway.

"A cop on my payroll brought that to me. Apparently this woman head-butted the president's old lady, or so the story goes. Either way, this woman was about to be sold. She fought for her freedom and they killed her." In the few years I've known Roan, I've never heard his voice spike with pain. Sure proves the best of us are more human than I think.

I grit my teeth, close my eyes. Ivy would never survive something like this. I'd never survive if someone took her from me. It was bad enough living those years thinking she was happy with someone who wasn't me. This though would kill us both.

How the hell Chaz has lived with what they did to him and his little sister is beyond me. Fucking Christ.

Pinching the brow of my nose, I glare at the dark computer screens in my office. I'd shut my security off after watching Ivy pace a hole in the floor. Her brain spinning out of control trying to remember the night at the club. Frustrated beyond belief, throwing things when her mind will never give the information she wants. I couldn't stand to watch her anymore. Now I'm going batshit over not seeing her. Wondering if she's crying.

Christ, I want to hold her as she cries and trembles in my arms instead of standing helplessly as she lets loose of all that's swamped her mind. I want her to beat on my chest, let all that pain sink into my skin until she falls lax from pure exhaustion. I've failed her over and over when failure is all she's ever had.

Ivy has lived a nightmare life, yet she's holding herself together by a thread. Strength and courage. Sexy as all hell.

"You think even after I take out my brother, Ivy might not ever be safe?" I inhale, hold the smoke in my lungs until I can't take it any longer.

"That's not what I'm saying. Pretty sure you'll fight 'til your death to make sure she is. And, if it ever came down to that. Which, it won't. You have my word I'll take care of her. Honestly, Cade. I don't think these men drugged her. They have no reason to come after Ivy. I believe if they wanted revenge, they'd have already killed your brother. It wasn't that long ago you killed a man who tried offering up his daughter to me for payment. These men fall under those lines. They take care of the one who did them wrong. Sounds kind of messed up considering they kidnap innocent women. But it's true."

We both take a moment to remember that night. Roan set a meeting with the man. Had me tag along just in case the guy showed up empty-handed. When he walked in with his daughter, it made me want to feed the narc to the sharks. That young girl clung to the piece of shit, scared and crying even after he offered her up in his foreign tongue. "They usually take runaways, junkies and clean them up, only to pump them full of sex enhancers. Use those women like an assembly line to train into submission. Then again, your brother fucked up by losing a case he promised them he'd win. They have two of their men six feet under from being murdered in prison, so you tell me if she's going to be safe."

He doesn't have to say anything more. These men don't want Ivy. It's the other way around. They have someone in their possession we want. Someone Chaz has worked his own revenge to find. "I still haven't been able to locate Chaz's sister. I'll get with him about it before I leave." I nod. My finger twitching, hands craving those men's blood. Like me, my friend has suffered long enough.

"If they aren't the ones, then it has to be someone inside my brother's personal circle. Someone I'm missing. He's hiding something. Whatever it is has been hidden well." I may never find out who did this. Drew has more enemies than friends. He might be good at what he does, but he's also lost some fairly big cases in his career. "This is why her disappearance hasn't been reported to the cops. He knows whoever did this wanted revenge in a different way. It's someone who works for him or someone else he's fucked over. One of the many women he's cheated with. Shit, I'm back at square one. Goddamnit. I feel like I'm chasing my own tail here."

I set my pipe in the ashtray, grab the photo, slide my chair and place it in the shredder. I've seen plenty of blood. Nothing is worse though than seeing it drain from the ears of a woman at war. They are beaten and raped in the dirty streets repeatedly.

Mutilated until all that's left is bones. Women don't hold any value to men over there. Ivy though, she's worth more than any amount of money. Any other possession a man holds in his hands. Fucks a man like me up with the possibility someone drugged her out of jealousy over a bastard who didn't value the gift he had.

"I'll continue to help out any way I can. If I hear of anything, I'll contain them until you take over." I appreciate him being as loyal to me as I am to him.

"Grateful Roan."

"There's something else I wanted to talk about. It's not my business. Butting my nose in whether you like it or not. I won't sit here and go into detail about my own brother. Our stories are a lot alike, Cade. My brother and I loved the same woman. Only his love was like your brother's. It was sick and all kinds of fucked up. That isn't loving someone. I might sound like a pussy saying this. Have that right I suppose after being married for twenty plus years to a woman who hated what I did."

I look him in the eye when he pauses and shifts to stand.

"Alina didn't want a part of my world at all. My brother hurt her, put the fear of a man's touch in my wife. I loved Alina. I wanted her, and I made her see what love was all about. Love makes you go crazy with wanting to protect. It makes you accept faults that you wish weren't there. It's able to forget. To forgive, but it's also one of the hardest things to accept in life. On the flip side, it's the most beautiful goddamn thing. Right now you don't think Ivy could love you for who you are. You're afraid to taint her, to let her hold your face in your crime filled hands. Don't go there with that crap. Give her the benefit of the doubt. Communicate. Fight. Play hardball, and hurt each other. But don't you ever give up. Love is putting someone else first because they mean more to you than anything else. You and Ivy might not be the same people you were. That doesn't mean you can't or don't deserve to love. Quit wasting time. You want her, then get her. I'm telling you right now if you let her go and she finds someone else. Someone who really loves her. You're going to go through a helluva worse than before." His grin slightly curves, and his eyes are a whole hell of a lot playful. Reminds me of something my dad would do and say.

I tamp my blazing temper down before I aim it at the wrong person. Roan means well.

"You going to let me walk away from this life?" I question. Knowing what he'll say before he even says it. Just like I'll be aware of every move Ivy makes for the rest of my life, Roan's aware of mine. I struck a deal to remain loyal, to do what he asked with no questions. Knew when I gave him my word if I tried to walk away I was good as dead. I admire this man who cares about me. But he'd put a bullet in my head if it meant protecting those he loves.

"No. You asking to walk away?"

"Never. I gave you my word. My word is the only good thing I got." I could have something a hell of a lot better than my word if I'd man the fuck up and go to her.

"Didn't think so."

"Whatever old man. I can't believe I'm sitting here listening to fatherly advice from a man I've seen blow someone's brains out. Alina was born into the mafia. She grew up around killing. Ivy hasn't." We shouldn't even be having this discussion. Ivy and I may never happen.

I've long forgiven her for marrying Drew when I realized she didn't do a thing but marry someone she trusted. It's me. It's the screwed up scared part of me that will die a thousand deaths if she looks at me in a different way once she finds out I'm a cold-blooded killer without an ounce of guilt.

"And I just told you she hated it. She took off and left her family behind after my brother raped her. She didn't want anything to do with them, but she loved them enough not to make them choose. From what you've told me, Ivy hasn't been able to choose what she wants in years. Give her a choice to make up her own mind. Don't make it for her. If you do, it'll be the biggest mistake you'll ever make. Take my fatherly advice or don't. I'm just telling you, women who love will have her man's back the same way he does hers. They learn and adjust. They do it for love."

I'm going to fuck this up. I can't do it. I have to let her go. I've only spent one night here with her being alert, and I'm already on edge. Her laying up in my bed. Naked and so fucking tempting. She deserves more than what I can give.

"I won't deny that I love her. I do. I have to let her go. It's the right thing for her. I appreciate your advice, Roan. Respect you even more for it. But, sometimes love is about sacrifice. I'm sacrificing how I feel so she doesn't have to live a life full of violence anymore. I'll never change. Got too much shit stored up inside. Too much hate to dump that on her."

"Yeah, well, nothing will bring your family back. I hope the beautiful thing called vengeance is enough for you. Just make sure it's a choice you can live with."

Ivy might be trapped in my head, but the choice to kill, it's trapped in my blood.

Chapter Twenty
Ivy

"My door was custom made to keep people out, Ivy. I won't be happy if you force me to bust it down. I've asked twice, not asking again. Dress warm and get out here. There's somewhere I want to take you."

My head spins from the sound of his angered voice. This is the second time he's asked me to come out. The idea of getting out of here set me on high alert at first. Even though he didn't say he was taking me to the gym, I'd still go just to breathe fresh air even if my body isn't ready for a workout. At least not on gym equipment. So where does he plan on taking me?

I was all set to go, even made it to the door. I paused after realizing just how rattled I was.

I'm on the verge of hysterics over what Cade told me I did at the club. Just thinking about the look on Drew's face as I played with myself in front of his clients had me storming in this room and laughing. Then after I collected myself, I became angry, so overwhelmed with what could have happened if Cade wouldn't have been there that I couldn't face him. Not until I gathered every bit of me and tossed the rotten eggs out of my basket. I needed to make a decision. This is my life, not anyone else's and it's about time I took control of it.

I'd be all too willing to kill whoever is responsible for drugging me. I'd be willing to walk out of his life once Cade seeks his vengeance and finds out who's after me if I honestly believed he didn't want me. Therefore, with every rotten thing that has happened in my life, I'm taking control and going after what I want. And I want Cade.

His reaction as he told me what I did and said proves he wants me too. The way his cock hardened at just the memory. Heat igniting beneath his gaze. It had my pulse fluttering out of control and my skin tingling. After everything I've been through, I should be afraid. I'm far from it. I'm coiled. Strung tight and if he doesn't relieve the ache, I'll continue to do it myself.

I'll play as dirty as I can to get what I want.

Cade would never hurt me, not in the physical sense. It's my heart, it's already destroyed, and he's the one who could shatter it into unrepairable pieces if he doesn't act on what's between us.

I don't care that we've spent next to zero time with each other. I don't care what he's done while we were apart. All I care about is here and now. Figuring out my life, and getting us back to one another.

There's too much time between us for me to think we will be the same. Doesn't mean we can't try, and it sure as hell doesn't mean we can't give in to our carnal desires. Mostly, it doesn't give him the right to kiss, touch, and stand there looking at me like he wants to fuck me until I scream, but scared I'm too much of a fragile, broken woman for him to try.

I crave every bit of his hard body. I want him no matter what it does to my heart. No matter if the reality of what he's hiding from me crushes me. And he is hiding. Not only from his pain but something else. Something he thinks I can't handle.

Bitterness has reared her ugly head. She screeches to lash out at him for his mouth telling me the opposite of his body. For him knowing everything about me when he's closed himself off from sharing the side of him he thinks I'm too delicate to handle.

It might only be days since he saved me, but I'm tired of being weak, tired of men telling me what to do, and tired of Cade pushing me away out of his own kind of fear. He wants me, yet there's something holding him back, and I'll be damned if I let him treat me like the weak woman I used to be.

I felt his reluctance slipping when he touched me. His need obvious where his cock pressed so massively against the black fabric of his sweats. It screamed out as apparent as the wild thump in both our pulses that blazed between us. The power that rolled in sharp, sturdy hooks that stabbed my soul.

He wants to protect me, but he doesn't want me. He knows more about me than I do him. The unanswered questions keep piling up, and before I know it, there will be a mountain of them too hard for me to climb.

I'm on such shaky dangerous ground. I can feel it move

underneath my feet.

There's a side of me so bare that I shiver even though I'm warm. I want to close my eyes and go back to a time when my life was peaceful. When sadness wasn't always digging a little farther into my bones. No heartache filling me up during the day and running over me when I sleep. No shame building walls around my heart. I'm suffocating, and I don't know how to gasp for the breath to make me stop.

A race of tremors flaps through my chest as I stand and head toward the door. Dizziness swooshing through my system.

"Screw it; he's worth the risk. I'm going to find out what he's hiding and why he wants to send me away."

Thundery, conflicted eyes fall on me when I fling open the door. I will never tire of seeing him look at me this way. I feel his energy from here. It's pulling me toward him, tugging at the tattered strings on my heart. Sucking me into a world that's sure to gut me.

Black energy about to swallow me whole.

I want it.

"You ready?" His deep voice set in an order he expects me to follow.

"No. Not until we settle a few things. I want to call Casey." I try to make a conscious effort to toss my tone back just as strong. I don't think it works when his brow quirks up as he shifts his body to where he leans against the doorjamb and crosses his arms over his black leather covered chest. He's covered in leather. Every inch. Sweet Lord, he's heating me up with a mouthwatering intensity that strikes me everywhere. My mind has gone to the tempting dark side as I look up at him. I could stand on that side with him forever.

"You can call her as soon as I'm one hundred percent certain she didn't drug you."

"She didn't. I know she didn't." For one split second, she crossed my mind. Casey has no reason to want to hurt me. She would do everything to save me if she knew what was happening behind the walls of my house.

"Non-negotiable." Ugh. I can't decide if I want to wipe that smirk off his face or punch him.

Damn, my deceiving body goes up in flames when he glides his fiery glare down my figure. My nipples harden. Sweat forms in between my breasts. "You're an asshole and a coward. What are you hiding about yourself, Cade?" I feel a push and pull coming between us. I take the few steps to stand directly in front of him and realize instantly it was the wrong move. Because, shit, he smells good.

"My life isn't any of your concern, Ivy. I told you." His grin is smug, and reeks of power meant to scare me. Good to know he underestimates me. I'm a survivor. A woman scorned by the man she thought she'd spend her life with, and we all know hell hath no fury like a woman who wants something.

"Yes, it is!" I interrupt. I quickly glance down at his finger. It's twitching. "I don't care what you told me. You're lying. Lying about how you feel about me, lying about who you are and worst of all, you are hiding things from me. Things I have a right to know. I'm sick of being treated like shit. Sick of not being able to make my own choices. I want my life back, and whether you want to face the truth or not, you want me. It's not just to fuck me out of your system. It's not just to help me and let me walk away. Quit trying to protect me from the man you are."

The room becomes eerily quiet as I study his posture which is stiff. His expression hard, and the way his eyes haze over in shock.

"You don't want to know the man I am. I've done people wrong, Ivy. Blood, there is so much of it on me you'll never scrape it off." Cade's nostrils flare, fists clenching at his side. If I didn't see the frightened man behind the mask, the beard, the tattoos, I'd be cowering on the floor with a foot to my gut. He looks as pissed off as his brother. This isn't Drew though, this is the man who might have changed, might be sharp around the edges, but underneath it all, he's still the man I fell in love with. He just needs a reminder.

I'm going to lay it all out for him in full color.

"I'm not afraid of you or what you've done. I'm trusting you, Cade. Trusting you to keep me safe. Trust me too, please."

"You're asking too much of me, Ivy. Jesus Christ." He pushes off the door, staggers back and runs a hand across his beard.

"You know, I hated the way Drew said my name. I wanted to carve it out of his vocabulary the way he did yours from mine. But you, the way you say it. It lights me up. It makes me love myself again. It makes me want to break down your walls and tell you I'm not afraid to get to know the man who had everything stolen from him in one night. Those tattoos aren't a reminder of who you lost. They are a reminder that I was waiting for you even though I had no idea I was. We have a road to travel. It's a long one. I'd rather do it by your side than travel without you any longer."

"You are so goddamn fucking gorgeous. Your name is as much a gift as you. Ivy, you don't know what you're fucking walking into. Don't have a clue. I want to protect you, not hurt you. Jesus, woman you are stubborn as fuck."

My patience breaks. At that moment, I'm blinded by a ten-course serving of rage that's too much for me to swallow. Years of it has been simmering into a low boil that's now running over my veins. I want to punch him in the face. Instead, I draw back my fist and aim for his chest, his stomach. I hit and punch with everything I have in me.

Rage and anger.

I feel guilty, but I can't stop. So many years of abuse I don't blame him for, but need to unleash, come raging out of my bones. It adds a justifiable seasoning that helps bring an end to the angry plate of disgust I was served. I know I should stop, apologize before I make him mad, but I just don't have it in me to put an end to my wrath.

"Do you feel better, baby? If not, I can take more. Let it out and hit me. I have rage in every cell of my body. I shake with it. When you're done unleashing yours, I'll let mine out in a way that will make you see that I'm fighting what I feel for you. Fighting to not only protect you from danger. But from me. I want you so goddamn bad I can't think."

No, it's not all I've got. I have years to make up for. Yet I don't want to argue with him anymore about it. I want to move on. Live and do my best to put it all behind me. His words of rage, of wanting me, of keeping me safe from him thump me like a hard finger poke to the chest. He is out of his ever-loving mind if he thinks he'll scare me away.

My chest heaves.

I take a step backward to take him in as his expression shifts through a thousand emotions.

Regret.

Sorrow.

Lust.

Love.

I see them clawing to get out. They can't because they are trapped behind his fear.

And there's desire. So much of it that I want to cage it inside of me and never let it go.

Longing vibrates through my body. I want to crawl inside him. To rip every secret out of his chest.

"I'm sorry. I don't want to change who you are. I want you. Just because we've been separated doesn't mean we can't try. You loved me before you left. Why can't you love me again?" My lips tremble. My heart hurts.

He rushes toward me, cocking his head sideways, eyes a blizzard of an ice storm.

Rough palms take hold of my face, his touch burns like fire down my skin when I pull back slightly, grab them and kiss across his knuckles. My heart is filled with agony from missing him. "Why can't you see that I don't care what you've done? These hands won't hurt me. Only sending me away will. Maybe part of you died with your family. You're not dead, Cade, and neither am I."

Before I have the chance to back away, to give him time to adjust. Those warm lips I've missed so much come down on mine, slitting my mouth open and kissing me deeply. His tongue is leaving no spot in my mouth untouched.

He eats and devours.

Licks and sucks.

Takes what he wants.

And I love every bit of it.

"I'll show you who I am. Is that what you want? You want the monster in me to surface. You want me to fuck you until you break? Because that's what I want to do. I want to claim you again, Ivy. I want to slam into your pussy hard and fast. I want to fuck your mouth until you gag on my cock. I want your ass. I. WANT. ALL. OF. YOU! Is that the kind of man you want? If it is, then have at me. I'll give you what you want and then when you see the real me, the man underneath my skin. You'll run before I know you're safe." Closing his eyes, he groans. A string of explicit words flies out of his mouth.

"I won't run. I'll never run from you." Opening those black irises wide, he studies me intensely. Eyes flickering back and forth between mine. Seconds whisk and beat incredibly slow as my heart pulses loud in my ears.

"Better be sure about this, Ivy. If I lay you on my bed, I'm either coming inside of you or coming all over your creamy white skin. I'd prefer the first, don't think you're quite ready for the kind of fucking I do. Only know my mouth needs to be on your pussy. You want me; then you do what I say. Strip out of those clothes and plant your sweet cunt on my fucking face."

My nerves are shattered as I watch him strip out of his leather jacket and t-shirt. Those tattoos temp my lips. Desperation to lick them coats my tongue.

"Quit putting words in my mouth. You don't know what I'm ready for."

Simply put, he does. I can tell by the way his brows quirk up he knows I'm not ready for sex. But I do want to feel what it's like to have him touch me again. To light me up until I can't take anymore, to allow every good memory of the two of us surface. What we had was left hanging in the air. We aren't nor will we ever be finished.

Drew flashes in my mind. I lost interest in sex after the first time he hit me. I definitely lost the taste for it after he used the knife and once we were married, he never went down on me again. Thank God.

I debate no further before shrugging off my jacket and boots, yanking the sweater over my head and rolling the leggings along with my panties down my legs. If I wasn't already aching for him, his words alone would drive a primal need through my overheated body.

"Fucking Christ. Look at you. Nipples hard and tight

underneath a deep purple lace bra. Pussy trimmed and inviting. Do you have any idea how sexy you are? I can picture you now. Those long legs clenched against my head, face flushed, chest heaving, pussy pink, and that tiny little bud that sets off is dying for my mouth. Isn't it? You tempted me enough earlier by getting yourself off. You do it again without me stroking my cock where you can see me and I'll blister your ass. Get over here," he nearly growls. Swings an arm out, grasp me by my wrist and drops us on the bed.

His dominance along with the fact he saw me shoots a quiver between my legs.

It's foreign.

Desire.

Longing.

Craving.

I've forgotten what they've felt like.

"Pussy now, Ivy." He doesn't wait for me to straddle him. The big powerful brute pulls me up his body, positions my legs on the sides of his head and takes a long lick.

I scream and buck like a wild mare who has never been taken on a ride.

"Damn, you taste good. Glistening. Wet. For me."

I squeal when his tongue flicks against my clit, and he sucks it into his mouth. Hard.

 Pain and pleasure.

"Ride me." My hips move at the command of his gruff voice. The way his tongue and lips go at me, it's as if he's waited years to eat me. And, I'll bet he has. The man always had an appetite to eat me.

"Please, Cade." It's been so long since I've had this kind of pleasurable feeling between my legs. I want to beg for mercy. I want to turn around and drop my mouth on his cock.

Rough hair scrapes across my inner thighs, tingles my pussy and on instinct, I squeeze my legs around his head. Another groan followed by a hiss of a zipper. A growl when skin meets skin.

I hear him begin to stroke himself. I want to see, but I'm unable to move.

He's licking, sucking and lapping up every bit of me. Relentlessly assaulting me.

I'm. On. Fire.

I don't want it ever to fizzle out.

Chapter Twenty-One
Cade

As a kid, my favorite thing to do was play with guns. I had every kind of fake one we could find. Drew and I used to play army. Our parents bought us all the cool gear, black combat boots. Fatigues. Helmets. Night vision goggles. We had it all. Then my obsession with knives took hold. Had every size and color in both pretend weapons by the time I was ten. I'll never forget the year I turned eight. Our parents stuffed our Christmas stockings with camouflage face paint. Drew and I couldn't wait to use it. We painted ourselves up that day and played outside in the snow.

It seemed every weekend we gathered up the neighbor kids, split into teams and tossed a coin in the air to see what team would be the United States. Drew's taunting and teasing used to piss me off when he would win the toss. It wasn't until I got a little older, I figured out why he would tease me. He was trying to throw me off my game. It never worked. I was faster, and so much quicker to find them. I was quiet when I snuck up and drew my gun. It didn't matter what team I was on; I always targeted my brother first.

I always beat him.

And I'll beat him again. This time with a real weapon.

As a teen, I still had my obsession with guns. There was nothing like holding a real one in my hands. Nothing better than the sharp, pungent, metallic flavor after firing that sat on the roof of my mouth.

When I met Ivy, the smell, the taste, the addiction came second to the taste of her pussy, her mouth, her skin.

"I can't believe I'm going to shoot a gun. I haven't held one since..." Ivy casts her head down, walks ahead of Nick and me to the table where at least fifty handguns wait for her to choose.

After I tasted her a week ago, I put this off so we could spend time together. The first few days all we did was talk. Then boredom set in. I took her out late at night driving around the city. Hitting a few of my hangouts where I knew no one knew her. We've driven by the cemetery. I wouldn't let her get out. Even though she told me Drew's never been, I didn't want to take my chances of him having someone stalk her dad's or my parents' graves.

"Since when?" I slide my gaze to hers, so fiery and tempting, edged by curly hair stuffed underneath a beanie and hanging down her back. She's a gorgeous distraction. One I need to get out of my head and focus on the task ahead. Too damn beautiful for my own good is what she is.

I haven't fucked her yet. Not from lack of her trying. Definitely not from me wanting to. I keep telling her she isn't ready. It's me. After the night I caved and ate her pussy I told myself I'd never lie to her again. I can't take her, or claim her before I tell her what I do. It's too big of a thing to keep between us.

Nick hands me a beer, lifts his chin and smirks. Smart ass knows something powerful occurred between Ivy and me. I also think he could tell I had a lot on my mind since he spent the entire ride to this warehouse keeping Ivy occupied by making up a bullshit story about his life. Fucker was all happy and shit while I sat there with a cyclone destroying my goddamn brain.

"Since the time I went with you and your dad." Motherfucker. That was one of the best days. About two weeks before they died. Dad was teasing her about the way she stood when she held a gun. Her stance didn't bother me any. I was hard as steel over it. I've jacked off many times to visions of the way she always stood with her legs spread a little wider than normal. Her back straight, shoulders rolled back enough to thrust out her tits.

I can't seem to move from my spot by the door as I watch her fingers lightly touch my guns. Well, honestly, they aren't mine. They belong to Roan. Before he left my apartment, I asked him if we could use his indoor gun range and if he'd drop off a supply of handguns fit for a woman Ivy's size.

I had every intention of making sure she could take care of herself once she got settled. Not that Drew or whoever is after her would be a problem. Not much they can do when their remains are underground.

But after she let out her rage, and begged me with words that dug deep, eyes pleading and so full of me I couldn't resist her. My body lit up like a match that went straight to my dick. The decision not to fuck her roared inside my head, cluttering my plans around until I couldn't think straight. I'm not equipped to fuck her slow and gentle like she needs. I don't even know if I should keep her with me. After seeing the way she opened the door, demanding me to tell her my secret, I've no doubt anymore she can't handle it. It's me who is all fucked up in the head. I can't fathom her despising me over what I do.

Her demeanor has done a complete one-eighty. Like me, she'll always have demons striking her at any moment. Now though as my finger twitches when she shucks off her jacket, runs her palms across her ass I know I have to tell her.

Because I can't let her go. I can't be the same man either. But I can put her wants and needs before my own. As long as she doesn't hate my guts once I tell her there will be times I'll be slipping out of my bed to go kill someone without a word to her.

I haven't wanted to get out of my bed all week. It's been hell and heaven having her body up against me without taking her. A few hours earlier was the hardest. I had just gotten done feasting on her cunt when I hopped out, my dick straining against my jeans. I gave her a swift glance, mumbled she had a half hour to clean up and meet me by the door. I wanted to fuck her until she came so many times she blacked out. The way she squirmed, moaned and said my name when she coated my beard with her release about had me blowing before I flipped her over and marked her gorgeous skin. I've no doubt she hasn't gotten off like she has this past week in years. Pisses me off and places a wicked grin on my face at the same damn time.

I might not be the same man but I sure as fuck would never leave her unsatisfied. Then again, after the things he did to her, it doesn't surprise me. Makes me want to keep her in bed for days, pleasing her in every way instead of making sure she's prepared to kill on instinct.

On the ride to the warehouse, I called for burgers from a joint I frequent whenever I hit this side of town. Even after eating, I can still taste her sweet cunt on my tongue. There isn't a thing I'll put in my mouth that tastes as divine as her.

"I'm not going to ask what you did to convince her to do this. I am going to ask if you think her body is healed enough to shoot."

"She's healed. When it comes to saving herself, she needs to be prepared at all times. Hurt or healthy."

A wave of concern collides with my skull as I grit my teeth. I took her bruises into consideration before setting this up. I see them changing colors every day. Ivy is tougher than I give her credit for. I knew that from the start. She needs to toughen up a hell of a lot more if she's going to stand by my side. I just hope she can remain upright because the devil in me is corroded with corruption.

"I agree. I'm heading out. I have a date." I glance his way, wondering if Nick has gone and lost his common sense. The man doesn't date. None of us do.

"With who?"

He grins. Bastard.

"Her friend Casey. Don't know why but my intuition tells me something is off with her. I followed her into a coffee shop the other day. Kind of bumped into her so she'd spill the coffee she just bought. Played like I felt bad, bought another one, and the next thing I know, I'm asking her out. Chaz is going to check out her place while she's gone."

I shift my stare to Ivy who is still looking at the guns as if they've suddenly amused her. A smile tugs at my mouth when she lifts her head, tugs off the beanie, smiles wide and picks up a pair of head muffs.

Her soft, excited expression causes me physical pain. A part of me hates to be the one that'll break the news to her if Casey is involved. It'll crush her.

"Don't fuck her, man. If she isn't the one it'll complicate things."

"I won't. Might have her blow me though. The woman has the perfect fuckable mouth." He laughs as he tosses me a set of keys.

"Don't touch her, Nick. Get gone. I have work to do here." Appreciate everything he's doing for me. Just don't want him around while I try and control my cock from talking me into laying Ivy in the middle of the table and fucking us both out of our misery. Shit, the thought of her legs spread wide, guns ready to go off all around her has me hard. Fairly certain we'd explode with a louder bang than the bullets.

"That the one you choose?" Knew she'd pick that one. I saddle up behind her, nuzzling her hair out of my way and lick up the side of her neck. "Choose wisely, Ivy. This gun and my dick are the only two things your hands will be wrapped around for a long time."

She gasps.

I nibble.

"Stainless Steel with an Amethyst coating. It's lightweight, cute, but it's deadly. You should have no problem hitting the bullseyes singled handed. Be careful. It's loaded, Ivy."

Fuck me; I love saying her name. Love it more she likes hearing it.

Tracing my hand along the delicate slope of her neck, I pause before I bite down. Her pulse picks up, her breathing labors but she doesn't move away.

Tilting her head back to look at me, those eyes wide with desire and not terror, I open the door to our unknown future a little wider "Tell me you want me." My question slides out in a bumpy tone. Still having a hard time believing she isn't flinching when I touch her. From both her past and knowledge of my soiled hands.

Her bright eyes flash with so much bravery I could drop to my knees and weep. Something about her change challenges me to keep pushing her, and I will, as soon as she answers.

"I want you, Cade. The good and the bad."

Nearly laugh. There isn't an ounce of good in me. If she can find it, it's all hers.

"Yeah. Remember that when I decide it's time to tell you everything. Got another question. You on birth control? I know the doctor did blood work. You're clean. I'm clean. Which means when I fuck you, Ivy, I'm not putting another layer between us. Not when we've peeled so many away."

Her face falls, eyes fill with tears. "I'm not on anything. I've never been on anything. Drew wanted a baby. A son. He was just as obsessed with having one as he was with me. The only way I know I can get pregnant is because he forced me to be tested."

Good thing she isn't tied to the man any more than she is. "Need to remedy that quickly. You good with seeing the doctor again?"

"Yes."

Fuck that simple answer had my dick throbbing.

I need a taste.

"Do you remember how to shoot? If you do, flip the safety and aim when I tell you." This time I don't wait for an answer before slamming my mouth down hard on hers. At the same time, I drive my hands into her hair and tug. I twist her hair tight in my hands, yanking her head back to grant better access to her mouth. Talk about a fuckable one. This woman has it. Lips plump. Mouth wet and inviting. Fuck, I'm caving. Not sure I have it in me to wait. I'm drowning in her exotic beauty. I never want to come back up for air.

A needy sigh escapes her mouth. Tiny pinholes pricking full of hunger wind me tight.

I groan when she sucks my tongue into her mouth. Toying and teasing until I damn near lose control.

Hot as hell.

"Flick the safety and concentrate, Ivy. No matter what I do stay focused," I coax at the side of her mouth. "Show me if you still have it. The recoil on this isn't much. Stop if it is." She isn't going to stop. I saw the determination in her eyes when I told her where we were and what she was doing.

Ivy is much more than a survivor. She's a goddamn fighter.

I shift to sit on the table, settle her between my legs, and position her juicy ass against my dick.

"It's hard to concentrate like this."

"Sure is, you can do it. Think of someone you hate and pull the trigger." The gun goes off just as I extend my hands and let them skim down her sides. My own target in mind.

"I missed." Yeah, she did.

I didn't.

"Keep shooting, Ivy. Don't talk. Pull the trigger and kill the fucker."

I press into her ass. Ivy's snug little body discharges more heat than the gun she keeps shooting off.

Scorching flesh.

Beautiful and healing.

Mine. Always will be.

"See, my gift still has it. Aim a little more to the left." That nickname hung out to dry for years. Now it swirls through the air like an aphrodisiac.

A sweet and tangy scent that I want to inhale. Let it curl into my lungs.

Hooking my thumbs underneath the waistband of her leggings, I slide my hand inside. Her stomach tightens, breathing picks up, but she keeps her aim nice and steady.

"I want you, Ivy. Need to get you off. You good with that?"

"Everything I have is yours, Cade."

Fuck that blows right through my veins. It should have only been mine all along. All of her should have belonged to me, the same way I should have belonged to her.

The ten-year war I've been planning to end screams at me to finish it. My stomach coils, my black heart clenches in its cage. Biting the silky flesh on her neck to hold my tongue, I close my eyes as she continues to shoot.

"Good. When I shove my finger inside you, I want you to scream my name." My twitchy finger that's been dying to get inside of her pussy all day flicks her clit before slipping inside.

She wobbles.

"Cade," she screams. It's music to my ears.

"Stay still." If she wasn't hurting, I'd spank her ass for that little wobble. Instead, I finger fuck her hard. My finger curling until her body shakes, her ass grinding into my pulsing erection. Teasing her this way is a bastard move on my part. She'll appreciate the outcome on both ends.

This beautiful woman, the most valuable gift I've ever held in my hands hit her target several times.

Wonder how beautiful she's going to be once she finds out how many times I've hit mine.

Dead center between their eyes.

Chapter Twenty-Two
Ivy

For what seems like the tenth time in the past two days, I've wandered around Cade's apartment trying to figure out the man behind all this black.

I've watched television, which I never do. Ellie brought me a few books and magazines. Chaz took me to the gym and even roamed around the mall inside this building. After hours, of course. I've seen the doctor, and even though birth control pills aren't additive, to me their still medication. So, we decided to go with an IUD. The one person I haven't seen since we returned from the gun range is Cade.

A gun range that had many thoughts running through my head as to why we were there other than him making sure I could take care of myself. And, why this particular warehouse that was set deep on the property of The Diamond Estate when Cade told me all he did was live in their building. Of course, I've never been to their immaculate home, but I know where they live. I'm sure most everyone in this city who has heard of them knows. And the guns. There were dozens of them. Cade has always had an obsession. Still, I've never seen so many and to top it off; I know that's what The Diamonds do. They smuggle guns.

I should have asked him. Made him demand to tell the truth. He works for them, I know he does. I didn't because my body was still floating from one of the most intense orgasms I've ever had, and my emotions were clogging my throat.

When we left, I told him how good the gun felt in my hands. How natural and how my heart rate kicked up from pulling the trigger.

I felt alive holding that tiny gun. More alive than I've been in years, and even though it should have scared me that I was holding a weapon of death in my hands, it didn't. It had me on a high like never before. It had me wanting to bolt like a strike of deadly lightning up the driveway of Drew's home and blow his brains all over his pristine white floor.

I take a seat on a barstool and glide my fingers across the smooth marble island in the middle of the kitchen. My gaze traveling to the windows. I don't think I'll ever tire of the view. Something tells me that wherever Cade just up and disappeared to in the middle of the night is the reason I should get used to this view. He's not going anywhere. This I can feel deep in my bones.

"Where did you go and why didn't you wake me?" I will the questions to stop screaming at me, to stop piling up, and yet they prattle on trying to search for answers.

I can barely sleep. My concentration is higher than the other night when Cade used his hands, mouth, and words to detour my focus.

Since he tore me wide open by asking me to tell him things about my past. Telling him about the beatings, the guns, the pretending stripped away another piece of it and leaving it behind.

Except my past is still out there lurking. He's looking for me; I know he is.

Trembling, I grip the edge of the chair to keep myself from falling to the floor. "What if he finds me before Cade kills him? What if he shows up here while he's gone?" Panic claws at my stomach. Knowing Chaz is sleeping down the hall doesn't do a thing to stop the anxiety blocking the air to escape from my throat. It swells until I can barely breathe.

I squeeze my eyes shut. Hate, hate, hate trembles and spreads. Remembering what Cade said when he told me to aim and fire.

All I saw was Drew.

His malicious decision to rob me blind of the person I was. Drew twisted the knife in my back until he shattered my spine, yet I'm still walking. Still breathing and as long as I continue to remind myself of that. I'll get through these attacks that come at me out of nowhere.

I hate him more than I ever thought I could hate a person. I want him destroyed, a massacre of his cold-hearted blood to stain my hands. To seek my own vengeance for not only taking from me but killing his family. Hurting Cade, and becoming my ruin.

I open my eyes and slowly lift my head when the door opens.
Tension.

It tightens the air in this room.

The thundering beat of my heart heightens until it rumbles like a roll of thunder in my chest.

Worried and tired dark eyes stare back at me. The mysterious man rigidly stiff and as he peels off his jacket, tattoos I still haven't gotten a close-up of hiding behind his blood-splattered shirt.

Tears roll down my face, and I blink past them, trying to see Cade completely.

"Are you alright?"

"I'm fine. Wasn't expecting to see you sitting there at three in the morning. You look good there, Ivy. Like you belong." He drops a black bag by the door. The same one he took with him the night I found out he was alive.

Pain clutches hold of my being, sending some wicked emotions of turmoil through me as I clutch harder to the barstool. "Whose blood is that?" We haven't talked about when he was going to kill Drew. After shooting the other day, I was hoping Cade would let me be the one to draw Drew's last breath. However, I don't believe that blood is Drew's.

My pulse hammers when he rips the shirt over his head. A wide range of muscle with a rippling effect of abs from chest shooting below the waistband of his jeans greets me, perfect bone structure and all man. His perfect body has me fighting not to strip right here. To lay on this island and have him take me every which way he can.

"It's not Drew's." His tone wavers on the edge of disappointment that it's not. My mind rattles and shakes. I have no idea whose it is, only have a feeling in the pit of my stomach I'm about to learn exactly what kind of man Cade is.

Powerfully, he steps toward me, grabs his pipe and tobacco off the table. Eyes directed down while he packs his pipe.

The man is sinfully beautiful.

Raw and hard.

Handsome and brutal.

Framed in threats.

Bleeding in danger.

Smoke curls around his face, flowing upward in a curly ribbon. His eyes full of worry and want and need and desperation land on me.

"Tell me, please. I see you, Cade. You're there. I want you to see me too, see inside of me and never let me go. I want us to secure ourselves to each other and support each other and fight off anything or anyone who dares to stand between us. But I can't fight off you. I don't want to, you have to tell me where you've been." I know where he's been. I can read his lips before the words come out. I can see it in the way his Adam's apple bobs.

In a blink of an eye, his gaze changes.

Fear.

It stretches across his face.

Fear of losing me. Fear of what I'll think.

That bitch strikes at the most dangerous times.

"I'm a cold-blooded killer, Ivy. That blood was from the man I beat to death."

Chapter Twenty-Three
Cade

The night I found out the hell Ivy had been going through. Hearing her say my name instead of my brother's, a part of me knew there wasn't a chance I'd ever let her go. I kept trying to convince myself she was better off without me when in truth she would have been miserable. The same as me.

My busted up soul wouldn't have been able to survive, wondering what she was doing, who was touching her, if they were treating her right. Yet, I kept telling myself she had to get gone. That my life wasn't a place for a woman who deserved more than I had to offer.

I'm not a saint. I'm a sinner. One at the top of the chain. One the devil himself is probably counting down the years, months, days, hours, and minutes until he welcomes me in his lair. I'll never be what she deserves, but I'll be damned if I free her to live the rest of our days without me.

I may drag her into hell with me, but it's a choice I'm giving her to make.

She's the only woman I'd allow to walk out my door with the knowledge I'm about to tell her without killing them before they made it through the threshold. Could be why I didn't burn my bloodied t-shirt after Nick and I chased some rat bastard motherfucker through the streets of New York.

I hadn't even gone to bed the other night before Roan called and told me the man he'd been searching months for, finally surfaced.

I grabbed my go-to bag where I keep a change of clothes, a few emergency items, guns, and everything I need to kill someone. Then I settled in to watch Ivy sleep until Chaz got here. I left the minute he walked through the door.

Guilt had never eaten away at me so hard. But I had to shut it down. Had to focus on getting my job done. A job that should have brought me back home before Ivy woke up.

The dirty punk had a woman in his bed. Fucking her, her squealing her brains out when we entered the crack house where he was hiding out. I don't think I'll ever get her squawking high pitched voice out of my head. Won't get the stench of the place out of my nose, or the people passed out half dead all over the filthy floor. It's one thing to wipe the scum of this earth off the bottom and kill them. They don't deserve to breathe. It's a whole other thing I can't comprehend when you shine a flashlight into the lids of a teenager who doesn't give a shit whether they live or die by putting poison in their veins.

Only saving grace I got is Roan took the teenage girls from that house. Have no idea where he took them. It's not my job to find out. As long as their safe from someone raping, killing, or snatching them to be sold, then I'm good.

After waiting for the fucker to get his dick off, Nick and I snuck back out and waited in his truck. It was there he told me what he found out about Casey. The bitch is just another person that took advantage of a gift and was hell-bent on destroying it. Haven't quite decided how I'm going to handle the knowledge Nick slid my way. I think a call to my brother will be the deciding factor.

Minutes led to hours while we sat there and waited for signs of life in that house. By the time people started rolling out, it was daylight. We sat in our vehicle and waited. The minute our target emerged. All clean shaven and looking like he hadn't just strolled out of a house full of drug addicts, he climbed in his car and led us across the bridge into Jersey. Took us another day and a half to wait him out. By then I was tired as fuck, angry and when we finally caught his ass, I beat him to death. Then we viciously tore every limb off his body before disposing of his remains.

"What exactly are you telling me, Cade? Are you an assassin for The Diamonds?" I sip on my pipe, pulling the smoke in my lungs. Not sure how to take the tone of her voice. A part of me swears there was a hint of amusement; another part heard uneasiness. The stroke of dread that had to surely be twisting up her nerves.

I've trusted three people completely since my family died. Three out of the hundreds of men and women I served with. No one knew the truth as to why I enlisted. No one knew the truth as to why I never hesitated to pull the trigger.

Shoving my sweat coated hair away from my face I graze her composure. Chin up in defiance with a slight tremble. Shoulders pulled back. Determination shining in the mist of her glossy eyes. Not only is she my weakness, but she's also my strength. Right here, as I spill my darkness into her pure heart, I can see her light beyond the wreckage of my life.

It's time she knew the real truth buried beneath my ink.

"Yes." Slowly, I slide my eyes up her body. Purple fuzzy socks on her feet, black silk sleep pants, nipples showing through the baggy white t-shirt. Hair piled on top of her head. Fiery and inviting. A vision of crawling inside of her after I return home from a kill, shoots straight to my dick. It wasn't but a few weeks ago where I sat outside the house she shared with Drew, thinking something good might come of my life. Never in my life did I think I'd be sitting here telling Ivy I kill people. Never in my life did I think she would still be sitting here looking at me the way she is now. Like she wanted to go along for the ride with me. Like she wanted to pull the trigger and kill someone. One guess who that someone is has my dick knocking on my zipper. "I don't have any regrets about it, Ivy. I am who I am. I won't change for anyone. Including you." This I've told her. Doesn't hurt to toss in a reminder.

We enter into a stare down. A war she and I have already won versus the beginning of a battle I hope she can win on her own. Losing her again just might be the end of me.

The screwed up thing is, I can read most people's minds. Been trained to do it. Detect repulsion when I see it. Smell fear from a mile away. I see neither of those in her eyes. Her mind might be racing against what I told her, but she isn't running. She's thinking. Those once broken down wheels in her head are cruising in my direction at full speed. Gears shifting, whipping her gorgeous mind around the dangerous curves until she slams on the brakes and stops directly in front of me. Opens the door and silently lets me inside.

"I would never try to change you, Cade. We haven't spent near enough time together to really get to know each other again. I doubt it will ever feel like we've made up for lost time. I couldn't stop loving you when I thought you were dead. Couldn't stop thinking about you. I dreamed about you all the time. Day and night, I always strummed up what our life would be like. Marriage, family. Our dream jobs. But that's all they were. A tortured figment of my imagination. Reality is much better than any dream, Cade."

I fight tooth and nail not to smile. Couldn't seem to help the one that felt foreign as fuck on my face. Never put much thought into getting married, sure as hell never thought about kids. Not sure if I'm equipped with bringing any into this screwed up world. Sure as shit wouldn't be able to deal if my child knew what I did. It's hard enough standing here telling the only woman I've ever loved.

Placing my pipe in the ashtray, I stand, spin her stool around and tug her hair out of the band. Those messy curls fall around her face. I wipe the drying tears off her cheeks and lean my forehead against hers. "I had dreams about you too. Mine had you on your back, legs over my shoulder and my mouth on your pussy." My fucking cock twitches at the slight smirk she tries to hide. "Jesus Christ, you are so beautiful. Trying really hard not to bend you over my couch and fuck you. We'll get to that soon enough. I need to rip these last few layers away first." She gasps. A slight sound that in this short time I've decided turns me the fuck on.

"I need you to understand something. You mean everything to me, Ivy. You do. My vengeance is in an entirely different category than what I feel for you. I have to put it first. I've waited too damn long to get it." She silences me with a hand over my mouth.

I want to draw her fingers in and suck.

"Stop. Don't say any more. I understand. Let's continue day by day, and when this is over, that's when we can officially say we're starting over too. I need you to hold me, love me, and protect me. I don't need you to put me before your vengeance. It's yours."

"Shit. Brains and beauty."

She follows it up with a shrug.

I back away, examine her eyes, stare so deep down into her soul while remembering the last time I was inside of her. Light pants and moans fell easily from her mouth. Used to drive me about as crazy as her taste. I loved her more than I could begin to describe. I cherished her, wanted to give her everything when I had nothing to give except a young man with dreams to make the woman he loved happy. It was enough for her. I was enough. She needs to be sure I'm enough now.

"I had intentions of having this conversation with you tomorrow, if you choose me, choose the life I can offer you, this is the only time we will talk about this, Ivy. There will be no more questions from you about this part of my life. As cliché as it sounds, the less you know, the better. I told you I had blood on my hands. More men's blood than I want you to know. There will be times I'll slip out the same way I did. Other times I'll tell you, but you won't know where I am. Who I'm with and you won't ask any questions when I return. Do you get me? The only people I'll tell you about are those that deserve my wrath. You want to know how I'm going to kill Adam and Drew, then I'll tell you. My life is black and white, Ivy. Either you take me as I am or I'll finish getting my vengeance and let you go."

Her decision to be with me has already been made. Still, I want her to know she has a choice. One I want verbalized.

Christ, her calm, soothing expression punctures my soul. It tears me right down the middle. Scattering parts of me everywhere.

"You want to kill him, don't you? Not sure if I can let you do that, Ivy. Not because I don't want you too. You deserve to draw his last breath. Wanting to kill someone and actually doing it, is two different things. You might be ready to move on, but baby, we're talking about taking someone's life. Brutally. Not just a bullet."

I reach up and swipe through the frown lines on her forehead, letting her take in the sincerity of my words. She might be strong. However, murdering someone the way I want to take care of Drew, is something I can't let her be a part of. Just like I'll never come home and expect her to ask me how my day went. I won't apologize if she's sitting here, lying in bed, or if she chooses to work and her mind is wondering where I am. If she'll get a call telling her I'm dead. I won't apologize for the agony I'll put her through. I'm just not wired that way. Not anymore. "If you broke after killing him, I don't think I'd have it in me to fix you. Not that I wouldn't want to try. I'd be the wrong man to do it. I need words, Ivy. You going to talk or are you in shock?"

"I've thought about killing Drew about as long as you have. I tried once. Stabbed him in the leg. We both know how unsuccessful that was. As far as the monster you seem to think you are, I'm trying to figure out what to say. I'm not in shock, Cade. I should have seen it all along. I'm just trying to decide if you really believe everything you said. I see you, you know. The man you keep telling me isn't there. I don't need sunshine and rainbows. Flowers and jewelry. All I need is you. I don't like what you do. I hate it. Violence in any form makes me want to crawl into myself. As long as that violence isn't extended to me, I can live with just about anything. Well, except sharing you with others. Then again, I'm still waiting to claim you as mine. So, there's that we have to talk about too."

The part of me that wants revenge for her wishes she would have killed him. For shit's sake though, if I touch on how she tried killing him any further, it's going to shift my mood to borderline animalistic. I know damn well he didn't let her get away with it. I dare to guess he hurt her in ways I'd rather not know about.

"Not only is she a gift to be cherished, but she also has her own gift of bravery. Warning you, Ivy, I don't plan on sharing a thing when it comes to you." A bright smile crests her mouth. Damn. She's even more stunning when she does that.

I love how she can see right through me the way I see her. This stunning fighter has the power to corrupt me in her own way. The only person to make me beg for forgiveness. There was still so much she needed to know, so much standing between us. Yet, here we are. My gift and me about ready to drive a little bit farther toward the end of one road and the beginning of another.

"I am a fighter. So are you." She's testing me. Tripping me up on edge with her sensibility and understanding sweetness. Christ, I need to get her between the sheets and fuck the feistiness back into her.

"Damn right we are. You might see me in there somewhere.

Get this through your head, Ivy. I don't do sweet, tender, or any of this deep-talking emotional shit with anyone. This is all you're going to get. Don't try and push the old me out." Not about to share with her that if she chooses the only life I can offer her, I'll bend a little in her direction since she's crossing the line to live in mine. Lord knows as well as I do if anyone deserves kind words, it's her. The only thing I won't do is what I said. I won't change who I am. That goes both ways; I won't change who she is either.

My head swims with emotions I haven't felt in years. I want to scoop her up and kiss her tenderly. Except I won't. This is about as tender as I'll get. I'm this close to losing my patience with being tender.

I need to walk in a circle full of rough.

With her.

Not just one of my fingers twitch, they all want to shred her t-shirt down the middle, giving me the access I need to pull those tight nipples into my mouth. Biting them hard. Hearing her whimper in goddamn pleasure. My balls are busting and blue. Fuck, I need to be inside her. Need to stake my claim. Take and give and just plain fuck her.

I'm a raging ball of lust.

Pure fucking hard.

"A weak woman would pack her bags and run. I have nothing to run with, nowhere to go even if I did. Can I forget what you do? Probably not. Can I live with it, can I love you when you walk through the door after knowing where you've been, can I stand by your side with a genuine smile on my face? Yes, Cade, I can. Do you know why?"

Almost afraid to ask. "Why?"

"Because I've never stopped loving you and no matter if I never hear you say it back I will always know you love me too."

I do love her. Just unsure if I can say it.

The edges of her lips lift ever so slightly.

Need compresses against my tongue. It sharpens, seizes hold, and breaks past my parched lips.

I capture hers with mine before she has a chance to say another word.

Chapter Twenty-Four
Ivy

Cade doesn't have to prove anything to me. My stance on violence will never change. I hate it. But I also hate people who think they can take from someone and get away with it.

I'll never know who or why he kills. I'm not even going to try to learn. If he can live with it, then I need to as well. Because living without him isn't an option anymore. But there's one thing I do know, and that's he wouldn't kill someone unless he thought they deserved to die. It's a crazy notion to swallow.

I'll forever be uneasy over it. Will I be worried, anxious, pacing the floor until he walks through the door? Sure. Will I be scared? Hell yes, I will be. More times then I'll care to count.

Still, I'm a believer that love trumps every emotion. It lives and breathes inside of Cade and me. In one heartless night, our love was stripped away, and because of it both of us are different people. I'm going to fight with, for, and beside a man and do whatever it takes to get what I never thought was possible to find.

My freedom.

In all honesty, I'll never be the same woman I was before. Too much of her was deprived of the oxygen she needed to stay alive. That doesn't mean the woman I'll be once Drew is gone won't be someone new either. She may fight demons along with Cade, or they may be gone.

I either live with it or don't. I choose to live. This savage man gave me that choice and no matter what path he chooses to walk down, I'll follow. I want him and everything he has to give. For him to brand me, have me, heal me. To give me new memories that erase the bad.

I pivot when the bathroom door swings open. Steam follows Cade. The man fresh from a shower stands in the doorway with his hand wrapped around his dick.

Stroking.

It's long and thick, begging to be taken inside of me.

I weep and whimper.

My breath hitches when I take a leisurely stroll up and down his body with my eyes.

Black energy zips and soars.

Tremors pulse in my body. Cade's intense words for me to be naked by the time he was done have me dropping my shirt to the floor.

I'm naked. Excited and dripping wet.

He moves toward me where I sit on the edge of the bed, dark and menacing. Powerful and prominent and pushing my breath right out of my lungs. Those sparks he started when he kissed me in the kitchen flicker and blaze. Wrapping me in arousal filled with desire.

A wild rush of invited need between my legs.

"You're so fucking beautiful. Do you have any idea how beautiful you are? Tits and ass and a face a man would kill and die for." He gazes down at me with the same look the night he took my virginity. Eyes full of love. He's crazy if he thinks I don't see him hiding in the shadows begging to emerge.

The thing is, he has every right to shield, to protect and defend his mangled heart. I assume he's done a good job at keeping it hidden from everyone else. Me though, I knew it was there all along. Just as I've known his vengeance needs to be completed before he could truly give me his all.

Shivers trail behind the goosebumps on my flesh, an ecstasy like never before carving a path through my senses and winding me up as eagerness swirls in my stomach.

I need him to devour me.

Everything that has happened before tonight is long forgotten when he removes his hand from his cock, glides it up my back, gathers a handful of my hair, and inflicts the right amount of pain that shoots hunger from my head to my toes. Prying my thighs apart with his leg, he leans down and licks up my neck. This curls my toes and drives the urge to touch myself. His presence, his touch, his smell has me squirming and grinding my ass into the bed.

"I'm going to feast on you before I fuck you hard, Ivy. Please you in ways you deserve. If you need me to stop," I cut him off by circling my hand around his dick.

The fierce man growls like a beast.

"Fucking Christ, your hand feels good."

It's been so long since I've touched him that I want to devour him too. I want to take him as far into my mouth as I can. I ache for it, and that is something I never thought I'd be capable of doing again.

"So does yours. I'm not going to break. I need this as much as you do. Don't ask me to tell you to stop again. I'll never ask you to. Now do as you should have been doing for the past ten years, Cade." My voice crackles in the air. I need him badly.

"I won't break you, Ivy. Trust me though when I say I'm going to split you in half. I promise you right now by the time I've fucked every hole in your body, you'll be coming hard, heavy, and all over my tongue, fingers, and cock."

I shudder as he twitches in my hand. I fall apart when he gently runs a finger over one of my nipples before he pinches and twists, sending a fire of need to my core. White hot fire scatters all over my skin. I have never felt this kind of hunger before. It's the beginning of something wonderful. The way it should have been all along. My brain screams to be worshipped by his rough hands. My body descends into orbit when he pushes me back on the bed, slides his hands down my sides and spreads me open.

My ankles tingle when he grasps them and runs his hands up my calves and thighs, tongue licking a warm trail behind them.

He stops at my scars. Kisses and licks across them before kissing up my body.

My back arches, body fevers as he pulls a nipple into the warm well of his mouth, and works his magic tongue in a circle. Just when I feel that grind to explode between my legs, he moves to the other one. Agony simmers and boils as he tugs hard, biting and causing pleasurable pain as I've never felt before.

It feels so good to have someone give me what I need, and he hasn't even gotten to the best part yet. Although, this tortuous foreplay is building a burning desire that's going to ignite and combust once he slips his thick cock inside of me.

My expectations of being fucked as I deserve are skyrocketing.

"Please, Cade. I need to come."

His body slides down mine. The intense way he fixates on my pussy has me mesmerized. "I've tasted this several times since you've been here. Need to taste it again. Never wanted something this bad, Ivy." His voice is hoarse. About as thick and heavy as his cock.

I'm swollen.

Throbbing.

Desperate.

Worshipped in the way he says my name.

My heartbeat quickens, my breathing turns into pants. I nearly hyperventilate when he palms my ass and runs his tongue between my folds.

A moan escalates from deep inside of me, escaping without warning, and I come with one hard suck of my clit into his mouth.

"Oh, my God!" I cry out and look down at him. Tears of joy fall down my face. I'm delirious. Overwhelmed and still in shock that Cade. My Cade is between my legs. Licking and sucking and feasting on my pussy. I'll never be tired of it.

My legs squeeze tighter around his head. His beard doing a fine job of sketching marks across my skin. Marks that are welcome to stay there forever.

I can't wait to feel him inside me, to finally be thoroughly fucked by the man who in such a short time has become my reason to live. I won't let anyone ever pull him away from me again. I'll kill them if they do. Demons of doing so be damned.

I feel his wicked grin as he eats me with his tongue, nips me with his teeth and builds up another surging orgasm inside of me. Combustion isn't a big enough word to describe what I'm feeling. Not sure if there is one. All I know is my brain freezes, my core clenches and every part of my body goes numb except between my legs.

"You're fucking soaked." His rough inked fingers pinch my clit, dip inside and cause me to spiral upward instead of down. I'm limp and floating and so in need for him to keep his mouth right where it is that I can't speak.

I hold my breath at the unexpected touch of a finger sliding down the crack of my ass, circling the puckered hole before smearing my juices and without doubt, slowly sinking inside. I felt dirty and used before. Now in my own twisted fate, I find my voice and scream out his name as he slides his finger in and out of my ass as violently as his tongue is my pussy.

Penetrating, feverishly probing as every lick, suck, thrust, and nibble undoes me.

"That's it, come one more time, and then I'm fucking you until you black out all over my cock." Good, I'll gladly blackout from him fucking me. At least this time it will be from pleasure and not pain. I grab hold of his hair while he fucks me with his fingers and tongue without objections from me at all.

I can't grasp onto this feeling. I truly thought I hated sex. Any form of it made me want to curl in a corner and disappear into my own little world. But this, this erotic euphoria is better than it's ever been. Better than any wild dream or fantasy I've had.

"I want you on top. Need to see my cock sink inside of you. Need to watch your face when you come." His husky voice sends desirable shivers up my spine.

My entire body vibrates with his words. All I can do is stare as the energy in this room ricochets off the walls and bounces back and forth from me to him.

Sinking into my skin.

He flips onto his back, muscular body covered from neck to ankles in tattoos I want to explore before I straddle him.

"Let me touch you." The man is insanely handsome. Decorated in so much ink I could stare at him for hours.

Sitting up, I inspect the colorful inked flames of fire roaring up his legs. His parents' and sister's names are intricately woven throughout. Guns, knives, horses, police shield. His entire lower half is a dedication to his family.

I want to bust out and cry.

Instead, I lean over and kiss their names. Place my cheek against his leg and gaze up to find his eyes matching the licking flames. His nostrils flaring. Lips spread into a smile instead of a frown.

"It's beautiful, Cade." Nothing more needs to be said between us. Pain is etched in our hearts as well as his skin. It's just him and me. Drawn into a world of pain for one heartfelt moment.

"Get up here and ride me, Ivy. Waited too long to sink in your cunt." Once again, I'm stricken with something dark from my past. I hated that word when it came out of Drew's mouth. It was derogatory and meaningless. With Cade, it's his way of telling me how badly he wants me. How much he wants me to connect with a part of my body that has always been his.

Suddenly, my brain unfreezes with the upswing of the need to ride his cock until I do pass out. I'm not frightened one bit if I lose control of my senses. Because it's *him*.

Cade.

By the time I crawl up his body, my wide awake eager legs straddling him, his length sliding along my folds, I'm practically slobbering like a lovesick idiot.

"Do I have control?" I murmur, feeling braver than I have in a long time.

"Never. Ride it. Fuck it. Milk it dry, just know once you sink down. I'm plowing upward until you feel me for days. Won't stop with just one fuck, Ivy. Plan on me fucking you long after the sun rises."

I'm glad to hear that. Right now though, I need him to make me come alive again.

My skin burns like being in the fiery sun all day when his big hands palm my breasts, fingers pinching my nipples. I wiggle my hips, grasp the base of his dick, and center it at my entrance.

I swallow my gasp as the tip of him stretches me.

I nearly come because my God, seeing his irises turn the darkest shade of black as he watches has got to be the most erotic thing I have seen in my life. I bear down, shivers of happiness heating up my muscles.

"Jesus Christ, Ivy. You're squeezing the hell out of my cock. So tight. Fucking hell, you are incredibly tight." His voice sounds like gravel.

Black energy.

It spikes the air.

Grabbing my hips, he plunges upward in one hard thrust causing me to suck in a sharp breath and exhale from the fullness stretching my walls.

Placing my hands on his chest, I begin to grind up and down his cock. A pleasurable cry leaves my mouth when he lifts me slightly and slams back in. Hard.

Sweat breaks out in between my breasts; my thighs burn, pulse beating in my ears.

I won't ever be the same after this.

This right here is worth every second of pain I've endured. I lean forward, press my lips to his, opening when he bites my bottom lip.

He bursts upward again and again; long, languid strokes are filling me completely. While we both continue to slam and grate and moan, our bodies begin to break out in a sweat. I'm not chilled to the bone like I'm used to being. I'm hot, needy and sweaty. I'm wanted for me.

He groans as he cups my ass, squeezing hard, while his eyes, they never once leave mine.

It's when I clench my walls that his eyes leave my face and drop to where we're connected. He grunts and groans. Turns absolutely animalistic.

In one swift move, he grips my hips, flips me over, and hikes my ass in the air. That hollow spot inside of me wants to scream for him to get off me. Except I don't. Not when his vanilla breath pants in my ear. Not when his twitchy finger pushes on my chin, commanding my head back, and begins to ravish on my mouth. And definitely not when Cade St. James slams into me from behind, fucking me wild and deep.

Mouth dropping open, I scream out his name as I clamp down around his length. My whole body coming alive as my orgasm rushes through me. Cade stills, twitching inside me and shoving his face into my neck with a groan. Somewhere around dawn, I fall asleep peacefully in my protector's arms.

Chapter Twenty-Five
Cade

Living on my own, I never paid the view of the city much attention, until now. There's a quiet peacefulness from up above compared to down below. The eerie glow of the nighttime starless sky. The tall buildings lit up. It's stunning, but it's deadly as hell.

There isn't a place in New York City where a person is safe. This building included. Drugs and power. Gangs on every corner. Thieves. Women and children are stolen in broad daylight. Murderers like me who can make a person disappear.

Monsters during the day and night. We are everywhere.

There's as much corruption being done by those who should serve and protect as there are homeless people on these streets. The screwed up thing about it is, I've dragged a woman worth so much more right into the middle of my messed up way of living.

Not one time during the past week has Ivy complained about being locked away in my apartment. The only time she's left is when we hit my gym or the gun range. This concerns me more than bothers me because it won't be long until the man behind the reason is going to be dead, giving her the freedom to do what she pleases.

I have to give this woman a choice to be herself. A sense of freedom she's still battling her pretty little head over.

The strong woman could do so many things with her life, and here she wants to be with me.

Hell, after everything I told her, there's no way she should be sleeping peacefully in my arms. Making me dinner, and decorating my place for Christmas. Helping me do paperwork while staying secluded in my office at the gym. She's a powerful woman who is quickly reining herself in.

There sure as hell is no way she should be letting me touch her. Yet she does. I don't deserve her love, but I'd be the biggest fool not to take it. Cherish it, and give her my all.

I'm a monster. A man with not an ounce of nobility in my

body. I have no remorse for the unjustifiable things I do. Not even taking one of her biggest fears to bring both of us pleasure. The kind of pleasure I've no doubt will relieve her from another fear.

As I watch her move from the window to the chair, the emotions on her face are hard to decipher. There's a sadness about her. Something more than the loss of her father. Something deep. It's as if she's missing something she's never had. Something within her reaches, yet too far for her to grasp.

"I wanted to come to you the day your dad died. I felt your pain from here. You've had a lot thrown at you lately. Have you thought about what you want to do once this is over?"

Her eyes narrow the same way they used to. Like she's trying to figure out why I'd ask such a question instead of giving me an answer.

"Not really. I need to find a way to get my identity first. I have nothing to prove who I am."

That's an easy solution. I could bust in there with Drew sitting in the next room and slip by without him even knowing I was there. One of the many useful talents the military teaches a sniper that I've taken full advantage of. At this point, I wouldn't care if he was there. All I'd do is torture him in his home. Vengeance for me. Retribution for Ivy.

"I assume there are security cameras around Drew's house. Tell me the code, and I'll come back with everything you want." I was planning on breaking in there, regardless if she gave me the easy way in. I want my knife.

"All I want is my wallet. It was inside a silver clutch the night you took me. I'm sure he has it. Where, I don't know. Probably in one of the safes in his office. Burn the place down when you're done."

I frown, can't do that like I want. It's a family neighborhood. Might be snowing like a sieve outside. Doesn't mean I'll chance a fire when there are kids around unlike my brainless fuck of a brother.

"I can't leave here, Ivy. If you want to be with me, whatever you do has to be done here."

I think she'd do just about anything for me. Including living in a town that has brought her nothing but heartache. Total bullshit on my end to think I have the right to breathe the same air, live in the same space while waiting to carry out my vengeance and not right my wrong when it comes to Ivy. She needs to know where I stand in order for me to get on the road to making things right before I warranted anything more for myself.

The thought of her giving up her dreams to take care of her father, then given no choice to follow them, punctures me like an arrow.

Can't stop the commotion in my mind. The idea of where she'd be if she didn't marry Drew and went to college. Would she be happy? Have kids? If so, she wouldn't be here with me. Ready to give up more.

My insides clench.

In fault.

In blame.

In redeeming my wrong.

Then there's the news about Casey. I haven't decided how to handle what I've learned about her friend. The woman is a conniving bitch who doesn't deserve to have Ivy as a friend as far as I'm concerned. Not my choice to make. It's Ivy's.

"You can do anything you want, Ivy."

"How about a job at the gym. I don't know; maybe you'd tire of being with me."

Fuck. Me.

I let a grin tweak up one side of my lips. "I have a lot of time to make up for. Hanging out with you was never, nor will it ever be a bad idea. You give it some thought. If that's what you want, then I'll put you to work."

"Okay."

She clears her throat, widens her eyes, and swings those long fucking legs over the arm of the chair. Her gaze parking on my mouth. My mind shifts back to sexual proclivities in an instant.

Her face is still free of makeup. Hair an untamed mess of curls.

There's such a raw honest purity about Ivy. One that captures your attention. One that lures you in and once she has you, those eyes burn with fire. The woman has been back in my life for weeks, and she's already slain me. Incinerated in her innocence.

Drawn in by her hidden carnal appetite.

"You wore your hair straight, fancy clothes and makeup for him, didn't you?" Ivy is one of those women who was blessed with natural beauty. She hated her curls. I loved them. She wasn't into makeup. I could have cared less. Might have noticed her face and body first. Those weren't the things that kept me coming back. It was her inside beauty that did.

I take one last sip on my pipe, place it down and travel the length of her body all the way down to her chipped red polished toes. Fuck, I want to drop and worship her. Suck her toes in my mouth, and lick up her leg until I dip my tongue, and dig my fingers between her thighs.

My cock stirs with the need to dirty her in a pleasurable way everywhere.

To erase another piece of Drew. To do something I've always dreamed of doing with her.

She gifts me with one of those I-know-what-you're-thinking grins she picked up in the last few days. It develops into a smile so bright that actually tightens my stomach in yearning to see it every day for the rest of my life.

"Yes. The woman you saw wasn't me. She was programmed to do what she was told out of fear. I took the only choice I had."

"Give her a choice to make up her own mind. Don't make it for her. If you do it'll be the biggest mistake, you'll ever make."

There's that word again. *Choice.* We all should have one. It wasn't my choice to live this kind of life. It dropped in my lap. It wasn't her choice to be left behind. It wasn't her choice to beaten and tortured to give her dad what he needed. I'm about to give her one now.

The choice to lay all her fears and nightmares to rest.

"Do you trust me?"

"Yes," she answers without hesitation.

"Come here."

I groan when she swings those legs to the floor, and I catch a glimpse of the neatly trimmed triangle through her panties.

She peers down at me with heavy-lidded eyes. Grabbing her hand, I yank her down on top of me, running the pads of my fingers over the soft curves of her hips and legs.

"I want all of you, Ivy." Her body shivers as I grab the hem of the shirt and whip it over her head. Tight hard nipples stare me in the face. Lush tits I want to slide my dick in between. A long neck and throat I want to jet my streams of cum over.

I draw one nipple into my mouth. Suck and lick until she arches.

"Oh God, please."

My dick is ready to explode.

"I want this, baby. You going to give it to me?" I place my hands on her ass, push the lace aside and slide a finger down the crack.

The rational side of me knows not to push her this way. I can't seem to help it. I want to give her pleasure at the same time I take away her pain.

"I want you in every way, Cade." Fuck, this woman. I'm not worried about dying by someone else's hand. Not when she's slowly killing me with her strength.

Poison fucking Ivy I'd gladly roll my body in every goddamn day.

Pouncing. I sweep up and draw her bottom lip between my teeth. She lifts a hand to my hair. The other tugs on my beard. Mouths closing over each other's. Tongues darting out and in one swift movement, I flip her to her back, my cock pressing into her pussy. She liquefies enough beneath me that I take over the kiss. Claiming her mouth with urgent strokes.

My hands hold her face as I steal her breath by plundering her mouth with my tongue. Each lash is a choice to surrender. Each stroke is a choice telling her she can work by my side. Go to school, not work at all. I don't fucking care as long as whatever she chooses is being with me.

"Cade."

Goddamn, every time I hear her say my name. Every time I sink into her tight body. It fully redefines my way of thinking from the first night she thrashed around in my bed. Her mind so oblivious to what she was saying.

I'll never tire of hearing my name being spoken in clarity. Out of sexual need for me in her right frame of mind.

I love her. Fuck I do.

On a growl, I launch up, taking her with me and marching us down the hall. What I have in mind needs to be done in my bed.

Chapter Twenty-Six
Ivy

Cade gently skates his free hand up the side of my stomach and over my breast, and with one finger, trails up the center of my chest until he reaches my chin. He cups it for just a few moments before moving over to my cheek, his rough hand's stroke tenderly.

The room is eerily quiet as he continues to stroke my cheek. It's a loving and caring touch to calm and soothe me, to convince me to let him do this. This is something I have never done of my own free will.

Even so, I'm not frightened.

"Thank you for saving me." My voice is hoarse. My words are coming from a spot inside me I never thought would see the light of day. My inner self. Me. The Ivy I've missed as much as he has.

He nods. That's as much of a thanks as I'm going to get. I'll take it. Hold onto it along with everything else this man gives me. Like a job. A job I'll think about later.

Leaning his head down. His expression is close to savage as he brushes his nose along mine. Stares deep enough into my eyes I can feel him slip through my soul.

I angle my hips upward. He needs to finish what he started. I'm desperate for more.

"You sure about this?"

"I'm always sure when it comes to you."

"Fuck, Ivy." His mouth crashes down on mine with enough force my body shakes. His tongue taking over so easily I surrender a little more with every sharp whip of his tongue.

My panties are ripped away. His shirt is tossed over his head. Jeans yanked off, and I'm flipped over, ass tugged in the air before sucking in a harsh breath when he plunges two fingers into my waiting core. Fingering me until I'm on the cusp of splitting apart.

Goosebumps feasts on my flesh. My body ablaze.

Trembling, my hands fists the comforter.

I hunger for him and everything he wants to give me. He's already marked me, scared me in good ways for life, and taken away so many bad memories. He's about to take this one too. If only I could get past the one where Drew forces me on my hands and knees.

I hitch my breath and tip my head forward when I feel him running the tip of his cock up and down the crease of my ass.

A tattooed hand drags up my thigh over my pussy before skimming along my sides to palm a breast.

"You're mine. All of you belongs to me the same way I belong to you." Those words rumble his black energy in my ear and right down my spine.

"He forced you to do this? Did it when you were knocked out?"

"Yes." I close my eyes, my breathing labors.

"I'll never force you. This is me and you, Ivy. Say no."

"I would have if I didn't want to."

He groans, kisses the shell of my ear, his chest crowding my back.

Just like when every time he's taken me from behind, it thrills me. Spiraling into a need to have his skin against mine. To have him push me further with just a touch.

"Your body responds to my touch the same way mine responds to yours. You got desires floating around in that gorgeous head of yours as much as I do in mine. You want this, baby?"

He already knows I do.

"This is what I've always wanted. To feel a deep fierceness with you. To dangle on the edge until we fall."

I suck in a sharp breath or stop breathing altogether; I'm not sure which when he rubs my juices around the rim of my ass, prodding a little deeper with every swipe.

"I want you in my bed, in my house, working beside me. It's driving me to the point of insanity that we've barely spent time together and here I am wanting so much from you. I lied when I said vengeance comes first. It doesn't, Ivy. You do. You always will."

The pain in his voice matches what lies in my heart.

"We have all the time left in the world."

His response is to press a finger inside of my ass. I tense briefly. Relaxing when he snakes his free hand up my back, pulls on the ends of my hair, and runs his tongue up my neck at the same time his thumb glides across my clit.

"Oh God. Cade." My body melts right into his. I don't have a clue how he manages to do what he's doing. He continues to stimulate my pussy with the quick push and pull on my clit, swirling more of me around my hole, plunging inside and stretching.

My skin burns with an urgency to let go and spin out of control, losing myself in the dizzying pleasure. My breathing becomes heavier. The walls between my legs close in. My orgasm trips right through me. I welcome it as it climbs higher and higher with every stimulating movement he makes.

I'm met with heavy breathing in my ear along with something large and demanding when he releases his hold on my hair, reaches down and grabs his cock, and nudges it slowly into my ass.

"Oh," I whimper as he begins to push into me.

"Relax, Ivy. I'll make it feel good. In order to do that, I have to be buried deep in this tight little ass."

He inches in a little farther at a time. God, it hurts, yet it feels good at the same damn time. I squirm underneath his touch. My body is fighting him every step of the way.

When it hurts to the point I'm ready to ask him to stop; he begins strumming my clit in circles. "You wait until you come, baby. I swear to God I'll make you come so hard all you remember is how good this feels. Fuck," Cade whispers gruffly, pushing in farther. "Tell me you're okay, Ivy."

"Yes." I don't know if I am or not. All I know is I want all of him the way he wants me. I want this darkened forbidden part of my past lifted from my spirit.

He pushes in deeper, stretching me in sweltering pleasure, the pain heating me from the inside out. I moan as he seats himself deeper. I'm shaking in a turbulent desire I never knew existed. Dirty and hateful memories are vanishing as he sinks all the way in.

"Oh, God," I scream out when he starts to move. It does feel good. So good that I flop my head forward. He plunges a finger into my core while slowly moving in and out of my ass. I'm bursting. Overflowing to the point where everything inside me catches fire. White hot flames fly in front of my face, and my release builds up as he works in and out of me in a way that has my body buzzing. Never in my life did I think it could feel this good. This full feeling that all of me feels all of him.

"Cade," I scream. "I'm close." I swear to all things holy I'm going to combust. He grunts, beginning to move faster, keeping up the rhythm with his fingers.

I scream when the sensations of my orgasm rule my entire body. It's all making me dizzy as I completely fall apart underneath this man who is stripping away my tortured past one touch from his tattooed hand, masculine body, and traces of the old Cade, at a time.

Chapter Twenty-Seven
Drew

"So you're telling me someone walked right in last night and handed the security guard an envelope for me and left? And you people can't get a read on his face. Is that what I'm hearing?" The head of security on the other end of the line needs to be fired right along with the piece of shit who didn't ask whoever dropped this nice little surprise off for me who they were. I mean, who the hell shows up at the crack of dawn completely covered from head to toe in black winter clothes with a ski mask and hands someone a plain white envelope, then walks out the door without being suspicious.

"That's exactly what I'm telling you. We have armed security everywhere, Mr. St. James. This building also holds apartments. Packages are dropped off at all hours of the day, and it is winter. In New York, I might add. It's cold out, in case you haven't notice. Criminals aren't the only ones who wear masks to cover up their face when it's below zero, sir. If you think you can get a read on the person, I'm more than happy to send up the footage." Cocky little bitch might want to slow down her mouth and think about who she's talking to before I barge down there and show her with my fists what disrespecting me means. I'll get her ass thrown out, and then she can carry on about masks, cold, and winter.

Speaking of winter, there are only three weeks left until Christmas. My house should be decorated by now. Ivy should be doing all kinds of shit around this office like she does every year. Goddamnit.

"Send them to me." I slam the receiver down. Huff out a breath and pour myself more scotch. Doubt I'll have a clue who it is. Besides, if it was Cade, he wouldn't have shown up here, he would have tracked me down to end our war. No, this is part of the game he's playing to drive me further insane. To let me know he's stopping at nothing to ruin me.

"Nice move, Cade. There's no way Casey would give him that

information. She knows what will happen to her and her precious fucking brat if she does." I should pay her a visit. If I do, she'll be more suspicious than she already is. Bitch showed up here the other day demanding to know where she is. I had to shut her up by writing a big fat check when what I really wanted to do was slice her open from top to bottom.

"And here I thought she was a timid little mouse only good for a random fuck." Women, they truly are only good for one thing, and most of them aren't even good at that. And if they are, they make it way too easy to get it. Fucking whores. All of them.

I exhale in disgust. Peer down at the information I'm sure was sent to me by Cade and rip the sheet of paper in half.

Information that could destroy me if it gets into the wrong hands. Information that should have never been so goddamn easy to find.

"You're starting to piss me off, little brother. Where's my wife, you goddamn thief?" Bet she's in his bed with him. Her dry as a bone cunt is nice and wet for him. Smiling and laughing. Fucking bitch.

I tip back my scotch, glare at my wedding picture sitting on the edge of my desk. "I wonder if you didn't drug yourself just to get away from me. Have you known he's been here all along? Should have waited until I knew you were in his room and burned you too." Should have done a lot of goddamn things. Then I wouldn't be sitting here before the milky gray clouds hover across this city. A city where I can't find my wife.

My fingers dig into my palms as my fists squeeze with the rage at how long I'd let Cade live. I should have found a way to have him killed behind those enemy lines instead of starving to look him in the eye before one of us kills the other. That ravenous need has eaten away at me for years. Now I'm going out of my mind wondering if he's touched her. Speculating that he has, and pissed the fuck off that my wife would let him, and enjoy it.

The malice I've felt toward my brother since the day Ivy walked into our parents' home behind him. Her sweet laugh echoing through the house when she sat talking to Rachel, and the way my parents took her and her father in has haunted me just as long. It should have been me introducing her to my family. Me who she should have been staring off into space for what felt like hours thinking about when in truth it was only minutes. Minutes that bent me up inside until the raw anger had me trying to beat or fuck him out of her system. Every damn time I brought her to her knees I wished like hell it would be the last. Prayed to the devil he'd make her stop looking at me vacantly and finally look at me the same way she did him.

My cell phone rings. Just like last time he called, I know it's Cade. The shrill ring torments me. I debate for a bit before I pick it up and hit the green button. His heavy breathing echoing in my ears.

"Thieves get caught, Cade. What all did you take when you broke into my house?" I grit, breathing slowly through my nose to calm the anger bubbling in my blood.

Prick broke into my house last night and tore it the fuck apart. The only thing left of my bed was the frame. The word vengeance carved into the expensive wood.

"Not my problem if you can't figure it out. I don't have time for an interrogation. Especially from you. Got a question for you though. Remember the time I snuck up on you and that chick who was giving you a blow job in your car? Scared her so bad your dick fell out of her mouth. You about beat my ass because I wouldn't stop laughing. You thought I was laughing because I cockblocked you. Man, you were after that girl to go out with you for a long time. Think you might have been obsessed. Know why I was really laughing?"

Don't know why he thinks I fucking care. I got what I needed after I shoved him to the ground and told him to get his punk ass back inside.

Bitch wasn't near as good as Ivy's warm and wet mouth.

"Are we taking a stroll down memory lane? Because if we are, I can tell you all about the first time I fucked Ivy. How about the first time she sucked me off on her hands and knees." I laugh. Can almost picture his veins popping out on his neck.

"Feel free to talk all you want. Ivy isn't a pawn. She's a queen. She might get taken down, but we all know she gets right back up ready to spring into action. She wants you dead, Drew. Get what I'm saying? Back to my story. It was because of the size of your dick. It wasn't any bigger around than a baby dill pickle. I still laugh. Used to laugh about it when I sat in the desert plotting your death. I'm laughing harder now that I've been fucking and pleasing Ivy. Her pussy is tight, warm, and mine. She tastes like heaven with a heavy dose of sin. Her mouth. Goddamn her mouth is sweet. You should see her when I take a sip of my pipe and blow the smoke in her mouth. Swear to God there's something in the tobacco that turns her on. She can't stay off my cock. Wants it every chance she can get. And fuck it's a beautiful sight when she comes. You wouldn't know what she looks like when she comes now, would you?"

I grind my teeth through a clenched jaw, trying not to flip the fuck out on him. That's what he wants. Goading little shit.

"How long are you going to stall this out? Come at me, Cade. Let's fight this out brother to brother."

I sit in my chair, my fingers digging into the empty crystal glass. Squeezing until my knuckles burn. He took something away from me I can't live without. I'd already lost my mind when I started taking my anger out on her flawless skin. Marking it with all I had. I couldn't stop once I started. That primal need to break her until there was nothing left of the woman who couldn't love me overruled my love for her.

If he's had her, which I've no doubt he hasn't, there won't be anything left of me. I live daily with endless reminders of mistakes and regrets, the things I could never change. But I needed to do those things in order to save me from killing her the same way I killed my family. A family I once loved.

I needed to fuck every woman I could. Needed to be the best in the courtroom. Needed the control because no matter what I did to Ivy, I couldn't control her heart or mind.

"Let's get something straight, Drew. I'm not your brother. My brothers are the men I fought beside. The men who had my back. You think I want to fight you? Man, you are more oblivious to what I've already done than I thought. You think I don't know where you are right now? That I couldn't look through my scope and put a bullet through your head? That I can't stand over you tonight while you sleep and suffocate you without anyone knowing I stepped foot in your house? I want your blood, Drew. When I take it, it's going to be with my fists and weapons. That last breath you draw is going to be with my knife. The one I'm holding in my hands. Technically, it wasn't stealing since it's mine. Need to finish this call so I can get back to Ivy. Drew, you should see her. Her ass is high, tight and juicy. She's running on a treadmill in my home gym. Thought I'd spare you the worry too. You know from the bruises and sexual abuse you inflicted. Ivy's nice and healed. Only marks on her body are my fingerprints from grabbing her hips and slamming into her tight pussy so hard I lose control. Taste so sweet I've been eating off of her. You were right about her being nice and tight. Don't think that pounding you did with your pencil dick did much."

His laughter blares in my ears.

"I knew you were in my house. I could smell Dad's scent. Is that where you stole the papers from?" Cade's hitched breath, and sudden silence has me releasing a dark chuckle. Must be he doesn't want to talk about dear old dad.

Fury swiftly replaces every emotion, every sensation, and every bit of antagonizing word coming out of his mouth.

"You want to know, go check your safe for yourself. By the way, you haven't found out who drugged Ivy yet, I see. I did. Found out all kinds of information since we last talked." My blood starts vibrating a little close to my liking.

"I already did check, and I know who drugged my wife. He's been taken care of." My sneaky brother stole a half million dollars, and the box of a few personal belongings I stashed away before I torched the house. Along with Ivy's clutch, her passport, and my life insurance policy.

"Taken care of how? Did you kill him or don't you have balls to take someone's life anymore?" Damn, he's a nosey little fucker.

"Who and what I did to him is none of your business. Just like my wife isn't your concern. You share that information you found out with Ivy, and it will hurt her. Is that what you want? I'm going to kill you, Cade. I don't need a weapon. Not when I've been waiting to do it with my hands. Tell me where to meet you, and I'll be there. You don't need to surprise attack me. Not when I want you as dead as you do me."

"Shit isn't going down like that. It happens when I say. I'm the one out for vengeance, Drew. Vengeance you made me want. Vengeance that doubled when I found out what you've been doing to Ivy. My Ivy. The woman who has always belonged to me. You have no say in when I kill you. You have no say in what I tell Ivy. I'm going to say this once. I got my eye on Casey and her daughter. If you so much as touch them, look in their direction. You'll die before your time. Gotta go fuck my woman and take her to buy a Christmas tree. Next time I talk to you, it'll be in person."

I throw my phone after he hangs up. Shattering it against the wall.

I killed the little bastard who dared to drug my wife. His admission on his deathbed was something I should have seen. Little pricks of this world always want something that doesn't belong to them. Always wanting more than what they deserve.

"I need a drink. I need my wife," I yell. Kick my chair so hard it smashes up against the window.

Feet moving to the bar in my office. I swipe up the bottle of scotch, take my hand and sweep the rest of the shelf clean. Clattering the bottles to the floor. Glass breaking, liquid pooling at my feet.

"Goddamnit. Motherfucking son of a bitch," I roar, tip back the bottle and chug. My throat starts burning, stomach churning and anger boiling into a rage I need to fuck some willing pussy to get it out. Even then it won't subside. Not until I meet Cade face to face. Thief and his wise talk have a fire burning holes in my veins.

Every damn thing I've worked hard for is crumbling at my feet. I need her back in my life. I can't function without her. Everything else can go to hell. Without Ivy I'm nothing.

I push the couch over that I've fucked many women on. The chair where my clients sit, everything on my desk goes crashing to the floor. I swing at the air. Wishing every punch was my brother's face.

"Fuck you both," I scream at the top of my lungs over and over again, until my throat stings. And my chest heaves. "She's mine."

Dropping to my knees, glass digging into my skin. I pick up the broken framed picture and tug it to my chest.

"I'll get you back, and when I do, I'm going to kill us both."

Chapter Twenty-Eight
Cade

Ivy slows from running to walking on the treadmill, her chest heaving up and down.

"Son of a bitch." Her words blending with his enclose in my chest, squeezing tight. So incredibly tight. I feel them digging deeper, twisting like precious ivy up my spine.

"I've thought about killing Drew about as long as you have. I tried once. Stabbed him in the leg. We both know how unsuccessful that was."

"All I want is you."

"She sucked me off on her hands and knees."

This woman placed her trust in me, let me push her a little farther out of her comfort zone by giving me what I thought was the last of her demons. Before that, she knew I'd bolted from the kind of lifestyle I wanted to live. She still let me in. Still cares about the man she sees, and here I stand with my dick hard getting ready to push her through the final step to free her beautiful spirit.

Her confession about killing Drew was spoken with as much vengeance as I have. Those words slamming into me with such force they've been living in the shadows where only the evilest of thoughts have lived.

My lungs constrict and seize.

The same night I slid into hell, Ivy wasn't far behind.

I curl my lips upward. I have to give her the vengeance she deserves.

I lied to Drew about taking her to get a tree. I had already gotten one. Sent Ellie on a shopping spree for decorations and now my home is lit up with the first Christmas tree I've had since my family died. Could care less if I have one, it makes Ivy happy, and that's all I care about.

Funny how two people who used to love the same things turned into opposites and yet they still find themselves attracted to one another.

One thing I didn't lie to Drew about was her staying off my cock. She wants me as bad as I want her. Shit, the minute we're alone, I'm inside of her before we hit the bed.

There was something in Drew's voice that doesn't sit right with me. It has to do with whoever drugged Ivy. Not sure if I believe him or not. If the other information Chaz found out the same night he snooped through Casey's apartment is any indication, then Drew is telling the truth. Guess there's only one way to find out.

Reaching for my phone, I shoot Nick a text with my plans, wait for his response and shut it off when he sends me one of those stupid thumbs up emoji things. I hate those fuckers. He and Chaz use them all the time. Fucking assholes.

"Don't move," I call out from behind Ivy causing her to whirl around. She's sweaty. I'm about to make her soak in it. Incapable of running for the next couple days if I have my way.

Dimming the lights, I make my way toward her as I grip my cock through my shorts. "Used to watch you through the glass of my office when you worked out. I jacked off dozens of times watching you. Dreamed of you dropping to your knees and sucking me off." Bastard fucking move on my part. Shit needs to be done. I want all of her fear gone.

Her features twist in pain.

"She sucked me off on her hands and knees."

Fucker forced her to do it. Just like he forced her to do everything else.

"Tell me?" I clasp her chin between my thumb and my twitchy finger to guide her face up. I know how much this is going to burn my ass about as much as it's going to hurt her to say it.

Her eyes fill with tears, but she holds them back. "He made me crawl to the end of our bed and forced me to take him in my mouth on my hands and knees."

I swallow down her pain while my hatred for Drew grows. The man is going to die on his hands and knees. Penance for what he made her do.

"I'd never force you to do anything."

"I know that."

I stare into those eyes that trance me every damn time waiting for more, but she slips out of my hold, takes off her shoes and socks, tugs her sweats and panties off and drops to her knees.

"Stand up, Ivy. You don't have to prove anything to me." I glare down at her, feeling the air inside my body burning with anger.

"No. I want to do this. I'm proving to myself I can do it, Cade. I want him out of my life before you kill him. Don't pity me. Love me. Drop your shorts." Her mouth screws into a rebellious expression as blood rushes to my dick. The air in my lungs ceases when she drags her fingers down the front of my shorts and grabs my balls. It's gut instinct when my eyes close and I fight to keep in a moan.

"I don't pity you. I admire the fighter in you." The stubborn woman shows more strength every damn day. "If you want this, you're going to have to pull me out yourself."

With lack of hesitation, she yanks my shorts down and grabs the base of my dick. My eyes roll. I'll never be tired of her hands on me. A pleasure a dirty man like me inhales every chance I get.

My mouth drops open to ask her if she's sure. However, before I get a word out, Ivy leans forward and pulls my entire length in her mouth. "Holy Fuuuuckkkkk," I roar so loud I wouldn't be surprised if the machines in here don't wobble.

Her hands slip to my ass as she teases and taunts my slit with her tongue. My hips thrust forward, my hands begging to grab hold of her head and fuck her mouth with my own pace.

Fast and furious.

I clench one fist, take hold of the handle on the treadmill with the other while she sucks me so hard into her mouth, it makes me wish I was capable of going easy on her.

I peek down to her watching me, her pupils are dilated, her tongue darting out, and our eyes convey a type of trust I never thought I'd see again. It's written all over her as she licks the underside of my shaft, digs her nails into my ass and fucks my cock with her mouth and tongue.

Sliding my fingers toward the back of her neck, I lightly grip, causing a moan to escape through her plump swollen lips.

I about blow into her mouth when she spreads her legs, inserts a finger into her dripping pussy, and fucks herself in sync to her bobs on my dick.

"Damn, Ivy." She thrusts in another, never taking her eyes off of mine. "How wet are you?"

"I'm dripping," she mouths around my cock.

I smell the heady scent of her in the air. Those fingers wet with her arousal. I want them in my mouth.

"Suck on them, but don't you dare take my dick out of your mouth." Pulling them out slowly, her juices smeared all over her fingers; eyes hazed over in lust, she wipes them on my dick and licks.

I groan and watch in approval as she darts her pink tongue out, runs her perfect mouth up and down my ridge tasting herself. Not a bit of wavering.

Naughty fucking woman.

My *gift.*

"Christ, baby."

Heat from her warm mouth sizzles through my cock.

I can't hold back. Shoving my hand into her hair, I thrust forward while she deep throats the hell out of me. I fuck her harder, deeper, and rejoice in the sexy submission of her greedy moan.

A grunt speeds through my brain as my spine tingles letting me know I'm close. I'm not blowing in her mouth. Not this time.

"Get up here." I step back, my cock aching, her mouth hanging open. I need inside her now. Bending, I grasp her by the waist, step onto the treadmill and hoist her onto the angled display and spread her legs over the bars. Perfect alignment for me to thrust right in.

Her breasts are heaving up and down in the confines of her sports bra, her nipples hard as hot little rocks.

I palm my hands on her sweet little ass until her pussy is aligned with my groin.

"Tonight I'm going to make good on my promise of fucking you raw."

Tilting in, I take her by that feisty mouth. Diving in to taste her with the first sharp swipe of my tongue. I'm not usually a man who takes my time. Always have with her though.

When she bites my lip, I know it's time to fuck her.

"Hang on tight, Ivy. I'm not taking mercy on your pussy. I've fantasized since the first time you walked in here to fuck you after you worked out." I slam into her hard. Her body jolts backward, fingers digging into my shoulders. Her pussy clenching my cock for dear life.

I pound into this woman's tight body so hard I can't even fucking think straight. She feels goddamn good.

Silk and seduction.

A temptress.

"Oh, God, I'm going to come, Cade." My name is bouncing off the walls and hitting my chest.

"Fuck, yeah, you are. Take it, take all of my cock and coat him with your pretty pussy. Play with your clit. I want you coming until you can't fucking think, Ivy." I lift her ass just enough for her to place her fingers right where I can see them. I want her to feel me slamming into her everywhere.

"Jesus fucking Christ if you could see yourself right now. Your greedy pussy is pink, wet, and swollen. It's gripping the hell out of me, screaming for more. You love this, don't you?"

"Yes. I love it." She pants, tits bouncing, nipples so tight I wish I would have pulled her bra down so I could pinch and twist them.

Like her, I can't get enough of hearing her say my name.

"Say my name. Scream it, Ivy." I growl, grabbing the ends of her hair, pulling it until her back arches, her body strung taut in my hands. Those eyes directed at me.

"Cade, Cade, Cade," she yells. I feel her hard, desperate breaths in my lungs.

Her body bucking wildly against mine with her fingers moving over her clit has my hips thrusting as hard as they've ever done before. I want to fuck her wild. Make her insane and dip right back in for more.

Gorgeous woman is giving as good as she's getting. Her striking eyes are glazed over in so much desire I can hardly see the white around their color. The more I thrust into her, the tighter my balls become. I'm sweating my ass off trying to hold out to get one more release out of her sweet little cunt. I've never fucked a woman so hard in my life.

"You better give me one more before I fill up this pussy of yours." I slam into her hard, my legs burning. My thighs are clenching, and when she clutches her walls around me, I spill into her on a wild roar. Her name is falling from my lips. I milk my cock until it's dry.

My cock starts to harden again the minute I pull out of her and watch my cum drip down her slit to the puckered hole of her ass. Fuck me that is hot.

In her weakness, she found her strength.

Chapter Twenty-Nine
Ivy

It's only been about an hour since I woke to a cold chill hit my back when Cade climbed out of bed and whispered for me to get up and showered before slipping out of the bedroom. I have no idea what's going on. I hurried through my morning routine with an unsettled edge in my gut.

I'd always known Cade was a straightforward man. What you saw in him was who he was. He's potent. He's honest, but the man unknowingly took the last bit of fear out of me last night with just one loving look.

After he plowed right through my insecurities and I took him into my mouth I could feel my strength to stand on my own deriving from him. I'm no longer afraid, and that is something I never thought I'd admit to myself.

A mixture of unease and discomfort twists through my body as I make my way down the hallway. I inhale the scent of vanilla mixed with pine, and it calms me a little knowing this will be one of the best holidays I've had. If only my dad could be here with us to see just how happy I am. I can't wait to get out of here to visit his grave.

My uneasiness comes to a screeching halt when I round the corner to a familiar head of blonde hair sitting on the couch across from Cade.

"Casey, what are you doing here? Where's Molly?" Excitement grows in my stomach. I'm so happy to see her that I could cry a river full of happy tears.

I want to kiss Cade and tell him thank you for bringing her to see me. That is until I round the couch and the look on Casey's face tells me this surprise visit isn't one she wanted to make.

Unease builds again. A bind of something ugly claws at my insides, trickling slowly as it spreads through my veins like a deadly virus.

"Molly's in the game room with Nick. I'm glad to see you're okay. I've been concerned about you. To be honest, I've been troubled about you for years. Almost five to be exact. That, plus jealous." She prattles about things that don't make a lick of sense to me. Long gone is her friendly voice, kind eyes, and gentle nature. In its place is hostility bristling with anger. Anger directed at me.

My chest screams with confusion. Her strange greeting thickening the air to my lungs and triggering a wire in my brain that crackles and hisses and breaks.

What in the ever-loving hell?

"What are you talking about?" The chaos running through me isn't that chaotic to think maybe I didn't hide what was happening in my home from her as well as I thought. But that's not what bothers me. It's the last word she spoke that does. Why would anyone be jealous of me? Especially my best friend.

Warily, I jerk my head toward Cade who glares at Casey as if she's a threat to my beating heart. As if he knows what she's talking about and wants her to spit it out so he doesn't have to look at her anymore. As if the sight of my best friend makes him sick to have her in his home.

He looks like he wants to kill her.

"I'm talking about your husband. The father of my daughter."

"What?" I shake my head. "Her father? No!"

Her eyes shed the truth.

Betrayal and anger brew deep in my being, bubbling like lava. They roil within, hungry to spread a layer to protect me from the only friend I thought I had. If I would have known about this while I was still with Drew it would have broken me because I trusted her.

But not anymore.

"You have got to be kidding me. If I hadn't lived with abuse for years by Drew's hand, I would beat the shit out of you. I could care less who that vile man sleeps with. It's you, you who took me for granted. You played on my friendship, Casey, and that is something I will never forgive you for. I cried to you about my dad. I shared intimate details with you about how I couldn't let go of Cade. We traded secrets. The man you called a loser was my husband? Well, at least you got that part right. I took a fist to the gut more times than I can count because Drew threatened to take Molly away from you if I didn't do what he said. And let me tell you, some of the things he made me do would sicken even a little bitch like you. I know all too well what it feels like to be beaten down until your brain fogs. Tell me, did you share the things I told you about Cade?"

God, the sight of her makes me want to lunge at her and claw her eyes out of her head. Except, there's a little girl who needs to be protected from a sick man. A man who happens to be her father no less.

"Yes, I did. I loved him. I thought he loved me too. He told me he needed time. That somehow we'd make it work. He knew you were still in love with a dead man. Leaves me curious if he knows you're alive." She stops as if she's waiting for one of us to answer. I'm not telling her a damn thing. "It doesn't matter if he does or doesn't. Drew stopped coming around to see her when she turned one. Told me it was going to be hard on Molly if he kept coming and going. I begged him to leave you and move in with us. Then about a year ago, he quit coming to me altogether. He told me we were over, and he wasn't leaving you. I didn't know what to do so I confided in my brother. Ryan became irate when I told him who Molly's dad was, he told me I fell for the oldest trick in the book when it comes to affairs."

She sure did. I can't believe I trusted a conniving little tramp. If she's looking for sympathy, it won't be from me.

"I'm sorry he put his hands on you. I suspected it. I even drove to your house about a year ago after you supposedly gotten another one of your headaches, to confront you. I was going to confess everything because I missed him. He stopped me. Threatened to take my baby girl from me. I stood up for myself and told him if he tried, I would tell you about us. That was the first and only time he hit me."

I should be a better woman than she is and toss her an olive branch. Tell her I'm sorry he hit her. I'm not going to. It's Molly I'm concerned about. Not her. Not anymore.

For the longest time, I trusted only myself. Learned that lesson early on in my life, and it took a long time for me to comprehend what that word meant. Trust is always broken. It's taken for granted. On the one hand, we lie to save someone from pain; on the other, we will stab them in the back, shove a hot poker up their ass if it saves our own. People misuse that word more than anything when it should be one of the most sacred things in their life. And all this time she shoved my trust in my face.

"I suppose next you're going to tell me you're the one who drugged me for some reason too. You don't deserve my sympathy or friendship. Molly does. Drew is a bad person. A dangerous man. You need to keep her away from him."

Horror etches across her face. An indication she knows just how evil of a man he is.

"I never drugged you. When Drew and I first started our affair, I wanted your life, but then when I realized what kind of man he was, I felt sorry for you. I've been blackmailing him for money with the threat to tell you and the entire city about the man we both despise. Every dime he's given me has been stashed away for my daughter because her father doesn't want a thing to do with her. All it would've taken was one press of a button from Ryan, and Drew would be exposed for having an affair. I honestly didn't want you to find out this way, Ivy. I didn't want to hurt you. I'm not going to stand here and tell you it just happened because it didn't. But now I want him out of my life because I know what he's done. I feel it in my heart he's the one who, God, I can't even say it."

"Say what?"

She drops her chin toward the floor. At the same second, I notice Cade tense up a little, like he knows precisely what she's holding back from saying.

"What the hell is going on? What did Drew do?" I challenge, my voice rising.

"You want safety then you better keep talking. You have no one to blame but yourself, lady."

A silent tension brews between her and Cade.

"How dare you say that to me. I won't apologize for having an affair with Drew. He gave me Molly. I didn't know about Ryan. I've already told you that."

"Not talking about Molly. Quit your goddamn stalling." Cade's eyes drop closed. He wants me to know and at the same time wants to protect me again.

"I kept waiting for you to find out. For you to finally put me out of my misery. There was a time when I hated you. Since then you've become important to me. I felt guilty. Wanted to say the hell with it and tell you. Even though I kept telling Ryan I hated how Drew treated me, how he wasn't there for Molly, he knew I was lying. He knew I would take him back to give my little girl a family because he and I never really had one. He said to let him handle it. By him handling it, I didn't think he meant drugging you."

A stamp of struggle stretches all over her face when she glances up at me. The only thing registering is what she said about Ryan. The disturbing words grate down my throat.

Suffocating silence swallows us while I glance at Cade to see if she's telling the truth. By the way his muscles in his jaw flex, his hands balling into fists, I believe she is. The man looks like he wants to leap out of the chair and choke her. Every muscle in his body is strung tight. I dismiss this bitch who I could give two shits about anymore and move to stand in front of him. To think I wanted her to know I was okay makes me want to kick my own ass.

"How long have you known it was him? How long have you known about Molly?" I don't believe for a second Cade knew long at all. This is why he has them here. Not only for her to tell me, but he's protecting her. Protecting Molly.

"Several days about Molly. I wasn't sure how to handle it. It wasn't my place to tell you. It was hers. Found out last night about Ryan when Nick went to tell Casey to pack their bags and show up here today or I'd find her brother and kill him. The bitch had her bags packed and was ready to flee. Her darling brother confessed to her that he drugged you. He was going to rape and kill you, Ivy, so that his sister could have what she wanted. Think you better tell her the rest and make it quick before I take my niece and make sure you never see her again."

The combined nerves, betrayal, deceit, and lies mixed with the black energy Cade holds along with a thick slick of shock bounces off the walls between us all.

I can't believe any of this. It's like a nightmare taking on an unwanted twist.

"You think you can resurface from the dead and threaten me? You are just like your brother. My daughter is innocent in all this. A child who doesn't know you. Leave her alone. Haven't you and your brother done enough to me? To her?"

Her body falls to the floor, eyes close, and face pinched in a painful grimace. Her sobbing and screaming rake across my skin. It's the trueness of a person consumed by a pain that has no beginning, end, or limit.

The old me would have been there by her side, soothing her, telling her everything was going to be okay. Instead, I stand there and let her wallow in her pain. If it weren't for the fact I honestly believe she would do everything in her motherly instinct to protect Molly, I would beg for her to drown in it.

"You are wrong. You know nothing about Cade, lady. By the sounds of it, he's protecting her from a man who is insane. Tell me the rest so I can get you out of my face and get Molly safe."

Every inch of me feels as if I've been beaten again. Like my flesh is covered in bruises. I know the agony comes from the idea of Drew getting his hands on Molly. Of Ryan being out of his mind that he'd attempt to harm me. Of watching a woman I cared about battle her guilt.

"Ryan's body was found yesterday morning by a man ice fishing. Someone picked through the ice on Lake Herriman and then left the ice pick in my brother's skull before pushing him into the water. Ryan is dead. I know Drew killed him for drugging you."

Dizziness creeps through my awareness, an awful brew fermenting in dread that this is the beginning of a violent storm shoots straight to my brain. It clouds my vision until my knees threaten to give out.

None of what I feel matters. It's a little girl who does. A young girl who loved her uncle with everything she had in her.

Chapter Thirty
Cade

"I can see why a man would move down here. Seventy-three degrees in December. Chicks I'm not going to be able to see running in bikinis down the beach. Oh, and friends who own homes and a goddamn speedboat that goes ninety miles an hour over the ocean. You owe me, fuck face." Nick continues to piss and moan sarcastically right before another wave of nausea hits him. He doesn't make it down below this time before another round of bile has him turning white. The pansy ass shoves his head into a bucket. Hot tears spilling from his eyes as useless whimpers for help spill out of his mouth.

"Jesus, dude. Where were you raised again?" Vomiting was already a nasty thought but actually seeing it only made it worse. I could feel my own bile climbing up my throat from hearing him retch. How the man can have anything left in his stomach beats the hell out of me.

"Miami, asshole. My family owned a restaurant, not a goddamn gut-wrenching machine," he argues over his dry heaves.

"Your story, pussy." I chuckle when he flips me off and shoves his head back in the bucket.

"Don't tell Roan this, but he isn't a fan of throttling this baby as fast as it can go. Now my wife, Anna, she's the daredevil of the family. The crazy woman used to gun it the minute we had the kids secure." Dilan Levy, Roan's cousin, not only offered to fly us down to The Keys where Adam owns a fishing charter business on The Diamond private jet, he also helped me get Molly and Casey out of New York undetected.

The little girl who looks like her mother still didn't have a clue Ryan was dead. How the deceiving bitch handles it isn't my concern. What bothers me is she's my blood, and I'll never get the chance to know her. It doesn't matter if I want to or not. The kid will grow up and wonder about her father and I sure as hell won't be the reminder she doesn't need of the son of a bitch who deserted her. Bastard keeps piling up reasons for me to end his life.

When Nick first showed me Molly's birth certificate, the first person I thought about was Ivy and what this information would do to her. It crushed her knowing her friend deceived her. I hated having to stand there and watch her remain strong while holding in her pain. Hated having to leave her behind with Chaz even more. This job needs to be done and even though she broke down in my arms after the two of them left, I've no doubt she'll be back to herself by the time we return.

"You positive he's home and not on his island?" The closer we get to shore, the more anxious to get this over with I become.

"Yup. Made sure of it before we left. He splits his time up from staying in his house here and the one on the private island he owns. Just so happens he's here this weekend. Makes it a hell of a lot easier for us." Dilan slows as we approach the marina, guides his boat into the slip in front of his house.

"Appreciate you moving this up a week."

"Doesn't bother us any. Gives Anna an extra week to decorate for Christmas."

Christmas. It's nine days away. The thought makes me miss my family.

I grit my teeth, shove my hands in my pockets and palm my knife in one, the black box holding my parents' wedding rings in the other and a ring I gave Ivy one year for Christmas. I'd all but forgotten about her leaving it on my nightstand earlier in the day that changed us all.

Had no idea my brother took them off their fingers before he killed them. Fucker couldn't even let them keep the sentimental bond of their wedding rings. Found the box in his safe when I busted in his house. These plus four family pictures are all I have left of my family.

About choked up when I pawned through the contents inside. Newspaper clippings taunted me until I picked them up and read them. Ivy knew I had gone there to get her stuff and my knife. She knew I burned the mattress Drew tortured her on. The only thing she doesn't know is about the ring.

I showed her what I read. We sat for hours researching the

web and came to our own conclusion that the story in the article is what triggered Drew to kill. A story I remember in vivid detail when our father explained why he was gone for five days straight.

"Sorry, man, I would have let you drive from the airport with Anna or waited till morning to get this out of storage if I would have known how much of a pussy you are. Don't know how you can stomach drawing blood from someone and can't take a little ride in a boat," Dilan taunts through a chuckle, reaches for my pansy ass friend's hand and helps him out of the boat.

"Six houses down. My men are waiting on the beach. Shoot to kill the first person you greet if he doesn't use the word 'lights.' They'll clean up and dump bodies in the middle of the ocean. Adam isn't a fool, Cade. I'll guarantee he's waiting. He's like a mafia king down here. People love to hate him. Go do your thing. I'll have your back in the shadows and hopefully get you home by the time your woman wakes."

I'd known all along he wouldn't go down without a fight. There were times when fear hit me dead center just thinking about coming up with a new plan to take him out if this one didn't work.

I'm used to staring fear in the eye. Lived and breathed it for years.

Fear creeps at the worst possible time. It stole my breath in the desert. Out there being able to draw my weapon before someone else drew theirs used to put the fear of the unknown in me. I didn't fear death. I feared I wouldn't survive long enough to get my vengeance. So, yeah, I stared fear down. I shit that bitch out, and the only fear I have now is the fear of losing Ivy.

"He'll lose more than his life if he tries ambushing us. If I die, make sure you follow through with the plan of burning his island. Send those documents to the IRS. He'll wish to God I killed him after he spends his life being someone's bitch in prison." Asshole owes the government millions in taxes. He's a scammer. A sneaky fuck who doesn't claim half his earnings.

My focus turns gritty, and the urge to kill damn near makes me lose control when we step off the dock and hit the sand. My finger twitches in frustration. I pray like fuck I don't have to pull my ace out of my sleeve and use it. Guess it won't matter if I'm dead.

The urgent need to pull the trigger has me pulling my gun out of my bag, attaching my silencer as we walk down the beach.

A never-ending line of mansions crawling up each other's asses prevents me from torching this heartless son of a bitch who used his part of the money to start a fishing business down here. Turned himself into one of the wealthiest men in Florida.

"He has a fuck ton of lights on, so be cautious." My muscles tighten as I shake the hand of one of Dilan's men.

To be honest, I expected him to be on his island several miles from here ready to blow my ass up the minute I stepped onto the sand. The private one he paid fifteen million dollars for only two years after my parents died.

Anger scrapes at the raw spot in my chest Adam helped leave behind as we approach the house, crouch down and scale between the bushes and palm trees decorating his pool. The goddamn place is lit up brighter than Times Square. The guy was always flashing his parents' money around. Goes to show what kind of greedy person he is. Can see nothing has changed.

A slinking sensation crawls up my spine, mocking my instincts, one that feels all too familiar. Like my days at war where women and children were just as much a suspect as a man. One of the reasons why I won't kill a woman is because I've had to shoot my fair share before she shot one of my brothers or me. The worst fucking feeling in the world to snuff out a life of a woman. Even worse to take a child.

"Something's off. I can feel it." Nick's words strike me in the chest, sprouting those nightmarish wounds a little farther.

Movement from the top deck of his three-story home catches my eye. I smirk, aim my gun toward the open door the soon-to-be-dead fucker just entered. Finger on the trigger and eager to squeeze when my breath catches in my throat as someone walks out the balcony door. It isn't the person I want. It's a woman, her long brown hair blowing in the breeze.

A woman. No wonder my mind snapped back to the past.

"Goddamnit. What the fuck is it with men sacrificing women?"

"Beats the fuck out of me, Nick."

A few seconds later, a hand snakes around her waist, slithers up her stomach and palms one of her tits. The other slides south causing her to arch into the man behind her. My gut tells me it's Adam, but my head screams he knows we're here and this woman is about to die in this crossfire.

"Son of a bitch," I hiss through clenched teeth.

"She shares, Cade. Don't you, Alana?" the deep voice calls out from behind her. Her mouth gapes open; hands squeeze the railing, head nodding as her body hums and shakes from the dirty fingers pumping her pussy. "The Diamonds might own New York, but I own the Keys. You really didn't think I knew when you'd land on my territory? The first mistake you made was landing in the Diamond jet. I learned my lesson the hard way about mistakes, Cade. My biggest one is hiding somewhere in my yard thinking he's going to shoot me before I get my dick wet. Still, a dumb punk, aren't you? You should have come after me first. Tell me, how's Ivy? Left her behind, I see. Damn shame, I might have tried to work out a trade. Your life for hers. But now, seems we're both about to be fucked. Me by pleasure. You by giving me enough time to call your brother. Do you get what I'm saying? You led your sweet little lamb back to her husband by association." His vicious laugh scrapes down the hunched over ridges of my spine. Panic sinks its claws in my chest. The mystery he's executing weighing heavy on my brain.

Drew knows where Ivy is.

I feel that fear. Dead center in my chest.

My lungs are expanding from the craving they need to function. I fucking feel it seep through the blackness in my heart. The fear Adam wants me to drink in like an ice-cold beer that would normally quench my thirst. Instead, it makes my blood ice over.

"Text Chaz."

I left Ivy with a peace of mind knowing she was protected. Adam is right, in my need for vengeance, I made a mistake. One that could cost Ivy her life. One that could cost me losing a man who would sacrifice his to protect her. I failed her. I failed to protect the only woman who has freed my soul. Who has breathed life back into me. I can feel it in my bones, my brother knows where she is. It won't be easy for him to get to her. Then again, greed is an easy thing to accept when the price is right. One slip of a stack of cash to a security guard and he's in my private elevator.

"No response yet, brother. Stay focused and kill him, Cade. Let me message Roan." Needed to hear him say that because I was about a split-second away from saying fuck it and getting back on that jet.

I keep my eyes open while visions of what could be happening to Ivy roll in slow motion in front of my face. She'll never recover from this. The thing is, I don't think she'll have to. I think Drew will kill her after he's taken everything from her he can take.

My heart beats wildly, each thump louder, angrier. I can hear Ivy's screams frantically ringing in my ears. I can feel the leftovers of my soul beginning to spoil any chance of living somewhat of a normal life. There will be no going back for me because if he gets to her, I'll carry the guilty burden of her death without being able to seek vengeance on anyone but myself.

Nick's hand rests on my shoulder. "Either you pull the trigger, or I am. Choose, goddamnit."

I blink. Focus and find my voice within my inner turmoil.

"You fail to forget something, Adam. I've had years to plan this out. I brought a trade for you. My dick is hard hoping you'll take it. Your brother, his wife, and kids living in New York. Another brother and his wife living on the other side of the island have men sitting outside their homes. All it's going to take is my finger to hit the button on my phone, and they'll be dead by the time you bring that bitch to orgasm. You have one minute to pull your finger out of her and decide between you and them. And drop that gun in your hand." I can see the glint of the steel through the glass of his deck. I'd been focusing on the thing until my mind drifted instead of his hand proudly palming a pussy I don't wish to see.

"You expect me to believe you'd kill innocent people?" There's a slight edge of fear in his voice along with eyes filled with panic and clarity from the woman as he removes his hand and clasps it over her mouth.

I stifle a laugh.

"Isn't that what you did when you participated in the death of mine? Isn't that what you're doing right now by forcing my hand to kill an innocent woman? Thirty seconds before all these lights go out and I put a bullet through both of your skulls. If that happens, you'll never know if I decide to kill them or not." He doesn't need to know I won't kill the women and children. I will kill his brothers though.

A vicious fucking cycle they've spun at the expense of my family.

The woman thrashes in his arms. I can smell her fear over the brine of the ocean. Her death will be blood I'll never be able to wash from my hands.

The lights flicker.

"Wait. Goddamnit. You motherfucker. Let me at least call them."

Not a chance.

"Why, so you can say goodbye? Did you allow my parents the same courtesy to say goodbye to Rachel and me? Don't remember them coming into my bedroom before the fire blew through my floorboards. Take this thought to hell with you, Adam. Out of the four of you, I thought you'd be the hardest to kill. Thought for sure you'd fuck me up a little. How wrong I was. You're the easiest."

The lights go out.

I pull the trigger.

Twice.

Chapter Thirty-One
Ivy

"Remind me to never drive during the holiday season again," Chaz grumbles. I'm exhausted and ready to climb into bed. The thought of sleeping alone has me wide awake in an instant. Wasn't that long ago I yearned to sleep alone, now I no longer wish for it. I wish to be held, to sleep on a hard chest instead of curled up on the edge of the bed stuffing pillows behind me as if they'd protect me from the predator lying next to me.

They never did.

"Adam might have one eye open waiting, but Cade can put a bullet through a man's heart in the dark. He's going to be fine."

I open my mouth to say something, anything, when I realize he's captured my thoughts.

"He's breathed for this vengeance. Fought in a war that killed men standing right next to him. If he can survive that, he can survive a rich asshole who might think he can take him down. It won't matter what I try to say to convince you not to worry. You will because you care. Coming home to a woman like you gives him a reason, Ivy."

Restlessness hammers through me, silence falling over us as Chaz continues to inch along in the traffic, allowing what he said to sink into my bones. Only it doesn't. A chill rips through the warmth of the vehicle. It whips in my face like a cold blast of air. The same kind of shiver whenever Drew was ready to bring me down, scatters across my body.

"You're right. It will be morning before we know it. Thanks for working out with me." Even though the man looks like a tall lumberjack with his long beard and hair, he's done a huge favor by taking me to the gym. An even bigger one by trying to soothe the worrying ache in my chest.

I stretch my aching legs, wrapping my arms around my waist to help the chill that has suddenly crept up. It's an unwanted feeling that reaches my cells, throwing me off balance and on high alert. "You always have a way of taking the worry off my mind. I'll whip up some of my dad's famous pancakes in the

morning. Thanks again for everything you've done for me."
During one of our many talks about anything and everything,
Cade told me how Chaz helped the night I was drugged. I'm not
prepared to talk about that night. I don't want to speak of it
again. The mere thought of it turns this cold sensation to ice.

"Don't mention it, Ivy. You take care of my brother. Stick by
his side is the only thing I want in return. He had my back more
times than I can count while we served. During those dark times
when I was ready to self-destruct, he always brought up you and
your smile. Talked about how kind you were. Told me things
about the two of you that made me laugh. Felt like I knew you
before we met. Have to admit, at first, I thought he was making
you up to calm me down. The first time I told him that he pulled
out a picture of the two of you. You were at the beach. The smile
on your face was brighter than the sun shining. I think that photo
helped him get through the years. It did Nick and me too."

Tears sting my eyes. A knot growing thick in my throat, so
abundant that I can barely breathe. I remember the day Cade
took that. The ocean scared the shit out of me. It looked so much
like Lake Michigan, but the thought of sharks and all the
creatures in the water freaked me out. Cade chased me down the
beach. Determined he was going to toss me in and drown my
fear. I gave up, turned around, and he snapped my picture. I used
to have a copy of that photo. Along with every memento I had of
Cade and me, Drew burned them.

I let out a sigh, leaning my head back and blink back my tears.
I'm glad Cade helped him, even happier he talked about me when
he had reason to hate me for marrying Drew.

"Fucking finally." Traffic is still ridiculously heavy as we
merge over two lanes just in time to dip into the underground
garage. Holiday season is beautiful in New York. It's also
beautifully tragic with shoppers everywhere.

The guard keeps his head down while tipping his hat. He
doesn't rap on the window like he's done before. I'm not sure
what it is about the way he looks at me when he lifts his head
and makes eye contact with me, but it causes an outbreak of
discomfort to prickle at the back of my neck.

As I'm studying him, I notice Chaz check the rearview mirror.

He goes to open his mouth, but doesn't have a chance to get a word out before the back and front of the SUV is smashed at the same time.

Confusion strikes. Bright lights blind me. My seatbelt locks with my chest thrusting me forward and backward. My neck snapping in a rush.

I scream. Before I can reach for my gun that's tucked away in my clutch, the back passenger side door opens, and a cold serrated blade rests on my throat.

"You fucking this one too, Ivy? Well, not anymore. Keep your hands on the steering wheel, asshole. You've broken way too many rules this time, you fucking bitch. You've left me no choice once again but to teach you a lesson. I'm afraid a beating won't be good enough for you, or a reminder fuck. It seems I don't have any patience left where you're concerned. Get out of the vehicle, Ivy." The voice I hoped never to hear again is the cause of the unease rolling through me.

"She isn't going anywhere with you. You've done pissed me off, motherfucker. Drop the blade, or I'll blow your brains all over the place."

All hell breaks loose as a bullet flies through the driver's side window, busting it to pieces. My entire body shakes as the blade cuts into my skin, and blood mixed with shards of glass from the window splatter all over my face.

Chaz lifts his gun, points and without hesitation shoots the guard when he sticks his head in the window. More blood splattering everywhere.

Men swarm the outside of the car. Anthony points a gun directly at my head. Eyes wide with anger and a fierceness so intense I stiffen.

"Ivy, run."

I bring my hand up and connect with a part of Drew that makes him grunt, shouting an ear-piercing scream that kindles from deep within my lungs. Vibrating inside my core.

I open the door to run when Anthony grabs me by the throat, swings me around and plasters my back to his front. His gun lodging against my temple.

Chaos erupts all around me.

Guilt crowds my thoughts.

Guns go off, bullets soar. Everything happens in a blurry vision.

The noise fades in and out right along with my heart.

Not even the darkness I succumb to will take away the sight of Chaz's bloodied body slumped over the steering wheel.

Chapter Thirty-Two
Drew

"This is where you want to die, Drew?"

"Ah, there you are. You've been awful quiet lately, Rachel."

I wait for her voice to taunt me some more. I'm met with silence. It's a good thing since my brain is screaming for it. The blizzard-like winds are whipping in a frenzy outside; the snow is coming down thick and heavy and creating all kinds of havoc outside while the one in my head swirls in chaos.

"I don't need your bullshit, Rachel. I'll choose when and where I die, the same way I chose for you. The same way I'll choose for Ivy and Cade. Stay the fuck out of my head."

I chuckle when I feel her floating out of my conscious.

Parking my car. I cut the engine and climb into the back seat to sit alongside my wife.

I pull the sheathed blade out of my coat pocket before adjusting her head in my lap. She doesn't move. Doesn't give me a hateful glare. Doesn't even realize she's minutes away from dying.

The edge of the blade gleams as I pull it out carefully and admire the wood. It's the exact same knife as Cade's. God, how I wish I had the time to fuck her with it. Time isn't on my side as it should be. The goddamn traffic getting from The Diamond building to here wasted too much of it. Left me with little time to play with my wife.

Lifting up, I pull out my phone. Shoot off a text to my whereabouts and hope Cade gets here in time to watch me kill her.

"You left me. I warned you what would happen if you did. I can't let you live, Ivy." I run the edge of the blade along Ivy's relaxed jaw as she remains unconscious. How easy it would be to slice her throat and end her life. If only I didn't need to see the fear in her eyes before I did. If only I didn't feel her disloyalty run like venom through my veins.

My mind screams out as the pain of not having her again

drives a knife filled with her poisonous betrayal through my back. It licks across my flesh like scorching fire.

Closing my eyes takes me back to a time in my life where I thought she'd be mine forever. Images so fresh from the first time I made her come. Her skin drenched in sweat. Her mouth agape, body ablaze and the sweet smell of sex in the air. It tears through my organs, bursting the vessels attached to my heart and causing an uproar in my chest.

This woman consumed me. Turned me irate. Made me insane, and forced me to make her bleed. I need to cut her poison out of my life. Need her as dead as the rest. I won't die unless she dies before me.

I'm a bastard. A murderer. A fool I'm not. I'd be the coward Ivy thinks I am if I didn't believe Cade could kill me. At this point, it doesn't matter. I'm as good as dead without Ivy as it is.

There's no going back for her or me. She'll never submit after being with him. She'll run and only force me to kill her. May as well do it here. May as well end my life right alongside her.

If I do, Cade will never get his vengeance.

"You wanted vengeance, little brother. This is the price you have to pay for it."

Chapter Thirty-Three
Ivy

Tears sting my eyes when I try to blink, and my lungs hurt when I try to breathe. My eyelashes flutter and stick to my skin as I slowly try to open them.

Either the bright light shining in my face is clouding my vision, or I'm scared to open them in fear of Drew punching me again.

I woke the second he pulled me by my legs out of the back of his car. My head and back smashing into the frozen ground. He beat me right there, grabbed my hair and dragged me through the snow into the cemetery.

A chill runs up my spine. I can't believe he brought me to his family's final resting place. Goes to show how out of his mind he is.

My memory of how we got here is unclear, but I know what happened, and I know I'm ready to fight for my life as well as Cade's.

The bitter cold air, harsh winds, and heavy snow seep into my skin, stealing the heat from my fingers and toes just as fast as the wind steals it from my face.

My hair is soaked, parts of it are frozen and sticking to my face and neck.

Vomit rises when I recall the bloody scene before I was knocked out. Guilt pricks my heart. All I have left of our attack is hope that Chaz survived.

"Cade's coming for you, Drew. He's going to find me, and when he does, I'm going to watch you die." I yell, opening my eyes and try to push my half-frozen body into a standing position.

I won't permit him to back me into a corner this time. I'd rather die first before I show fear ever again. Regardless if it's trickling down my bruised arms and legs, sending worse chills everywhere until I swear I hear my bones rattle.

I will stand my ground.

I'm going to survive this because I deserve a better life. Cade is that life and I refuse to give up. Not when I've endured this man's kind of crazy for as long as I have.

And boy is he crazy. If I didn't believe it before, then the newspaper articles, and the research Cade and I did on why Drew killed his family proves it.

"Oh, he's coming alright. I made sure he knows right where you are. I suspect him to be here any minute. Kind of fitting for him to die in the place he'll be buried. The two of you made a nice move by getting Casey and my daughter out of the way. You did me a favor by getting rid of them. I could give a rat's ass if I would have killed Casey, but selling my daughter to be trained for a man's personal debauchery wasn't something I wanted to do."

Drew raises his brows. He's waiting for me to ask him how I feel about him being Molly's father.

I'm not playing by his rules. Not anymore. "You're delusional if you think I'm buying into your bullshit that you care about that little girl."

"I don't care about them at all, Ivy. Them living isn't going to stop me from killing you and Cade before I turn the gun on myself. I wanted to torture your pure little heart. Wanted you to die knowing I killed your friend. I wanted you to beg me not to sell my daughter and watch your heart bleed out when I told you it was too late. Since you one-upped me, I'm going to plunge this into your heart, pull it out and stick it in mine. Now that sounds like a good plan. One that can't go wrong." He pulls out a knife. One so familiar looking that my insides curl right into themselves. No! I refuse to believe he found Cade's knife. It's a fake, just like everything else that is this pathetic man.

Anger snakes through my gut. I have to stall him. Kill him, because Lord knows I won't survive him using that knife on me.

"You're trying hard to scare me because your world is unraveling, you brainsick piece of shit. What kind of monster has taken up residence inside you to make you hate so much you wouldn't have a thing to do with your child?"

Ice sinks into the skin on my neck when he gets up in my face and dangles my gun he obviously took and positions it underneath my chin.

"Are you not aware by now that the three of us are going to die here tonight? Let me tell you something else you aren't aware of. The monster in me is you. You couldn't let Cade go. You couldn't give me a chance. You took residence inside of me. Driving the plan, I made haywire and poisoned my skull. Molly is a girl. I wanted a son. Our son. You fucked that up by not giving me a son, and I'll be damned if you live to give Cade one. Nice gun. What else did my little brother give you, Ivy?" He leans in, whiskey breath and all and licks right up the middle of my face. "I can smell him on you. Did you come for him? Did you?" He drills me with a look infused with fury. It seeps out of his dark edges, gloomy and bitter.

"If I ever have a child. It will be Cade's," I yell, violent sobs building in my chest.

I lift my leg to knee him in the balls when he reels his hand holding the gun back and cracks it against my face, knocking me back down with the sharp force of his blow.

The solid power from his strike kicks the air from my lungs, squeezes it in my throat until I'm gasping to breathe.

He drops to his knees. Foolishly lays my gun beside him. A sinister growl pierces the freezing air as he grips my throat. "You'll never be a mother, Ivy. I didn't want it to end this way. I wanted to destroy you before Cade hunted me down. Leave you weak and scared. Make him see you weren't the sweet gift he thought you were. The entire time you've been gone I've barely slept knowing you were spreading your legs easily for him. You think I'll let you live after that? My fucking wife getting off to my brother. Not a goddamn chance."

A menacing chuckle falls from his mouth. Eyes that used to scare me so full of ire and his crazy that death is the only answer to cure him. Even that is too good of a punishment for everything he's done. All his mocking and ridiculing do now is making me pity the demon living inside of him. How far gone he is that I can't imagine the things that are going through his head. That's the mechanism of a person driven by something they become infatuated with. They become so far gone that it takes over every rational thought. It all started with the story in the article.

"Let's talk about my brother fucking you. Did you get on your hands and knees for him willingly? Were you nice and wet for him?"

My blood freezes. Heart is skipping in a harmful loud beat as white spots that aren't snow, dance in my eyes. He's killing me. I can feel my blood slowing, my brain shutting down, my heart struggling to beat.

Malice is what I feel for this man, although he's not really a man at all. He's messed up in a way I hope I never understand.

With his hand still on my throat, he runs the blade of the knife back and forth across the seam of my jeans in between my legs. I freeze. Every part of me locks up.

"Kiss me, or I'll slice you from here to your skull."

The bitter taste of him gags me when he shoves his tongue in my mouth; I bite down as hard as I can. The sour taste of his tangy blood mixing with the satisfaction of fighting back riles me up.

I won't give up.

"There she is. The woman with a spark of life. Too bad she decided to appear a little too late. I warned you what would happen if you left me."

I can feel the blade slicing through my jeans. Any second it's going to cut me.

My lungs begin to burn, my hands instinctively going to his cheeks where I dig my nails into his face.

"You stupid cunt," he hisses, drops the knife and his free hand joins the other. He squeezes tighter until my vision blurs and those alarming spots cloud my sight.

"You'll never get away with this," I wheeze out. My lungs are closing. For the first time since he's struck me, I fear I'm really going to die. Pulled into blackness just when a few weeks ago I found the happiness I never thought would be found.

My lids grow heavy, my mind remembering how unfair life can be. It gives you a little of what it feels like to be loved before it shoves you through the gates of hell reminding you how it feels to live in the polluted air where the devil has all the control.

"I've gotten away with so much already. I would have continued to get away with it, unlike the man I copied if you would have loved me. You're to blame for every fucking move

I've made."

I'm not to blame for anything. It was his choice to kill. His choice to hurt me. His choice to do everything.

My hands try to find something to hold onto. There's nothing but the snow. Nothing until I feel the butt of my gun. With the strength I have left, I wrap my hand around it at the same time he yanks me up by my throat and slams me hard enough against the marble headstone that my brain tilts causing the gun to slip from my hand.

I'm going to die. Cade isn't going to get here to save me this time.

My vision tunnels as his fists connect with my face. I cough and splutter as the blows to my stomach rob me of my breath.

"You spiteful cunt. I'm going to kill you."

My thoughts cease when I feel Drew's hand begin to dip below the top of my pants.

This bastard is going to have to kill me because there is not a chance in hell he's going to take what he wants from me ever again.

"Fuck you. I don't love you. I never did." I spit in his face, my hand reaching down to grab his erection. I dig my nails into his sick, hard flesh, twisting the appendage with everything I have.

"Fucking bitch." He winces, doubles over in pain, hands flat on the ground. His breathing ragged as he fights for air. I scurry to grab my gun. Fingers numb as I scrounge through the snow.

He grabs me by the waist, flips me over and straddles me.

I attack, clawing and scratching at his face. I scream, I buck, and the entire time I am attacking him he's attacking me, but I am on a mission to kill this man before he kills me.

"You crazy bitch."

I flinch, blood flowing down my face, vomit lurching when the knife suddenly rests on my throat as he claws at my clothes.

"Feel how fucking hard I am for you?" He rolls his hips into me.

"You are a sick, evil man."

"And you're a dead fucking bitch."

Chapter Thirty-Four
Cade

"Get the fuck off my woman, Drew!" I lift my knife and fling it through the air. Target his skull. The snow is so damn thick I miss. Motherfucking shit.

"Don't take another step or I'll cut her beautiful head off and throw it at you." Unbalanced. His words are filled with it.

Darkness threatens to raid my vision as I shake my head trying to clear the fog shadowing my brain.

On the other side of town laying in a bed that's surely going to piss him off when he wakes is the mangled up body of a man who took several bullets to try and save my woman.

Chaz was shot in the arm, shoulder, and leg during an ambush where somehow Drew got away with Ivy. All I know from the dozens of calls I had while in the air with Roan is that Chaz killed several men including the bodyguard who followed Ivy around. The man is going to be hurting for a long while, but thank fuck he's going to be okay.

Kind of ironic when the last man I killed sacrificed the life of one, all because he thought he'd be the one to take me down. But I'm not like Adam, who's probably shark bait by now. I'm like my brother. The one who takes what he wants, when he wants.

Guilt trails down my spine. Ivy wouldn't be hurting if I would have made it here sooner. I had no idea where she was until Roan notified me about a text from Drew. He sent it to Ivy's phone. Prick must have left it in the SUV for that purpose only.

I should have known a man like my brother would find out. A huge goddamn mistake I made that not only Chaz could have died for, one that just might cost Ivy her life.

Difference between Drew and me though, I'm not waiting years to rectify my mistake. Drew should have taken me out the second he knew I was alive. He should have used his money to pay off someone to kill me instead of building an empire that's going to crumble to the ground.

My insides seize.

In agony.

In fear.

Neither showing mercy as they twine around my lungs, and squeeze until I can barely breathe.

Can barely stomach the attacking images of his hands on her. Of her screams as I ran through the snowbanks toward her.

This whole fucked up person my brother has become decays me from the inside out.

I should have taken him out the easy way. Should have just put a bullet through his head every time I looked through my scope from atop the building next to his instead of waiting to look him in the eye and get the answer to my parents' question.

Why?

"Fuck you, Cade. You couldn't stay away could you?"

My eyes deadlock with the man who has the same blood as mine coursing through his veins. He stands, jerks Ivy up by her neck, and slams her battered body against the headstone. A knife exactly like mine is placed underneath her throat.

"She looks like a sacrificial angel, doesn't she? Too fucking bad neither one of us will win her."

More recollections than I care to count flicker through my mind. The many talks I've had with my family every time I came to visit them here. The flowers I had sent every year for birthdays, my parents' anniversary. The tears I let fall when no one was looking. But the one standing out above all is how Drew snapped and became violent. How his chemical imbalance went missing from his warped state of mind.

Never really gave notice to the time Drew went from a fairly easygoing brother to one with so much pent-up anger for Rachel and me until I read the headlines in those articles. It all made sense to me then. The man he copied didn't want to share the life insurance he was set to inherit from his dad's death with his mother and sister. Mitchell Davies, a young college kid, studying criminology at NYU. He and a few of his friends beat, raped his sister, and burned the two of them inside. He ended up getting away with it. Collecting the money until the guilt ate away at one of his friends, he ended up turning them in.

Drew killed over that case. I remember how it drove my

father to tears thinking a teenager was that fucked up he'd commit a crime so horrendous over greed.

I was interested in hearing about it because I wanted to be like him. One Drew acted interested in because he became obsessed with it. Obsessed enough to conduct a copycat brutal crime.

My body shakes, my finger twitches uncontrollably and my stomach churns when I see the bruises on Ivy's face. A few minutes longer and who the hell knows what kind of damage he'd have done to her.

"Back away from her, or one of the dozen men waiting to clean this mess up will shoot you."

Drew's low rumbling sadistic laugh proves how off balanced he is. It contains a theory he's this close to snapping into a cyclone of wrath. To do his best to take care of the mistake he made.

Me.

I choke down my laugh and welcome him to try.

"Cade." My name falls from Ivy's lips like Drew just stabbed me through my heart with my knife.

"Baby, are you all right?" She has got to be fucking freezing and hurting. So incredibly hurt that once again I've failed her. It slashes right through my chest.

"Yes. Is Chaz?" Her caring about my true brother barely scathes the tiny surface of my anger. It makes me love her all the more.

"He's going to be fine. Giving you a choice, Ivy. You want to stay and watch this or have Nick take you home?"

Unraveling. I can smell Drew doing it before I see it.

I pull out my gun. This needs to be over before he loses it completely and kills her.

"She'll do what I say. Her home, the end of her life is with me. Ivy is my wife, you son of a bitch."

"She's about to become your widow, Drew." I pull the trigger. Hitting him in the leg instead of in the head where I want. His brains would splatter all over her. Not sure if she could handle that. Snow flies up in a white powdery cloud from where his body drops to the ground.

"Step away from him, Ivy." I wait for her to move before I inch in closer. "It won't be long, and that snow will be coated with your blood, Drew." It's oozing out of his leg already.

"Still determined to use a weapon on me instead of fighting like a man. Bet this wasn't how you planned to end me was it? Bet you wanted to burn me alive. Listen to me beg and scream the same way our dad did. You know he begged me to let you and Rachel go. Tried pleading with me that you'd all stick by my side and get me the help I needed. Had to laugh in his face before I slammed my fist in it. Stick by me, my ass. He would have put me in an asylum or prison just like what happened to Mitchell Davies. He wasn't as smart as me, was he? We should talk about that story, brother, don't you think? Goddamn, I loved that story. I beat that kid though, didn't I? He didn't get away with killing his family. He got caught, sent away for life. I studied that case until it was all I could see. I had it perfected. But then you had to go and survive."

Mitchell Davies deserves to die just like Drew does.

He'll get no response out of me until I make sure Ivy has it in her to stay out in this sub-zero cold until I finish. One blink from her eyes and I'll finish this now.

It takes her determined gaze not leaving mine for me to stand here and not squeeze the life out of him. He needs to suffer before I do him a favor by relieving him of his misery. There has to be all kinds of disarray running through his crazy head. How the fuck he hasn't snapped by now is a riddle I'll never solve.

Not a flicker. The only thing dripping from her is understanding of the choice I'm given her, and her trust that I'll kill him before he hurts her again. I'll never doubt this woman's ability to stand tall again. Her willpower is as clear as her love for me is. It shines brighter than the light casting all over her face.

Her bruises and scars that will last a lifetime are worth the decision I made. One she deserves more than I do to see this through. One that will prove I'll always give her a choice.

"You want to die from my fists? If that's what you want then throw the knife and any other weapons you have, I'll do the same. If you don't, the next bullet goes in your skull. After you're dead, I'll take Ivy home, get her cleaned up and fuck her until she's screaming my name."

Steam, it billows out with his loud white puffs of air. I could taste the end of my vengeance. After this, I'll have nothing except good memories to make and a long future with Ivy.

"It isn't going to work that way. She dies, you die, and I die. You fucked my wife! I should've killed the betraying bitch years ago and moved on. I'll be goddamned if I make another mistake by letting either of you live."

He pushes himself up so fast I don't have time to blink. The blood drains out of my face when at the same time I fire off another bullet and nail him in the shoulder; he plunges his knife into Ivy's arm.

Time stands still. Her bloodcurdling scream ripping from her mouth while she drops to her knees. I failed her again.

"Goddamn, that stings. Nice shot, brother, but take a look at her. She's on her hands and knees just like she should be." Drew's low rumbling words hold years of pain and torment.

I can't fucking breathe.

My lips curl over my teeth in anger, bloodthirsty for this fucker who will not steal another life from me.

My vengeance becomes a livewire. I dive at him. He howls in desperate agony as I take him down.

We roll and tumble. Two enraged men fighting to the death.

Brother to brother.

Black soul to blacker soul.

Arms, fists, and legs flying everywhere. Blood dripping from his wounds. I give the man credit for coming at me when he's profusely bleeding.

He lands an uppercut to my jaw. I nail one in his gut, another to the side of his head as we throw our hatred into every motherfucking punch.

I blink away the blood gushing from the severe cut to my brow. Circling my brother as he circles me. Each of us inhaling air cold enough to freeze our lungs, exhaling heavy white puffs of heated air.

"As much as I'd love to dance in a circle with you. I need to get my girl fixed up." I lunge at him. No mercy is given as I dig the tip of my finger into his bleeding shoulder.

"You're bleeding out from both wounds. It won't be long until you die."

"You aren't any better than me. Choosing to kill me over making sure she's alive." He's gasping for air now. Scrunched up features are starting to show his pain.

I can smell his fear. Feel his death drawing near. Fuck, it's about goddamn time.

"I know damn well my strong woman is alive. If I didn't, you'd be dead already. Ivy, you good. He's yours, get up baby."

A little rise in the corner of my mouth lifts at both ends. It's then he becomes aware of how I intend to seal his fate with the way his eyes shift to her.

"I say when your life ends, and it ends here. By her hand."

I wrap my arms around Drew's waist and take him to the ground, a rush of adrenaline filling me. I can smell his death. Feel Ivy's freedom and taste my vengeance.

My head snaps up. I keep my eyes on the rise and fall of her chest as I bind my legs around his neck and squeeze.

"Ivy is mine. She loves me, and you love her. How does that make you feel, brother?" I nudge. "Hell is too good for you, but wherever you end up, I hope you suffer eternally. There will be no penance for what you have done."

Drew's body begins to convulse. But it's not in terror; he's trembling in unadulterated rage, his face contorting to display the monster he's become.

"Fuck you," he shrieks out in pain. The urge to snap his neck off pushes my hate for him to my legs. I won't do it no matter how much I've planned and plotted and killed while I waited. This kill belongs to Ivy. Demons be damned. I'll fight them off if they dare try to haunt her.

"Ivy, get up baby. He's all yours."

Drew's body begins to flail trying to get out of my hold. His laugh a ghosting echo in the wind.

Chapter Thirty-Five
Ivy

I tilt my head to the side, doing my best to try and muffle the sounds of my cries from the pain in my arm. The numbness from holding still causing a surge of the worst discomfort I have ever had, to progress its way down my arm.

I remain exactly where I am, my eyes darting back and forth between Cade and Drew. Until finally they lock on Cade's eyes that capture and hold.

The man is hard and yet just like the boy I knew, he's showing his love by giving me his vengeance.

His look is chocked full of determination and unspoken love. Utterly convincing, it's impossible to look away. My heart aches beneath his stare that's filled with grief and regret.

Why would you give this to me? I blink away tears wanting to pour out of me. *Why?*

Because it's the only gift, I'm giving you to destroy.

My lids close and the weight builds and builds and builds. All the years of Drew driving my soul into the ground surface.

 Strong and intense.

As if he was abusing me all over again.

I open my eyes and stare at the man who holds more evil inside of him than the devil.

Drew laughs, coughs and sputters a malevolent sound. His good arm is tugging against Cade's legs that are wrapped around his neck. Feet and legs thrashing and stirring up the bloody snow. He freezes when his eyes fix on mine.

"Come on, pick up the gun or the knife and kill me, Ivy. I dare you. You'll be handcuffed to the bed while they stitch you up. Little miss innocent and deceiving will spend her life in prison." A glacial grin ticks up at the corner of his mouth.

I won't touch that knife or another one ever again in my life.

Fear blares inside my head so loudly I can hear it deafening my ears. "You expect me to believe Cade's friends haven't killed your men already? Your threats won't work on me anymore,

Drew. You have nothing left but death. If you had anyone alive out there, they would have already put a bullet through Cade to save your ass." I might have been a scared woman before. I'm not anymore.

"He might have had men here; I'll guarantee every one of them are dead and on their way to never be found. I think I told you I had brothers who would have my back. Let me mention you committed a crime on Roan Diamond's property. The man doesn't take kindly to people crossing him. Ivy, do you remember reading a story about a family being murdered in their home by a fire, and the only survivor was the oldest child? He went on to collect millions from life insurance. I came up with a plan on how you can kill your husband and get away with it. Pick up the gun and pull the trigger, baby, and I'll fill you in." Tears fall, and I wobble a smile. Cade's words are the last bit of strength I need.

I'm delirious and confused, but I notice the second reality creases Drew's brow before his eyes go wide.

I take in the snow coming down. The purity of the flakes promising something new. A sign of strength. A representation of a fresh start for Cade and me.

Laughter slips from my mouth when a cold gust of wind blasts through my body. "Whatever should I do with all the money my dead husband is leaving me? Cars, a mansion on top of a hill. His business. I'll own it all." I don't want a dime of it. I won't share that with Drew though.

"Fuck you, Ivy."

"No thank you. I have a man who gets me off just fine. He does it so well that he'll be inside of me before you hit the depths of hell. You're not so tough now, are you? I told you there'd come a time when I'd get a chance to kill you, Drew. Thanks to the man I love, I've been given a choice. Do you know how long I have waited for today? A long time. I've loved Cade ever since I can remember, and you took him from me, and now you're going to pay. Not only for that but for what you did to him. To your family. How does it feel to be helpless? To wonder when you're going to die?"

I drag myself the rest of the way up. Grab my gun that glistens in the snow like a symbol of hope. Hope I never thought I'd have.

I won't hate myself for drawing his last breath. What I do despise is doing it here. Over the top of his family's grave. But he's the one who brought me here. He's the one who copied a killer and committed the worst kind of crime.

"Look at you standing there. You don't have the guts to kill me, Ivy. You're weak. Pathetic. How many years did you let me take from you? Too many to turn you into a killer. Too many for you to forget."

I swipe at my bleary eyes. My legs are weak, my arm is throbbing, my face is swollen, and my vision is blurred, to say the least.

I edge forward, boots crunching in the snow.

I gulp down the bile that threatens to rise in my throat, the fear this crazy man has put me through threatens to bring me to my knees. I did it for so long when I stared into his vile and retched eyes that my legs wobble to fall.

Not this time. Not ever again.

Black energy trembles through me.

Dark and sinister.

Powerful and fierce and wanted.

Warmth skids down my spine.

Tremors roll as my conscience opens wide, my pulse fluttering, ease of comfort soothing across my skin.

I puff out a white clouded breath and slowly tilt my head toward Cade.

Pulled.

Those black eyes are giving me a choice to pull the trigger. To do it fast so he can tend to my wounds. Protect me and become my savior.

I blink myself away from his soothing face and turn my attention to the man who is turning blue from lack of oxygen to his messed up brain.

"Wrong, asshole. After tonight the memory of you, and everything you've done is as dead as you are."

I pull the trigger hitting my target dead center in his cold hollow heart.

Epilogue
Cade
Five Months Later

I watch Ivy shimmy out of her workout shorts, slip out of her tank top and climb on top of our shared desk in the office at the gym. A slight twinge in her face tells me her arm's giving her a fit today. Wouldn't have suspected it was hurting by the way she pushed herself through her own workout, plus taking care of two of her clients a bit ago.

The woman never complains about the scar tissue and the possibility of permanent chronic pain or whatever long-lasting effects she might have. Every time I bring it up, she bounces back with telling me it'll be worth it knowing the man who caused them is dead.

Not only did she choose to become a fitness instructor, but she also plowed right into it the minute the doctors gave her the clear. She leads clients in stretching, aerobics, and weight training.

The best part of watching her shine is the way she speaks her mind. Encouraging in a positive, motivating way.

Her voice is as welcomed here as her body is in our bed.

She's signed so many checks and documents over the past few months that watching her sign the final one earlier today, sliding it across the desk to her attorney unlocked the last chain to Drew to fall.

Ivy made a choice on her own to sell everything and donate millions to be split evenly amongst the many women's shelters in New York. The other million is sitting in a trust for Molly to do whatever she pleases. I still haven't a clue where they are, and neither does she. We both agree it's best to keep it that way.

We owe her being able to collect the money to Roan. He, along with Nick, and several of his men killed Drew's people surrounding the cemetery. Disposed of the bodies. Confiscated the weapons from the scene and stole a car from a dealership, parked and left it behind Drew's. It made his death look like a robbery gone wrong.

When I stole the life insurance policy, I didn't give two fucks about the money Ivy was set to inherit and neither did she. The thing is, we needed a body for her to collect it. Unlike Drew's copycat murder, ours took ten minutes to plan. It's a plan we'll get away with for eternity.

It was an easy lie for her to tell while lying in a hospital bed bruised, battered, and stabbed. After all, she was left for dead while visiting loved one's graves with her husband. I wish his death would have happened without Ivy being hurt, but at least the last time the sick fuck touched her, he was digging his own goddamn grave.

It hurt like a motherfucker not being able to go to the hospital with her. Nick went in my place. Her getting the proper care she needed wasn't a choice for her to make. It was mine. I made it perfectly clear while I held her until the sirens blared that when it comes to her well-being, I'll stop at nothing to make sure she's properly cared for. That included having to stay away while she was in surgery. Being questioned by the police, and disobeying orders by ripping her IV out twice. She received several swats to her ass for trying to heal without pain and antibiotics.

"I heard from Chaz today. He'll be back in town next month." I haven't shared much about his whereabouts with her when she asks about him. Chaz is healing the best he can while dealing with the information he was handed last month.

A group of hikers found bones in the mountains upstate. Forensics came back with positive results of them being the remains of his sister Chandra's. The man isn't taken it well at all. Guilt, like I've never seen, is eating away at the friend I once knew. Not sure if he'll ever be up to get the revenge he needs.

"That's great. I can't wait to see him." Nick and I can't either. Have a feeling Chaz isn't going to be the same man.

Enough dreary news. I need to be inside of her.

"Fuck, I missed you. Lie back and spread your legs. Need you to fuck my face, Ivy." I got home a few hours ago from a kill that took me several days longer than anticipated. I need to fuck my rush from pulling the trigger, into her sweet little cunt. Get her home and see what kind of color she painted our living room. I have more color in our penthouse than I do black anymore. What the hell ever. It makes her happy.

Her nipples harden as she watches me strip out of my shorts, make my way to her before grabbing her face and crashing my mouth to hers.

Her fingers tangle in my hair; mine skim up her thighs. Our teeth clash, breaths mingle as we grind into each other.

Pulling away and licking my lips, I stare down at the woman who fires me up at the mere sight of her.

I lower myself until my face is between her legs. Inhaling the sweet scent of hers that jacks me up every damn time I smell her. Palming my hands under her ass, I lift her and drag my tongue up and down her seam. Her body squirming in my firm grasp.

Her moans ricochet off the walls. So damn loud and inviting, I flick my tongue into her pussy over and over with such unrelenting fierceness to make her come.

I suck until she arches her back, her juices coating my beard.

Pushing up, I plant her feet on the edge and stare into those deep green eyes.

Even with her killing a man; Ivy's still untainted in a rarity I can't explain. Innocent in certain ways and sinful in others. I tower above her, loving how her smile spreads when she wanders over my face, my chest.

Tempting seductress about drops me to my knees when she swipes her tongue seductively across her plump bottom lip when her eyes land on my cock.

Her tight walls grip my shaft, warm and inviting when I slam into her. She feels so goddamn good, I don't want to move.

"Please, Cade."

My name on those begging lips has me moving slowly. Can't pull my eyes away from staring at my glistening cock between her legs.

"You are so beautiful. So brave, and mine."

I fuck her then. Hard and animalistic.

"Lift your hand." She does without question.

Our gazes lock on her ring instead of each other. The vintage ring I gave her years ago. I wrapped it up and re-gifted it to her for Christmas.

A diamond promise ring rests against her skin.

That's the best I can do at the moment as far as a commitment. Because the old Cade St. James doesn't exist anymore. He does to the only person who matters. As long as she continues to look at me the way she used to. As long as she continues to make choices on her own. And, as long as she knows I'll never hurt her, then my vengeance has been fulfilled and served.

"I love you, Cade."

"Know that, Ivy."

The End.

WANT MORE?
Sign up to receive an email when, WARRANT, Chaz's story releases.
Newsletter:
https://landing.mailerlite.com/webforms/landing/a6r6g1

Please consider leaving a review. Long or short, your review is always appreciated, and along with telling a friend about the book, it is the most wonderful gift you can give an author.
Thank you for reading my words.
Kathy.

45488560R00137

Printed in Poland
by Amazon Fulfillment
Poland Sp. z o.o., Wrocław